Praise for

Full of Wonder is charming and sweet, with a dash of humor and a pinch of zest. The fake dating trope is taken to the next level by combining it with an underlying theme of faith. No emotion goes unturned as Marco and Rosalina navigate their accidental romance. B.M. Baker delivers another delightful story with unforgettable characters, swoonworthy moments, and valuable lessons for us all. ~ Kaelin Scott, author of *Game Set Love* and *Worthy of Love*

Full of Wonder epitomizes the fake dating trope through a Christian lense. The characters grapple not only with their growing feelings for one another, but also with the consequences of their deception. With classy wit, dramedy, and swoon, Baker is sure to leave the reader... full of wonder. ~ Drew Taylor, author of *The Designated Friend*

B.M. Baker has done it again, blending comedy, sweet romance, and purity in one of my favorite tropes—fake relationships. If you're someone who appreciates some romantic madness, awkward moments, and you're a dog lover too, then don't hesitate to get this book—you won't be disappointed. Enjoy the journey as Marco and Rosalina accept each other's flaws and reveal their true feelings. ~ Lisa Renee, author of the *Bachelors of Clear Creek* series

Full of Wonder is the perfect light-hearted read that will have you grinning from ear-to-ear. Baker's unique characters deliver a delightfully fun story brimming with banter and hilarious situations. You can't help but root for the characters as they navigate separating their real feelings from the lies they've weaved. Full of genuine faith, warmth, and loads of doggy love, Full of Wonder is sure to leave you with a smile on your face. ~ Latisha Sexton, author of the *In the Midst* series

Baker delivers a romantic comedy without the spice, witty banter without borderline comments, and a sweet love story without anything explicit, proving this to other rom-com writers: you can tell a great story while keeping it clean. ~ Caitlin Miller, author of *The Memories We Painted* and *Our Yellow Tape Letters*

From meet-disaster, to fake dating, to falling unexpectedly in love, Baker delivers laugh out loud moments with these two imperfectly adorable characters. With just enough tension and swoon, you won't be disappointed by picking up this sweet read! ~ Dulcie Dameron, author of the *River Hollow Romance* Series?

Full of Wonder

A sweet romantic comedy

Full of Wonder

A sweet romantic comedy

B.M. Baker

Redeemed Writing Press

2023

Dedicated to Marie.
Thank you for your excitement about this series,
and for always asking how my writing was going.
It served as an encouragement to me every time I
wanted to give up on this book. God bless you!

Psalm 105:5
Remember his marvelous works that he hath done;
his wonders, and the judgments of his mouth;

Chapter One

July 10, 2019

It's hard to attend the wedding of the woman you thought you'd marry.

Marco Mendez folded the wedding invitation up for likely the five hundredth time since receiving it in the mail on Saturday from his high school crush, Lillian Harrison. It was only Wednesday and the creases were already looking worn. Marco doubted it would last much longer if he kept pulling it out of his pocket to glare at.

Why he was carrying it around to torment himself with, he didn't know. Maybe he liked pain?

Yeah, that's it. I like pain.

Marco rolled his eyes at his own pitiful thoughts. If only he had spoken up sooner, maybe things would have turned out differently. Why couldn't he have worked up the nerve to tell Lillian how much he cared for her?

He supposed he took it for granted that she knew what his feelings for her were. Hadn't it been obvious? They'd spent their entire junior and senior years of high school together.

Having attended a small Christian school, there hadn't been much diversity among the students. With Marco being Hispanic and Lillian Asian, they were both in the minority. So, naturally, they'd created a bond and had been best of friends.

But, best of friends wasn't a free ticket to the marriage altar. Now Lillian was engaged to marry a Vietnamese man. Lillian had often talked about wanting to marry someone who shared her heritage, so Marco figured he should be happy for her.

It was hard to be happy, though. It hurt too much. Now he had to attend *her* wedding and watch her marry the man who'd managed to win her undying love. A man who couldn't even stay awake while standing up, as he suffered from a neurological condition called narcolepsy. But Clint Bishop had been able to do what Marco never could: speak his feelings and declare his love.

If only Marco hadn't waited too long.

He sighed regretfully and proceeded to down the last of his carton of coconut water.

"Hey, you about ready to get back to work, *amigo*!" One of Marco's coworkers and best friend, José Torres, hollered from up on the roof.

Marco tossed the empty beverage in the bed of the utility truck. "I'm coming!"

He jogged back toward the house, climbed the ladder with monkey-like skill, attached his safety harness, and scaled the high-peaked roof without a single wobble in his knees.

"Were you reading that letter again?" José asked, an eyebrow raised in an expression that said his friend already knew the answer.

Marco grumbled.

"What's that?" José cupped a hand around his ear.

Marco sent José a glare. "I was." He grinned largely to hide the heart-wrenching pain he felt in his gut.

"You need to get over her, Marco."

"It's not that simple."

"She's getting married, for crying out loud! That means any fancies you held for Lillian are over. You had your chance, and you blew it."

"Wow. Guess I won't be getting any sympathy from you." Marco grabbed his roofing shovel and returned to the task of removing shingles. He put extra muscle into the job than he normally used and found satisfaction in the pulling he felt through his back. At least it momentarily took his mind off the pain in his heart, and the torture in his mind thinking about seeing Lillian at the altar with *that man*.

"You need to suck it up, bro."

Marco rolled his eyes while his back was to José, but then he turned around and flashed another of his big grins. "I'm fine. Really. See? I'm smiling."

José set his shovel down to point a stern finger at him. "Your smile doesn't fool me. We've been friends since we were in diapers. I know you wear that smile to hide what's going on inside. The bigger the grin, the deeper the pain."

Did his friend have to be *so* right? Margo growled and didn't bother keeping the grin on this time, but scowled and, for the first time, said words out loud he'd never admitted to anyone but himself. "I love Lillian."

Whoa. Those words were powerful. And saying them now made it feel as if his whole world had been rocked. Good thing he had his safety harness on, for Marco's legs gave out on him in his squatted position and he dropped to his bottom.

It's too late. How he hated those three words. As much as they hurt in this instance, he couldn't imagine how terrible it'd be to hear them from God on judgment day.

José shook his head, probably thinking of what a sorry lot he was. And maybe he was. A man in love with another guy's fiancée?

Yeah, that doesn't fly.

Marco clenched his jaw and worked on taking more of his hurt anger and frustration out on the shingles.

"Say, why don't I help you get your mind off of things?" José asked after a few minutes.

Marco was already panting from his exertion. If he kept up this pace he'd never make it through the day. He needed to get a hold of himself. He swiped the arm of his orange long sleeve T-shirt over his perspiring forehead and righted the brim of his tan sun hat again.

"Nothing will get my mind off it. It's a hard fact that can't be changed, and I need to learn to live with the reality."

"I think I know exactly what would help you, though."

Marco doubted it, but gave his friend his full attention. "What do you have in mind?"

"Join Regina and I for dinner Friday night." José got a silly lost-in-love kind of look. It was *not* becoming on him.

Regina was José's fiancée, and wedding bells would be ringing for them next month too—exactly a week after Lillian and Clint's wedding.

"Why would I want to join you and Regina for dinner? You two will be so caught up in each other. I'd be an annoying third wheel on your date."

"Ah, but you miss my meaning." José *tsked*.

Marco shook his head in annoyance and returned to scraping off shingles. "Then tell me what I'm missing."

"Let me set you up on a blind date."

"Absolutely not." Marco gave a hard shove on his shovel. "I don't want you setting me up with an unknown woman. If I can't have Lillian, I won't have anyone."

"Well, then you'd better learn to enjoy bachelor life. Because you ain't getting Lillian."

The man was no help. Not that there was any help for him. The engagement ring he knew was on Lillian's left fourth finger now sealed the deal. He knew Lillian. She'd not let a man put a ring on that finger unless she was serious. He should have known it was coming. In fact, he'd *seen* it coming, but had kept himself in a state of denial.

It all started that fateful day in May. Marco would never forget the scare Lillian had given him when she'd wound up in the hospital after a bicycle-versus-automobile accident. She'd been in a coma for two-and-a-half weeks. Marco had feared he'd lose her. He'd spent the days of her unconsciousness praying and working up the courage to tell her he did, in fact, care deeply for her. That they weren't merely friends.

But then one day when Marco had gone to visit her in the hospital, there'd been a man there. A *Vietnamese* man. Who looked exactly like the kind of man Lillian would fall for. And from the look on said man's face, Clint Bishop (he really didn't like the name right now), Marco had known right then he hadn't a chance. Clint clearly loved Lillian, and he knew Lillian would choose him in a heartbeat.

And she had.

To Marco's dismay.

Now he had around three-and-a-half weeks to come to terms with her decision before he had to witness the wedding of the love of his life to the man Marco felt no small kindness to at the moment.

God, help me.

José's eyes were locked on him and it was grating on Marco's nerves. "Will you quit staring at me," he hissed.

"I will if you say you'll come to dinner."

"Sure. I can say I'll come."

José growled. "You have to mean it."

Marco paused in his work. "I don't know if I can trust you with picking out my blind date."

"Ah, so you're considering it?" José's eyes took on a light.

"I said no such thing."

"Would you agree if I told you who the woman is?"

"I might." Marco rubbed his chin.

José nodded and inched across the roof to get closer, likely so Santiago and Javier, their fellow roofers on the other side of the steep peak, couldn't hear. "My cousin. Rosalina."

Marco raised a brow. "I didn't know you had a cousin Rosalina."

"Oh, didn't you? I guess I never told you about her." José shrugged as if it was neither here nor there. "Well, yeah, I have a cousin Rosalina, who happens to be completely unattached."

"José," Marco growled.

"What? Come on. This could work. Maybe you can hit it off and have yourself a date to take to the wedding. You know, as your plus-one. If you don't bring someone, and you're still wearing a face like you have been since you got the invitation, Lillian's gonna know you're harboring hard feelings. You don't want that."

Marco hated how right his friend was. He sighed and picked at the handle of his tool.

"Is she even from around here?" Marco couldn't believe he was considering the date.

"She lives here in Peoria. In fact, she lives with my parents."

"Why is she living with your parents?" Not that it mattered, but if Marco was going to do this, he figured it'd be good to know the woman's history.

"Well, mainly to help my mom with house chores with that bad back of hers. But also, Rosalina has her own up-and-coming dog-grooming business, and it helps her out with all those expenses not having to worry about cost of living too. Besides, Mom loves having her there. It's a win-win."

"Hmm." Marco rubbed his chin, the prickly stubble reminding him he'd fallen asleep as soon as he'd gotten home last night and, in turn, didn't get around to shaving. "You think she'd agree to meeting?"

"I can stop by tomorrow morning before work and ask." José used a sing-song like voice, which told Marco how pleased he was with the plan.

I can't believe I'm agreeing to this.

Yet, he couldn't let Lillian see how he was pining after her. Having a date at the wedding would be the best cover-up. He sure couldn't go with a big grin and expect to fool Lillian. Because, like José, she also knew how he grinned to hide any inner pain.

Would this Rosalina be distraction enough to put a true smile on his face though?

There is only one way to find out.

Marco gave a quick nod of his head before he could change his mind. "Okay. You can mention it to Rosalina."

José made a fist pump and then reached over to turn on the radio. With the Mexican music blaring, all conversation was brought to a halt and their work speed ramped up as they fell back into their normal day-to-day rhythm.

Chapter Two

While some people dreaded hump days, for Rosalina Torres they were usually a delight.

This Wednesday was no different. She smiled as she gave the Maltese a chin rub before sending the dog and his mom off. It'd been another successful dog party here at her The Pampered Poochie's Parlor.

She'd had around a dozen dogs romping and frolicking in the fenced-in back lawn of her establishment all afternoon, and she'd loved every minute of listening to their high-pitched yips and friendly growls, and watching their happy tail wags and exuberant zoomies around the yard.

The birthday party for little Gianna, the Maltese, had been a success in Rosalina's book. And by the big smile on the pretty pupper, she knew Gianna would agree.

With a final good bye to the last dog, a Silkie terrier, and his dad, Rosalina lifted her face to the sun one final time before turning around and re-entering her dog salon. The interior's painted tan walls and ivory floors with brown paw prints with yellow and turquoise bows served to lift her mood even more. It'd been a good day.

A satisfied sigh escaped her as she made her way through the building, turning off all the lights. It was time to close up shop and go home to a quick supper before beginning her evening job: walking other people's dogs. She needed every possible source of extra income she was capable of, and so Rosalina spent a lot of time dog sitting, dog walking, and babysitting. To be honest, she preferred the work with dogs over the babies. At least dogs didn't cry, or talk back like an unruly toddler.

A yip sounded, followed by the *click, click, click* of little toenails on the industrial tile floor. Rosalina spun around and dropped to her knees. "Well, hello, Queenie. Hi, darling." She proceeded to give her bichon frisé a chin rub. "You had fun during the party today too, didn't you?"

The smile on Queenie's fluffy white face was the undeniable answer. "Ah, come here." She scooped the dog up and buried her nose in the soft white hair. "I love you, doll."

Queenie showed affection by a long swipe of her wet, pink tongue across Rosalina's cheek, ending at the corner of her lips. Rosalina chuckled, set the dog back down, and wiped at the wetness with the back of her hand. "Ready to go home?"

One high-pitched, happy bark was the affirmative answer in dog talk. Queenie's nails took on a prancing beat as she did circles around Rosalina's forward march to the back room where all the dog toys were kept for the Wednesday—and weekend, by special appointment only—parties.

Her only other employee, Haven Denver, was back there putting away all the toys that had been pulled out today.

"Thank you for picking up, Haven." Rosalina helped organize the few remaining items scattered at her employee's feet.

"Of course. And what a party! I think those were some of the happiest dogs we've had in a while."

"I agree." Rosalina couldn't have held back her delighted grin even if she wanted to.

After the last pop-up tunnel and beach ball had been put in their rightful places, Rosalina settled her hands loosely on her hips. "I'll lock up, so you're free to go."

"You sure?" Haven angled her head to the side and ran a hand down the length of her light brown ponytail.

"Absolutely."

"Well, see you tomorrow. Have a great night." Haven grabbed her purse and was off.

Rosalina finished turning off the lights and set the alarm system. With a tap on her leg and a double kissing sound from her lips, Queenie came bounding down the hall and jumped into Rosalina's waiting cupped hand. She scooped the dog up and held her between arm and body.

"Let's go home, girl. I think we both earned our supper tonight."

Rosalina's good mood for the day evaporated like a single drop of moisture on the July-hot black asphalt of her parking lot when she retrieved the mail from the receptacle beside the front door.

The address on the top envelope took her breath away. Her landlord. She knew whatever the contents were wouldn't bode well for her. She was behind on last month's payment, and from her recent interactions with Mr. Truman Scott she doubted he would extend her much mercy.

"Am I going to lose my business?"

She cleared away the lump of emotion in her throat, but it did nothing for the frustrated tears of possible failure burning her eyes. Queenie licked at the salty droplets and then squirmed to get down. Rosalina didn't have the leash, however, so refused to give in to the dog's desire. She couldn't risk Queenie darting into the busy traffic and getting run over.

With heavy steps, she crossed the lot to her car. Queenie took full possession of the passenger seat, sitting in a regal stance fit for any queen of England, while Rosalina slumped in the driver seat until her forehead touched the steering wheel.

Save my business, Jesus.

With a tight chest, she added audibly: "If it be Your will."

Chapter Three

Rosalina woke the next morning with a tear trailing across her cheek. The sun wasn't yet above the horizon and the sky was that whimsical shade of blue between night and morning light. On occasion she would wake up this early and find beauty in the stillness of sunrise, but not today.

She rubbed the sleep and tears from her eyes, and her gaze landed upon the picture of her parents on her nightstand. A sob caught in her throat. Sometimes the ache to be held in her *ma-má's* strong arms was so deep it made Rosalina want to pack up her meager belongings and return to Mexico, where she could once more surround herself with the love and support of her *pa-pá* and *ma-má*.

Not that she didn't have love and support from her *Tía* Carmen and *Tío* Juan, who she'd been living with since coming to the United States post graduation from high school, but it wasn't the same. If asked, she wouldn't hesitate for one second to admit she was homesick.

Yes, she appreciated the opportunity she'd been granted to attend college and pursue her dreams. No, she didn't take her parents' monetary sacrifice for granted. But she wished with all her heart she could bring *Ma-má* and *Pa-pá* to America too. But they had to care for *Abuela*, and the old woman was staunchly against leaving her native land.

Rosalina couldn't fault her. Mexico was the only home *Abuela* had known for eighty-seven years. Not that she was hasting the woman's death, but, perhaps, at *Abuela's* passing, Rosalina could somehow find a way to talk her parents into moving to the States as well.

With a pitiful sigh that came straight from her sorrowful spirit this morning, Rosalina tossed the bedcovers aside and moved to a sitting position on the edge of her bed. Pining would accomplish nothing. Right now she needed to get ready to go into work, and be brainstorming ways to come up with the money she owed Mr. Scott—before he could kick her out of her building.

She wasn't sure how far behind she had to be in payments for that to happen. Didn't want to think about it. She had enough on her plate figuring out how to make up what she owed, on top of the next bill coming due in a matter of weeks. If only she wouldn't have had the unplanned expense last month of having to buy a new car when the transmission had gone out in her old beater Buick.

"Maybe I never should have pursued this career."

It hadn't been her original dream. She'd initially enrolled in college for a degree in elementary education, but early into her first semester the college had brought in some therapy dogs. Rosalina couldn't recall why they had, or how she'd ended up going into that room where the dogs had been, but it'd been a life changing experience. The sweet eyes of the golden retriever she'd petted had melted her heart, and the gentle way the dog leaned into Rosalina's hand and allowed her to hug it had worked as a balm to her hurting, homesick heart.

She knew right then that there was something extra special about dogs and the bond that could be made between a man and his canine. She'd taken up several more babysitting jobs then to be able to save up for a dog of her own. It'd taken months, what with having to pay her way through college too, but she'd succeeded, and Queenie was the result of all her hard work and late hours studying.

She'd also immediately switched her major to business, and here she was two years post college graduation and The Pampered Poochie's Parlor was the result of all her hard work. It truly was a dream getting to work with dogs all day every day.

But, apparently, she wasn't much of a businesswoman. Why did everything have to cost so much? She didn't even have a house payment, and yet Rosalina still couldn't make ends meet.

"What an irresponsible adult you are," Rosalina spat at herself in the mirror.

"Oh, Rosalina!" It was *Tía* Carmen.

"¿*Sí*?"

Rosalina's bedroom door opened and her *tía* appeared. "José is here to see you."

"José? Right now? The sun isn't even up. I'm not dressed."

"He says it is an urgent matter."

Rosalina huffed and looked down at her dog print pajama pants and oversized T-shirt that was borderline fit for the trash. She supposed since José was her cousin it didn't matter whether she was presentable, so long as she was covered.

And knowing José, he would be in a state of anxiety until he was on his way for work, so she shouldn't keep him waiting.

Running a hand through her sleep-tangled hair, she hastened down the hall to the living room, where José was standing right inside the front door in his standard uniform of denim pants and olive green shirt sporting white block letters that read *Torres Quality Roofing*. *Tío* Juan owned the business, and, naturally, José found his place in the company.

"What's so important you had to come bursting in here this early? Don't you know decent folks rise with the sun."

José gave her an ornery smile. "Maybe for those people who lean toward the side of lazy and don't begin work until ten o'clock."

"I start at nine-thirty, thank you very much." Rosalina plopped fists on her hips. "Now, what's this *urgent matter*?"

"Um," José darted his eyes to the red corduroy couch. "I think it'd be easier to bring it up if we were sitting."

"So, let's sit." Rosalina walked over to the couch and plopped, then turned an expectant look to her cousin.

He came more hesitantly and sat at an angle so he faced her easily, but he remained silent.

"Well?" She urged him on with a duck of her head. Whatever it was José had come to discuss with her, it sure seemed to make him uneasy. She'd never seen him so uncomfortable.

"Uh, well." He rubbed his chin. "Can I ask you a favor?"

"A favor?" Rosalina arched a brow and locked her arms over her chest. "What kind of favor?"

"Would you come with me and Regina to dinner Friday night?"

Rosalina wrinkled her forehead. "Why would that be a favor?"

"Um, well..." He rubbed his nose in that way of his that told Rosalina he was second guessing whatever hare-brained plan he'd come up with. "You see, I want you to come as a 'so-called' blind date."

"You want me to what?" Rosalina shook her head, not sure if she'd heard correctly. A blind date? Surely not.

"Please, Rosa. Just one date."

So she had heard right, and, apparently, José thought he'd try a little honey using his "sweet" nickname for her, because he knew she wasn't dating right now. She reminded him of the fact every time he dropped a line about how nice it would be to be able to double date and proceeded to name off a friend she could meet.

Well, her status had not changed. "No. I don't have time for a relationship. I'm trying to grow my business."

Normally, he abandoned the subject here, but for some reason José was being persistent. "It doesn't have to be anything serious. I only want you to meet him."

"Who is this guy?" As the words left her mouth, Rosalina wished she could unsay them. She wasn't seriously considering it, was she? After all, Friday night dinner...she could very easily get a last minute call for a babysitting job, which would bring in much-needed extra cash.

"A friend and coworker." José's words pulled her from her thoughts. "He's a great guy. I can vouch for his character."

Well, that was good to know at least. "What's his name?" Not that it played into her decision at all. But still, she might as well know a little about the guy she *might* be going on a date with Friday night.

"Marco. Marco Mendez."

"Mmm." The sound was all she could manage as she weighed her options.

"Well, what do you say?" José leaned forward, his anticipation palpable.

Rosalina shook her head. "I might have to babysit."

José shook his head, disbelief written across his face. "You'd rather spend your evening babysitting than share a meal with me,

Regina—whom I know you happen to love like a sister—and get to know a guy I think you will find to be likable?"

"I have bills to pay."

"You know what they say about all work and no play..." Her cousin leveled an irritatingly smug look at her.

She huffed. "But even God worked six days out of the week and rested on the seventh. I rest on Sunday."

"So you won't consider it?" Now he was starting to look upset. Annoyed.

She crossed her arms over her chest and met her cousin's hard gaze with a concrete one of her own. She was just as stubborn. The Torreses were known for their bone-deep stubbornness and Rosalina was determined to out-stubborn José.

"You don't have an ulterior motive in inviting me, do you?" She had a feeling there was some fine print she couldn't read.

José raised his arms in surrender. "No! No way."

Rosalina scrutinized him. Thought she detected a slight squirm. Was he lying?

She readied to open her mouth and say no, and yet she thought about the benefit of going to a sit-down restaurant. It'd been a while since she had the opportunity. Against her better judgment, she felt her stubbornness slipping and she let out a sigh. "Fine. I will go, but you're going to owe me."

"Tell you what, how about I pay what you'd charge for an evening of babysitting?"

What? Rosalina was stunned. "You'd do that?"

"I'm offering, aren't I? It's the least I can do."

She studied him another moment. He stared at her with a firm expression. *My, but he is serious.*

She supposed she could suffer through a meal—which she was certain would be delicious—with her cousin, Regina, and a stranger...and get paid to do it. "I will come with you."

"*Gracias*, Rosa. You won't regret it. I promise."

She waved a hand. "Be off with you. I know how you get work anxiety. I don't want you to run late."

José grinned and then it sounded like a stampede of half a dozen full-grown St. Bernard's as his heavy work boots clomped on the hard floor and out the door.

That cousin of hers would do well to learn another speed besides *hurry.*

Her stomach grumbled then and Rosalina returned to her room to change into an outfit for the day and pass a brush through her waist length black hair. Queenie was just now stretching and waking up in her fluffy pink princess bed in the corner.

"Well, good morning, doll. Did you sleep well?"

Queenie yawned large, revealing her small tongue.

"Are you hungry?"

That got the dog out of bed in a flash. Queenie danced at Rosalina's feet and let out an adorable whimper of anticipation. Rosalina measured out kibble and dumped it in the monogrammed stainless steel dish.

"Eat up, princess." She ran a hand down the dog's back before proceeding to the kitchen for some nourishment of her own. She knew she would only have time to pray and down a swallow or two of her morning coffee before Queenie would be done with her food and demand to go out and take care of business, but at least she'd be one step closer to feeding her own ravenous stomach.

Tía Carmen was already setting Rosalina's plate of scrambled eggs and hash browns on the table when she entered the room.

She sniffed deeply. "Ah, it smells so good. *Gracias* for always making me such a fine breakfast. You know you don't have to."

"Ack, I enjoy spoiling you. You know I never had a daughter, so having you here has made it feel as if I do have one."

Rosalina hoped her gratitude showed in her eyes. No sooner had she lowered into her chair than Queenie came barreling down the hall, skidding past Rosalina and not stopping until her little black nose bumped into the sliding glass door that led out to the patio and back yard.

"Wow, I guess it's an emergency this morning." Rosalina slid the door open and the dog ran out and squatted almost immediately, making Rosalina laugh.

Tía Carmen *tsked.* "You do realize you spoil that dog of yours, don't you?"

Rosalina shrugged one shoulder. "She's my baby."

Tía Carmen brought up a wooden spoon out of the dish water and shook it at Rosalina, soap suds and all. "You best be careful what you get attached to, child. Must I keep reminding you?"

Rosalina turned away lest her *tía* see her deep frown. *Tía* Carmen didn't understand the bond between a man and a dog. In fact, her *tía* didn't believe in pets at all—saying they were an unnecessary expense and a dangerous attachment for the heart because they loved so unconditionally and lived such short lives.

Rosalina understood that, and knew one day there would be a very painful goodbye—although she prayed Jesus would return before then. But she didn't have to think about that right now. For the present, she would love her dog and they would make all the happy memories together they could. She believed God blessed mankind with animals—dogs especially.

In the time between breakfast and heading in to work, Rosalina pulled out her check book and signed into her online banking to see where she stood financially, so she could have an idea of what she could propose when she called her landlord.

The numbers didn't look promising and the morning's eggs and hash browns settled like a ton of goop in her middle. But, Rosalina Veronica Torres wasn't one to give up. She would fight for her business tooth and nail. She'd worked too hard to lose everything.

Chapter Four

The evening of the dinner date arrived much too quickly, and with it came a passel of angry pit bulls in the middle of Rosalina's stomach.

Despite her nerves and strong desire to send José a text and tell him she wasn't coming, she pulled on a maroon summer dress with a smocked top and puffy sleeves, sprayed on some cotton-scented body mist, and approved of her appearance in the mirror with a nod.

"Time to meet Marco."

She smoothed her hands over the middle of her dress, willing the dogs inside to quit their fighting.

Because, seriously, what could possibly be nerve-wracking about going on a double date with her cousin and his fiancée to meet a nice young man of good character—according to José?

She knew why.

She was afraid Marco wouldn't like her.

Not that it mattered—because she had no expectations of anything coming from this date. Didn't want anything to come of it. But, still, there was the delicate female part of her that wanted to be accepted. Rejection hurt, and she was plenty familiar with the feeling.

"Supper is on the table, Rosalina." *Tía* Carmen stepped into her room and then let out an approving "Oh!" as her eyes passed over Rosalina's outfit. "I don't suppose you got all prettied up to eat with your *tío* and I, did you?"

"No. I'm sorry, *Tía*. I forgot to tell you I had plans for supper tonight."

"Ack, no need to apologize. It does my heart good to see you going out and enjoying yourself."

Rosalina wanted to say she likely wouldn't be enjoying herself, but she reproached herself for the thought. That was not the kind of mindset to have when headed to a date. Instead she asked, "Is there anything you need me to stop and pick up on my way home tonight?"

"Oh, no. I'll be going grocery shopping tomorrow. You go and have yourself a good time without a single worry."

If only...

Rosalina hadn't told her *tía* and *tío* about her situation with the rent and Truman Scott. Maybe she should, but she didn't want them thinking they had to help her financially when they were already doing so much for her.

Tía Carmen pressed a gentle hand to Rosalina's cheek then. She held her breath, praying her *tía* couldn't see the trouble in her eyes. But then *Tía* gave her a sweet smile and slowly left the bedroom.

With a sigh, Rosalina grabbed her purse and keys, said goodbye to Queenie, and headed out to her car—fighting herself the whole way. Because she wanted nothing more than to be walking the opposite direction. To the supper table with her *tía* and *tío*.

At least then she wouldn't have to fear being rejected by a man.

◻◻◻

"Where is he?" Rosalina leaned over the table to hiss at José.

José spread his arms wide as he lifted his shoulders. "I don't know. I told him to be here at six."

Rosalina huffed. Figures her first time trying dating again since starting up her business and her date would be late. She dipped a corn chip in the salsa bowl and bit off a bite with a satisfying crack and chewed forcefully. "I never should have agreed to this."

"Come on. Give him a minute. Something must have come up. He'll be here. There was probably an accident or something. Besides, it's only been fifteen minutes."

Okay, so maybe Rosalina was being a little impatient. But it had felt like far more than fifteen measly minutes had passed. Perhaps it was because of the angry pit bulls still fighting in her stomach mixed with the weight of Mr. Scott's recent letter. How she wished she would have waited until after tonight to open it. The amount he'd listed as what she owed was far more than what Rosalina had calculated.

Strange, that.

She shook away the dismal thoughts and focused on the other present problem. "Well, wouldn't he have let you know if he was running late?" Rosalina took another dramatic bite out of the large corn chip and took a moment to dwell on the flavor of the salsa.

The explosion of taste from the spices, peppers, and tomatoes gave her a momentary reprieve from her ill inner feelings. Although, what would really help would be her favorite snack: pita chips and guacamole. Now *there* was comfort food. Or even a package of Oreos.

"I—well, yeah, I think Marco would. But my phone hasn't gone off."

"Well, check." Rosalina reached for José's phone, which was sitting in the middle of the table, but her cousin snatched it up before her fingers could graze the dark green case.

"I will check." He gave her a steely look and Rosalina watched as he swiped the screen open. "Oh."

"What?" She leaned over the table again and stretched her neck to try and get a look over the phone and see what was on the screen.

"He did send. I never heard it go off. There *was* an accident at a stoplight and he's held up." A few taps of José's fingers on the phone screen. "Oh, then he sent again and said things were clearing up and traffic was starting to be allowed to pass through." José darkened the screen. "He should be here any minute."

Rosalina let out a relieved breath, but the minute it was expressed her chest tightened up as anxiety filled her.

What if he took one look at her and thought her ugly? She certainly didn't consider herself a beauty. She was short and...and most people thought her much younger than her age.

And what if Marco wasn't friendly? Just because he was José's friend didn't mean he would be nice.

What if they couldn't converse? It could be the longest dinner date Rosalina had ever been on—not that she had a lot to compare today with. She'd never been the popular girl by any stretch of the imagination. She'd practically had to beg Carlos Diaz to take her to her senior prom. Even though that had been six years ago, it still stung at Rosalina's dignity.

As her mind began to formulate more questions and she took a sip of her bottled Coke, the Mexican restaurant's door opened, and in walked a man Rosalina could only reason was Marco.

She choked on her Coke and the carbonation burned her nose and made her eyes water. She coughed to dislodge the discomfort in her chest, and by that point the newly arrived man stepped up to the table.

"Sorry I'm late," he said, his eyes having an almost frantic look like he must have ran across the parking lot.

"Not a problem." José stood and clapped Marco on the back. "Marco, this is Rosalina, my cousin." José swept his hand toward her. "Rosalina, Marco Mendez."

Marco came around to stand behind the empty chair next to her and held out a hand. "Nice to meet you, Rosalina."

Rosalina started to extend her hand, but when she opened her mouth to speak, a mighty cough erupted and a rush of burning liquid traveled through her nasal cavities and she knew she was in trouble.

She had to act fast or her date was going to see Coke come dripping out her nose. It wasn't the first time something like this had happened to her, although last time it had been when she'd choked on Jell-O at something funny José had said during supper when they'd had the pastor of their church and his family over.

She only hesitated a second as she considered which scenario would be the most humiliating, and decided dashing from the table for the ladies room would be the least embarrassing. And that's precisely what she did.

Leaving Marco, and his hand, waiting.

Chapter Five

Am I really so repulsive? was all Marco could think with Rosalina's hasty retreat.

He turned to José with what he figured must be a confused and wounded expression, because that's precisely how he felt. "Did I do something wrong?"

José looked baffled. "Not that I know of. It was a simple introduction."

If Rosalina couldn't survive a simple introduction, Marco doubted she could be the woman to come as his plus-one to Lillian's wedding.

José laid a hand on Regina's arm. "What do you think, sweetheart? Did Marco do something wrong?"

Regina shook her head. "No, not at all. I'll go check on her. I think she may have been choking."

"Choking!" Marco's eyes shot back in the direction Rosalina had fled. "Then you'd better hurry. If she ran off to the restroom, being alone in there and choking is the last place she should be."

Regina didn't waste another minute in pushing up from the table and hurrying toward the restrooms. Marco's eyes followed her departure, until he dropped his focus to his still outstretched hand.

So he was apparently repulsive enough to make a woman choke at first sight. Not at all reassuring.

What did I get myself into?

Marco dropped into his chair and stared at José. "Am I ugly or something?"

José choked on a laugh and roamed his gaze over Marco's face. "No, I don't think so. But I'm a man." He winked.

Marco sent him a glare. "You aren't helping things here."

A waitress breezed up to the table and Marco placed his drink order. José told the woman they weren't ready to order yet—the courteous thing to do, of course, since the ladies hadn't returned yet. Marco could have ordered right now, though, without even looking at the menu. This was one of his favorite restaurants and they had the best tacos. Even if he couldn't enjoy the date, the food would be worthwhile.

Minutes passed and Marco checked his watch. "You suppose they are okay?"

José shrugged.

He frowned and looked at the empty seat beside him. What if Rosalina had sneaked out the door and wouldn't be returning to the table at all? The thought stung.

Surely not.

After all, Regina hadn't come back yet, so they had to be together.

Before he could have any more doubts, Regina and Rosalina returned. Regina wore a pleasant smile, while Rosalina's eyes and nose were red and puffy.

Has she been crying?

Marco formed his lips into a smile and stood at the women's return. He offered his hand again. "Nice to meet you, Rosalina."

This time her feminine hand came to rest in his, and he gave it a gentle squeeze.

"Likewise, Marco." Her voice sounded hoarse.

Marco longed to ask her if everything was okay, but he bit his cheek against the question.

Everyone sat and the waitress returned to take their orders. At her departure, José and Regina seemed to think they were in their own little world as they increasingly leaned closer to each other until their noses were almost touching, their whispered conversation only for the two of them.

After their food arrived and Marco had tasted of it, he pulled at the collar of his orange button-up. He needed to find something to say to get Rosalina talking or this was going to be a miserable evening. But it was hard to feel confident in himself when one look at him had made Rosalina choke.

He cleared his throat and set his taco down before he could take another bite—which was the only thing that sounded desirable right now. "So, Rosalina, José tells me you own your own business..."

Rosalina's blotchy face turned to meet his. "I do. The Pampered Poochie's Parlor."

"Clever name." Marco started to pick his taco back up.

"And you work with José." It wasn't a question.

Marco nodded. "Been roofing ever since I got out of high school."

"Did you know *I* would be here tonight?"

He froze, not at all expecting that question. "I did."

"Hmm." She narrowed her gaze, looked at José a moment, then turned back to him. "I knew you were going to be here."

"Okay." He shrugged.

"Doesn't a blind date mean you don't know who you're going to be meeting?" She raised one of her dark eyebrows.

Marco felt the air between them grow tense as he took a bite from his food, not at all sure how to answer that one.

"What's the purpose in tonight?" Rosalina's eyes pierced him, telling him he didn't dare skirt the issue. She wanted answers.

Oh boy. She's a sassy one.

Figured.

"José wanted us to meet."

"Why?" Her eyes held his, gaze unmoving. Stern.

"I guess he thought we might hit it off." Clearly, José thought wrong. If Marco's first impression of today was any indication.

"My cousin knows I don't have time for a relationship. I honestly have no idea why he would have set this up. I don't even know why I agreed."

Marco bit down on his back molars. This was not going well. He cleared his throat. "Can't you simply enjoy a good meal with family and friends?"

"I can. Although, whether we're friends or not is yet to be determined." She narrowed her eyes.

"Maybe we should change the subject. Do you have any summer plans?"

Rosalina crossed her arms over her chest and twisted to face him, resting one elbow on the table. "I still think you and José are hiding something from me, and I want to know what it is."

There wasn't a single doubt in Marco's mind that Rosalina wouldn't like what he'd had planned to ask her tonight. She'd made it clear she wanted nothing to do with a relationship. But a fake one?

He took a fortifying drink of his lemon water, deciding he'd go ahead and lay everything before her. "I...well...you see— Actually..."

"Why, Marco! I never would have imagined we'd run into you here tonight."

It's a good thing Marco didn't have anything in his mouth or he'd be choking same as Rosalina had at the beginning of this evening.

He knew that voice as well as he did his own mom's. With a gulp, he twisted in his chair to look up at Macy Harrison, Lillian's mother. Lillian's father, Evan, was there too.

Could he shrink himself and crawl inside his taco and hide among the crumbly ingredients?

"Hello, Mrs. Harrison. Mr. Harrison."

Mrs. Harrison, never one to miss a thing, roamed her eyes over the table. She did a double-take when that all-noticing gaze landed on Rosalina. The older woman's face brightened. "Marco Mendez, I knew you'd find yourself a girl."

"Oh. Oh...uh." Marco couldn't get anything intelligible to pass his lips. Of all people who he could run into tonight, it had to be Lillian's parents. What was he going to do now?

He looked to José for help, but his eyes were large, expression blank—telling Marco he would be of no help.

I never should have agreed to this.

"Actually, Mrs—"

"Who is this lovely girl?"

Marco longed to cover his face and hide with the way Rosalina was drilling him with her eyes—eyes he was quickly learning were downright scary. "This is Rosalina Torres, José's cousin. You've probably heard me talk about José, my coworker. And that's his fiancée, Regina." Might as well introduce everyone so Rosalina wasn't singled out. Maybe he could distract Mrs. Harrison in doing so.

"How nice. A double date."

"Honey, we'd better get a table. The place is filling up quickly tonight." Mr. Harrison tugged on his wife's sleeve.

"You go save us one, dear. I want to hear how Marco and Rosalina met."

"Yes, Macy."

Marco wished he could call after Mr. Harrison as the man left and tell him to drag his wife away if necessary. Anything to stop this conversation he didn't want to be having.

To Marco's further discomfort, Mrs. Harrison pulled up an empty chair to the table next to Marco. "Now, how'd you two meet?"

"Uh," Marco shot his gaze between José and Rosalina. Neither of them offered up a word.

I think it's time for me to get new friends.

Marco decided the truth would work fine. "We met right here in this restaurant."

"Did you?"

At the light in Mrs. Harrison's eyes with that, Marco let his mouth run faster than his brain. "Yeah. In fact, it was right here at this table." He nodded at Rosalina, hoping she'd get the clue and play along.

Her lips were pursed, face hard. Not at all looking friendly—let alone like a girlfriend.

Nope, she wouldn't be any help either.

"Is that so? How romantic?" Mrs. Harrison pressed a hand to her bosom. "How long have you known each other?"

"Oh, um…" He never had been good making things up on the fly, but he needed something clever or else Mrs. Harrison would realize that Rosalina really wasn't his girl. And he couldn't have that.

Honestly, the timing was perfect, because now it wouldn't seem strange at all when Marco showed up at Lillian's wedding with Rosalina. "You know, I can't remember exactly when. Sometimes it seems as though we just met, and other times as if we've known each other our whole lives."

Oh, brother.

This was getting out of hand fast.

José's eyes bugged and he quickly hid his face in his shoulder.

Mrs. Harrison, on the other hand, feasted her gaze on Rosalina now. And Marco could only reason she wondered why Rosalina, the woman in this relationship, wasn't sharing all those silly details that girls seemed to never forget.

Marco, realizing this needed to look as authentic as possible with the story he was telling, reached over and rested his hand atop Rosalina's. He felt her stiffen beneath his touch. "Isn't that right, Lina?"

Lina? Where did that come from?

Something like Rosa or Rosie would have made far better sense.

Rosalina pulled off the fakest smile Marco had ever seen, but she surprised him when she laid her other hand on top of his.

Okay. Never mind. Not surprised. For she dug her fingernails into his skin as she answered. "That's right, Mars."

Mars?

Now that frosted him. Mar, sure. That made sense. But Mars?

Oh, they needed to have a talk after this meal...

Actually, scratch the meal. Marco didn't have an appetite any more. He didn't even care to get a to-go box for the food he'd been thinking about all day and had so far only managed to eat two bites of.

"Ah, I love it." Mrs. Harrison clasped her hands under her chin. "I can't wait to tell Lillian. Why, we were talking the other night how that now with Lillian finding Clint, we wondered how long it'd be until you found your true one."

My true one?

A cough lodged in Marco's throat.

This conversation couldn't get any more out of hand. And by the way Rosalina's nails dug further into him, Marco knew she was seething on the inside. He wasn't about to look at her again. That woman had a whole vocabulary with her eyes, and so far all the "definitions" were terrifying.

What more could Marco say that wouldn't get him deeper in trouble? How could he put a lid on this conversation and send Mrs. Harrison to join her husband?

He settled with, "Yeah, well, I guess you guys don't have to wonder anymore." Marco flicked his gaze to where he'd seen Mr. Harrison settle at a table. A waitress stood there now. "You know, I do believe they are ready to take your orders. You might want to join Mr. Harrison."

"Oh, dear." Mrs. Harrison gripped the seat of her chair and snapped her spine upright before covering her mouth with one hand. "I completely forgot. Yes, I should go. I've left my date to fend for himself. Now, you two enjoy the rest of your date. And I'm so happy for the two of you. Who knows, Marco, maybe you and Lillian will both get married this year?"

Beside Marco, Rosalina gasped loud enough he hoped with all his might Mrs. Harrison hadn't heard it too.

He pulled at his collar and laughed nervously. "Yeah, who knows?"

He wouldn't mind if he and Lillian got married in the same year. In fact, he'd've preferred it. The two of *them* getting married. Not Lillian to Clint Bishop. And the way Rosalina had been acting beside him, Marco doubted he had to worry about a wedding of his own this year. The possibility was laughable.

Being a bachelor for life wouldn't be the worst thing. Since he couldn't have Lillian.

Mrs. Harrison rose, laid a hand on Marco's shoulder, and bent to whisper in his ear. "To be honest, Lillian was worried about you—how you would take the news of the wedding. I have to say I agreed with her. I always thought you had a thing for Lillian. But, well," She peeked around Marco for a quick look at Rosalina. "I'm glad to see I was wrong. Everything is going to work out perfectly."

If this was perfect, then Marco decided that was the most warped word in the dictionary. He had no response for Lillian's mother, so did the only thing he could manage. Give her one of his cover-up smiles.

And with that, Mrs. Harrison ambled away to join her husband. Marco expelled a relieved breath.

Glad that's over.

Then he turned to Rosalina and any relief he felt disappeared when he saw her fiery eyes.

"We. Need. To. Talk." He didn't like the way she enunciated every word through her pinched lips.

Marco held his arms out, palms up. "Okay."

She eyed the two across from them at the table. "Alone."

Uh oh. Busted.

The only other person who could give Marco the impending feeling of doom he felt now was his own mom.

He was playing with fire.

By the name of Rosalina.

How did I let myself get into this mess?

Chapter Six

Rosalina whipped around to face Marco the minute she stepped onto the sidewalk outside the Mexican restaurant.

"What was *that* all about?" She locked her arms over her chest, drilling Marco with her sternest, most demanding gaze.

He scratched the inside of his ear. "About that..."

"Do tell." The gall of the man to talk to that woman as if Rosalina were his girl.

And to call her Lina? Well, that was a liberty she never would have given a friend—much less a stranger she'd only met a few minutes before.

Lina. Absolutely not.

Marco him-hawed on his feet.

"I'm waiting." She utilized the same tone she used when dealing with a disobedient child she was babysitting.

"Did José tell you why he set this date up tonight?" He asked.

Ah, of course. Answering a question with a question. The classic way to avoid confessing.

"To meet a friend. He thought I might enjoy myself. But so far this evening has not been enjoyable. Not in the least."

Marco grimaced. "That bad, eh?"

"Girlfriend? Lina? Feeling as if we've known each other all our lives? Oh, and let's not forget about that utterly romantic fact we met at this restaurant at the exact table we are sitting at tonight. Come on. What is this?" Her body was heating up, and it had nothing to do with the humidity of the summer evening.

Marco stared at the ground, and Rosalina took a moment to study him.

He wasn't at all how she'd imagined. For some reason she'd expected him to look like José, who was taller than her by a head, lanky, and almost still boyish looking because of it.

She couldn't have conjured up a more wrong image. By contrast, Marco Mendez was only a few inches taller than her four-foot-eleven frame, which was nice for a change. He was broad-shouldered and a bit stocky, but not so much that he appeared overweight. In fact, he was just right.

Just right?

What was she even thinking? She was mad at the man, so why on earth would she be appreciating his physique?

Speaking of *physique* he definitely looked like a roofer—what with his dark brown face and neck from all the sun exposure. His arms on the other hand were lighter, so she assumed he must wear long sleeves. José did the same, and Rosalina couldn't understand how a person could wear long sleeves in the middle of summer—not to mention on top of an oven-hot roof.

"Do you want the honest truth?" Marco finally asked.

His voice was deeper than José's too. Deep enough, Rosalina imagined she would hear him singing bass if they were in church together—unlike her cousin, who never witnessed a voice change with puberty.

What? Wait a minute. Why on earth couldn't she keep a rein on her thoughts. Singing in church together? Seriously?

Marco asked me something. Oh, right.

Well he took long enough in responding, Rosalina had to take a moment to remember what her question had been. She'd let her mind wander in too many directions, which should have been off limits, that she'd almost forgotten the question. But, *sí.* Now she recalled with perfect clarity. He was preparing to tell her what this evening was really all about.

She widened her stance and pointed a finger at him. "The honest truth. Or else I'll march in that restaurant right now and demand José for the answer."

"That's not necessary." Marco met her gaze and held it. Finally. For being on a so-called date, they hadn't done much true looking at each other. Only little moments of awkward acknowledgement...or, on Rosalina's part, to send warning messages. "You see, I need a plus-one to take to a wedding in a little over three weeks, so José thought you might be a good option, I guess."

I guess? Well, *that* built up a woman's confidence. *Humph.* Rosalina tried to piece together the conversation that had ensued inside the restaurant between—was her name Mrs. Harrison?—and Marco, and came to one conclusion. "Is this wedding by any chance for a girl by the name of Lillian?"

Marco ducked his head.

Ah, so she hit the nail on the head. She usually did.

"Yes. It's Lillian's wedding." He raised his head, but kept his face angled away from her, his face and neck muscles pulled taut.

"Why are you clenching your jaw?"

"I'm not." His comeback was far too hasty for innocence.

"You are."

Marco huffed and came a step closer. "Because, I've had a crush on Lillian since our junior year of high school and I thought I'd be the one marrying her. Instead, she's found the *love of her life* and is marrying him next month."

"Well! So you expect me to come along as *your plus-one* to a wedding for a woman you love? How incredulous!" Rosalina slammed her hands down on her hips and took a step closer to Marco.

"I don't want Lillian to know I still have feelings for her. The best way I can prove that is to have a date for the wedding."

"I can assure you, Marco Mendez, I will not be your date."

Marco worked his jaw and Rosalina could see the veins in his neck gradually start to bulge. She couldn't help but wonder how often a couple ended up in a shouting match on this sidewalk. They were probably the first. Er, well, scratch the "couple" part, because they decidedly were not *a couple.* But they had the shouting match part right. She only hoped there weren't any security cameras aimed at them.

"Look," Marco held his arms out in a gesture that looked a bit like an apology. Was he going to apologize? Rosalina doubted it. She knew enough about a man's ego that they liked to think they were never wrong—especially to a woman. "I'm sorry things got out of hand in there. I wanted it all to come about differently. I was going to ask you to come as my date for the upcoming wedding, but I wanted it to be your choice. But now—"

"Excuse me," Rosalina butted in. "I still have a choice, thank you very much. And I am not going."

"No, you see, you *have* to come. Now that Mrs. Harrison has seen us together and believed the romantic nonsense I spouted in there."

Romantic nonsense, indeed. "I don't have to do anything."

"Yes, you do. Mrs. Harrison thinks we're a couple. She's going to expect you to be on my arm the day of the wedding. She has probably already told her husband everything, and when she goes home tonight she is going to tell Lillian. If you don't come, they'll all know it was a lie and I'm going to be in worse trouble than I would have been had I gone to the joyous wedding by myself looking like a miserable man."

"Maybe you shouldn't go."

"I couldn't do that. It'd hurt Lillian's feelings. We've been the best of friends. She expects me to be there."

Rosalina raised a brow. If they'd been best of friends and Marco supposedly loved the girl, how did it come to be that Lillian was engaged to another man? It didn't add up to her. Maybe if she met Lillian and her fiancé things could be made clear. Perhaps, it could be worth going to the wedding as Marco's date so she could satiate her curiosity. But, still, the whole thing was absurd.

"So, I only have to go to one wedding with you?" She couldn't believe she heard her own voice ask the question.

Marco rubbed the inside of his ear in that uncomfortable way again and it made Rosalina roll her eyes. Was there some other technicality then? The man was exasperating and she'd only been in his company for less than an hour.

"Actually, don't you think it would be smart to spend a little time together before then? I mean, we should know each other better. That way when people ask us questions, we can have a plan of how to answer—rather than making things up."

"Like you did tonight, digging your own grave."

Marco's face hardened. "It doesn't have to be a grave if you'll play along."

"Humph." Rosalina turned her nose up and away.

"Well? Are you going to?"

"Going to what?" She wasn't going to make this easy on him.

Marco huffed. "You know perfectly well what. Play along. Be my fake date for three and a half weeks."

Fake date. Sounded horrible.

But, it could be fun—in a warped sort of way—and she wouldn't have to worry about anything serious coming of it. Because, as Marco said, they would be fake dating. She might not have time for a real relationship, but a fake one surely wouldn't require much time and effort. But, still, she didn't want to give in too easily. After all, look at what he'd put her through inside the restaurant during that conversation with his crush's mother. "I don't know. Three and a half weeks in your presence."

Marco threw his arms up. "So I am repulsive?"

"What?" Rosalina lost some of her sass. "What are you talking about?"

"Your hasty flight to the—*ahem*—restroom upon my arrival this evening."

Confusion clouded Rosalina's mind for but a moment before realization dawned. "Oh, you mean... Oh my." She threw her hand over her mouth and laughed.

"I don't think it's funny. I *didn't* think it was funny then, and I still don't."

Rosalina shook her head. "No, no."

"No, what?" For as silly as the man's smile was, he sure could have a hard face at times. Hard enough to make Rosalina consider cowering and growing serious.

"I was choking. True and simple. It had nothing to do with you being, uh, how did you put it? Repulsive?" Far from it. If Marco Mendez was anyone other than the man who pretended she was his girl tonight, *and* if she wasn't currently in a no-relationship time of life, she would find herself easily attracted to him. After all, he had a nice physique.

She cleared her throat to get her thoughts back on track. "I swallowed wrong because I was caught off guard by your arrival. My Coca-Cola was about to come squirting out my nose, and that is not the first impression I wanted to make." Oh, but shouting at him on their "first date" was so much better.

Great job, Rosa.

She mentally rolled her eyes.

"Oh, I...see."

The way he appeared to be fighting a laugh led Rosalina to believe he was surprised she was *so* honest with him. That had her wondering... Would most women not disclose so much information? Perhaps, she should work on her TMI content in the future. Well, at least for the next three and a half weeks.

Ugh, it was going to be difficult. She'd never really dated before. Wasn't sure what a man expected of his girlfriend.

Girlfriend?

Oh, dear. The reality of it all crashed over her as if she'd been mauled by a Great Dane. She had to pretend to be *his girl* for almost an entire month.

I know I'm going to make a fool of myself.

"Well, now that we have that cleared," Marco's deep voice pulled the imaginary dog off her and she sucked in a breath. "I guess it's all settled."

"Settled? Are you forgetting I have yet to agree?"

"Like I said a few minutes ago, disagreeing isn't an option any longer. Not after my big mouth. So, this can be whatever you want it to be."

Whatever I want it to be? Was he serious? She had to clarify. "You mean, we can do this fake dating thing at my regulation?"

"Seeing as how I have pulled you into this against your will, don't you think it only right you get to make the rules and boundaries of this, um, relationship."

Rosalina shivered at the word "relationship," but felt a slight softening at his thoughtfulness to let her make the rules. Hey, what girl wouldn't run with that? Every woman loved to make the rules. "Then, *sí*, I will *play* along." She was surprised by how easy the words came out.

Marco's smile stretched from one end to the other of his round, bubbly face. "Thank you."

"Promise me one thing?"

"If I can."

"Don't make up such silly romantic stuff again."

Marco choked on a self-deprecating cough. "I think that would be wise. If I'm not careful, I could have us getting married next."

Rosalina gasped, horrified at the thought. "That *cannot* happen!" This could *not* end up in marriage. Why, the very thought was preposterous. She had her business, and bills to figure out how to pay. The last thing she needed was a wedding she couldn't afford.

Marco held his arms out straight in front of him, palms facing her. "You have nothing to worry about."

Well, that was a relief.

Maybe.

It hit on her womanly confidence again.

And made her wonder why he wanted to proceed with this fake dating thing if he wanted nothing to do with her.

She sighed inwardly. The only times she'd been escorted by a guy for anything, she'd had to ask them. Why was she so unwanted? Was she unsightly? Comely? Or perhaps it was her mouth. She had a tendency to say exactly what she was thinking, no matter how it might be taken.

Hmm. Maybe she could use this as a learning experience so when she was ready for a real relationship with someone other than Marco—because he clearly didn't want her—she would know how to be the kind of woman a man did want.

Chapter Seven

"She is nothing like Lillian." Marco rubbed at his ear in frustration.

It wasn't fair to compare Rosalina to Lillian, but that's what Marco found himself doing while sitting in his truck the next morning outside his parents' house.

Now, there were some similarities between the two women. Like the fiery eyes. Oh, Lillian could be feisty. But they had always gotten along. And they certainly had never engaged in a shouting match outside of a public place.

Lillian and him, they were like—had been like—two peas in a pod. He could recall their easy banter while eating lunch together their junior and senior years of high school. He couldn't forget their evenings out to the bowling alley, where they had competitive games along with Marco's older sister and her husband, as well as his younger brother.

He longed to repeat the simple front porch conversations they shared at Lillian's little house...up until her accident and engagement to Clint Bishop immediately thereafter.

Marco sighed with regret. He'd always heard how memories were supposed to be precious. But for him, he considered good memories to be a curse. At least, in this case. Every moment shared with Lillian Harrison that he relived in his mind only reminded him he'd waited too long.

He would forever regret that, he was sure. No one would ever take Lillian's special place in his heart.

"God, take the ache away. If necessary, take the memories away too. Maybe I could get selective amnesia or something?"

What kind of prayer is that?

Marco gave his head a hard shake. "Maybe forget I made that last request, God. But I don't want to be pining after...another man's woman." My, but those words were hard to force from his lips. "Help me."

He had a feeling that would be his most common prayer over the next who knew how long. *Help me.*

With a deep grumble, Marco pulled the keys out of the ignition of his Dodge Dakota and then proceeded to load his arms up with his belongings to carry into his parents' home.

Now that stunk. For almost six years now he'd been living with José and another guy, but now that José was going to be getting married soon, he was kicking Marco and Julio out. How nice to not only lose a bachelor friend to marriage, but also lose your housing.

Marco supposed he shouldn't complain. It wouldn't be for long. He already had a contingent offer in on a nice house in a great part of town. He just needed to pray that the sellers found a place within ninety days.

But, he supposed there were worse things than moving back in with your parents at twenty-four years of age. He couldn't presently think of anything worse, though, for he knew he was going to suffer a lot of grief from his mom about his still single status.

"Ah-hah! Rosalina." He grabbed his suitcases and bags from the back seat of the truck, closed the door with his backside, and did a little victory hop. At least for a little while he could keep his mom's nagging at bay. He wondered how long he could make this temporary fake dating with Rosalina seem real.

He knew it wouldn't work forever, but if he could lead Mom on long enough for his contingent offer to be accepted, that would be fantastic.

Speaking of Rosalina, Marco made a mental note to send her a text later. Somehow, he'd managed to get her phone number from her after they had gone back inside the restaurant to finish their meal. She'd given it begrudgingly, with an expression that seemed to dare Marco to even think about contacting her. Sorry, but weren't a dating couple supposed to have each others' numbers?

He wondered what it would take to get her to agree to some sort of "date" tomorrow. One that would involve eventually introducing Rosalina to his parents.

Marco shuddered to think what that would be like, as the scenario at supper last night with Lillian's mother resurfaced. He and Rosalina would have to figure out what story they were going to tell his mom so he could keep his promise to Rosalina about not making up any more silly romantic stuff.

They would have to keep their story similar to what he'd told Mrs. Harrison, though. Otherwise, Marco knew the two mothers would get to talking, realize a missing link, smell something fishy, and come wielding pointed fingers, sharp tongues, and demanding expressions. Not a sight Marco wanted to see in duplicate form coming after him—especially when it meant getting caught in a lie.

A lie...

Ouch.

No one could find out this was fake.

When the wedding was over, he'd just need to make sure enough time passed before he and Rosalina staged a "break-up." Hopefully, by then Marco would be moved into his own place and not have to suffer nightly interrogations about when he was going to settle down and give his mom some *nietos*—grandchildren.

"Never," was Marco's answer to that, but he couldn't say that out loud.

And it wasn't that he didn't like kids. In fact, he loved them. They were fun. He just doubted he'd ever be able to care for a woman like he had Lillian, enough to want to marry and have children with. And he would never marry for anything less than love.

So the big question was: could he fall in love again?

Then again, was what he'd felt for Lillian truly love? If it had been, wouldn't it have come naturally to tell her?

That was a disturbing consideration.

Before he could think any more on it, the front door of his childhood home swung open and his mom filled the doorway. "Marco!"

Oh, boy. Here we go. He pulled off a smile. "Hey, Mom."

"Welcome home."

Marco frowned as he passed over the threshold. "You make it sound like I've been gone for a long time. I only lived five minutes away and visited often."

"I know, but I'll enjoy doting on you for however long you stay here." Then she leaned close. "Hopefully, the next time you move out will be because you found yourself a wife."

It hasn't been three minutes and she's bringing it up. Marco hid his face behind his load to roll his eyes. "You don't need to dote. I'm a grown man. And I already have an offer placed on a house."

"Nothing to say on the marriage front?" Mom cocked her head and raised a scrutinizing dark brow.

Marco only cleared his throat in response to that. Then he let out a moan. "You know, this load is getting heavy. Could we keep the questions until later?"

"Oh, yes. Come, come." She beckoned him to follow. "I set you up in Isabella's room. I didn't think you'd want to share a bedroom with your brother."

Marco barked a laugh. "Promise me the walls in Isabella's room aren't still that disgusting mauve."

"Don't go badmouthing the color. Mauve is a beautiful shade. But, no, Antonio and I painted the walls a neutral tan."

"Great. Thanks." He'd have to remember to thank his brother for helping with the painting later too. Marco happened to know Antonio had disliked the color as much as he did, so his brother had probably enjoyed painting over those unsightly walls.

"Now, I need to go work on lunch, but you let me know if you need anything." Mom gave his arm a squeeze before her ample figure bustled down the hallway in that way all church kitchen bosses seemed to move about. With authority. Brooking no argument.

Marco's mother was a force to be reckoned with. Another reason why he had to be sure she didn't catch onto this whole dating charade.

He groaned as he set his stuff down, but the sound came not because of the load but rather because of his frustration at getting himself into this mess in the first place.

"It's going to be a long three and a half weeks."

Chapter Eight

Sunday was supposed to be relaxing. A day for recharging to be able to start the next workweek refreshed. Rosalina did not feel any of those lovely "r" words this Lord's Day.

By contrast, she was anxious, worried, and a little mad.

Anxious because she had to meet with her landlord tomorrow during the lunch hour.

Worried for fear he would not be kind and understanding.

And mad at that conniving Marco Mendez.

Oh, just thinking about dinner the other night set her to fuming.

It didn't help, either, that right now she held her phone with a text from the man himself. It had come in as she was walking out of church. Thankfully, not any sooner, for she had forgotten to turn her sound off. *Ugh.*

She never should have given in and shared her phone number with Marco. Although...wasn't a dating couple supposed to call and text and do all the digital conversing? Not that she should care. In fact, she couldn't care less if this ruse was discovered. But...

But for some reason she had agreed and she still couldn't believe she had...yet here she was. Currently, trying to figure out what to respond to Marco's message. She read it for the dozenth time.

> **Marco:** Happy Sunday, Rosalina. Are you busy this afternoon? I thought it might be a good day to introduce you to my parents. I think it would be smart to not prolong it.

Now that was the wrong first request a fake boyfriend could make.

Meet his parents?

Rosalina would rather receive a facial from a St. Bernard.

With a sigh, she typed a message. Her fingers begrudgingly obeyed her brain's commands with every button touched:

> **Rosalina:** I suppose that would be fine. Church just got over, so I need to go home and let my dog out first. After that, yes.

Rosalina didn't expect a quick response. After all, this was fake. It wasn't like Marco was an overanxious boyfriend who couldn't wait to see her. Not that she knew what that was like. She'd never been the object of a man's romantic obsession. Most of the time she didn't mind. But she was female, and there were times her heart ached a tiny bit for a little tender affection and appreciation. For the present time, the only affection and appreciation she received was from a large number of the dog population in Peoria and some of the surrounding towns. And, well, she could include *Tía* Carmen too. But that was different. Nothing at all like *romance*. Or, what she assumed true romance would be like.

To her surprise, Rosalina's phone pinged before she could back out of her parking spot.

> **Marco:** Great. How about I meet you at your place??

Double questions marks. The man was uncertain? Nervous? It made Rosalina smile. They were going to have to be more persuasive in the audience of his parents if they had any chance of pulling off a believable relationship.

Rosalina: That works. I suppose you already know the address, since it's José's parents'??

She couldn't resist utilizing the same double question marks in return. If anything, this farce they were portraying was built upon assumptions.

Marco had assumed she'd be okay pretending to be his girlfriend.

Marco had assumed she would like being called Lina. And he'd better never call her that again, by the way.

Now Marco assumed she wanted to meet his parents. Okay, maybe "wanted" wasn't in the equation. Rather, this was something that had to be done. Any serious relationship had to eventually involve meeting the significant other's family, right?

Rosalina groaned. She'd signed up for way more than she'd thought. Why hadn't she considered what all this favor would entail?

Marco: Yep. I know the place. See you shortly. Then we'll make a plan.

Rosalina snorted. It was a little late for Marco to be making a plan. He should have created one long ago. Before he opened his mouth during their "dinner date." Boy, if José ever asked her to meet one of his friends again...

She didn't bother with a response to that text and wasting any more driving time. So with ponderings of what this afternoon would be like, Rosalina traveled the few miles to her *tía* and *tío's* home.

No one was home when she arrived, which was as expected. *Tía* Carmen and *Tío* Juan were spending the day with José and Regina going over last minute wedding preparations. But, Queenie was home, and that four legged white puff ball was the best welcome into a home a woman could ask for.

Rosalina scooped the dog up when it jumped at her legs.

"Hey, girlie. Are you happy to see, Mommy? *¿Sí?* You are? You are happy. Ah, *Ma-má* loves you, Queenie. You're the best dog in the whole world."

Queenie lavished Rosalina with multiple face licks, which she didn't mind in the least. She was at the point where dog saliva didn't faze her.

When Queenie squirmed, she set the dog down and they marched to the sliding glass doors, where Rosalina let her out to the fenced in yard.

Not at all sure how long it would take Marco to get there, Rosalina left the door open for Queenie to come in whenever ready, while she went to change into something more casual.

Easier said than done.

What did a woman wear when being introduced to her "boyfriend's" parents for the first time? She hadn't the faintest idea.

Rosalina pressed her index finger into her chin as she stared at her closet, its bi-fold doors wide open.

As minutes continued to tick by, she started to feel anxious with the time she was wasting.

In frustration, she flung her hand. "Oh, what does it matter? It's not like they're going to be my future in-laws."

With that solidified once again in her mind, Rosalina grabbed her favorite sundress, which had a tiny stain at the hem from some household cleaner, but it was barely noticeable. Besides, it was the embroidered top with white daisies in the turquoise fabric that would be the attention grabber.

She'd barely finished passing a brush through her long hair when the doorbell rang. Rosalina's hand paused midair on its way to set the brush down. "He's here!" She had no idea why she shouted, but she must have made it sound urgent, because Queenie's head popped up, eyes wide, and the dog took off toward the front door, barking at the top of her little lungs.

Rosalina took in a bolstering breath and ran her hands down the bodice of her dress before following after Queenie.

"You can do this. Nothing is at stake. Remember that. This is fake. Got it? Fake."

With one last indrawn breath, Rosalina opened the door and once again acquainted herself with the image of Marco Mendez. He was so unlike what she'd originally conjured in her mind, she was having trouble rationalizing the true him.

But he was the same as she recalled from Friday night. A tad taller than her, stocky and solid, and with a round bubbly face and cheesy smile that made Rosalina imagine he took nothing seriously.

Great kind of man to get tangled up with.

She mentally rolled her eyes.

Marco cleared his throat and twisted his finger around in his ear. "Uh, hello, Rosalina."

"Marco." Her clipped tone didn't sound friendly to her own ears, and Rosalina rebuked herself. The least she could do was be kind to the man. It could only help the next few weeks go better. "Do you want to come in?" She supposed that was the kind thing to offer.

Marco lifted one shoulder. "If you're ready to go, we can head on over to my parents'."

Rosalina's mouth went dry to think of the awkwardly silent car ride it would be. An idea materialized. "How far is their place?"

"Only a few blocks away, actually."

"How nice. Then, how about we walk? Would you mind? My dog could use the exercise."

"Walk? Hmm." Marco scratched the top of his head. "Well, I guess we could do that. I'll have to walk back here with you because I'll need to get my truck, but if that's what you want to do."

"It is." At least then she'd be in the company of one she appreciated. That *one* being her dog. Not Marco. "That is, unless dogs aren't welcome at your place. I know not everyone likes dogs..."

Marco raised a silencing hand. "Dogs are welcome. Not a problem."

Without saying anything more, Rosalina left Marco at the door to fetch the leash, which she promptly secured on Queenie's harness.

"Okay. We're all ready."

"Great." Marco plunged his hands into the pockets of his tan cargo pants.

As Rosalina stepped out and closed the door she noticed Marco squat beside her.

"Cute dog." He held his hand out to Queenie, who growled and nipped at the fleshy part of his palm.

"Queenie! No, no. Bad girl!" Rosalina tapped the dog's nose and gave her a stern look.

Marco stood, shaking his hand out.

"I'm so sorry, Marco." Mortified would be a more accurate word. "She's never tried to bite someone before."

To her relief, Marco laughed—although it did sound nervous. "No harm. She didn't even puncture the skin."

To Rosalina's relief. "I guess she needs to warm up to you first."

"I guess. What'd you say her name was?"

"Queenie."

"Ah, well, maybe I need to treat her like royalty before she'll give me audience."

Rosalina chuckled. "Perhaps. She is pretty spoiled. But that's the way we like it. Isn't it, Queenie?"

Queenie pranced in place, clearly ready to get this walk started. Rosalina was as well. "You lead the way." She waved her hand from right to left, not sure which direction they needed to go to get to the Mendez house.

Marco ducked his head, returned his hands to his pockets, and set out headed right. Rosalina fell in step beside him, Queenie romping on ahead. She *almost* felt bad for making it to where Marco would have to walk her back home to pick up his truck.

As expected, there was uncomfortable silence between them for the first block. Rosalina could feel her anxiety rising with each step. If Marco's parents lived only a few blocks away, they had very little time to figure out what they were going to tell his mom and dad.

"Marco."

"Huh!" He looked startled, as if he'd forgotten she was there.

Of course, she hadn't spoken in a soft voice either. She had a tendency to be loud...and blunt, so maybe she'd scared him out of his thoughts. "Don't we need to plan our story before we get there?"

"Oh, yes. But I think what we already told Mrs. Harrison should work...mostly."

"Key word: mostly. I don't want you exaggerating the story to ridiculous heights with that fanciful mind of yours. What do you do in your free time? Read unbelievable romantic comedies?"

"Ha. No. Do I look like a reader?" Marco turned his upper body toward her and pointed at himself.

Rosalina almost—*almost*—cracked a smile. "No, you don't."

"I barely take the time to read emails, let alone a book. And romantic comedy? No way." He grimaced.

"Okay, then. So I've learned one thing about you. You don't read."

"And I learned you have a mean dog."

"Queenie is not mean!" Rosalina stomped her foot down with the next step, although her words wobbled with a barely restrained chuckle.

"She bit me. If that's not mean, then I don't know what is." Marco leveled a serious look at her.

Rosalina sighed. "Give her time."

"I approached her the correct way. I didn't go touching her without warning. I let her sniff my hand first, which she bit...might I remind you again."

Rosalina shook her head. "She probably didn't like your smile."

"My smile? My smile! What's wrong with my smile?"

"It's too fake. Dogs are good at sniffing out con artists, and are an excellent judge of character."

Marco threw his arms up, spun on his heels, and started walking in the opposite direction.

Rosalina wheeled around, and the leash yanked at her arm with the abrupt stop by Queenie's continued forward march. "Where do you think you're going?"

"Taking you back home."

"Why?"

"Um, *hello*. You just criticized my smile. Clearly, this..." he shook a finger between the two of them. "...isn't going to work."

Rosalina rolled her eyes. "I already agreed and I don't go back on my word. Look, I'm sorry. Perhaps that was unkind of me to say." If only she could learn to filter her thoughts before they came out of her mouth.

Marco stopped but kept his back to her. Rosalina watched his shoulders rise and fall with a couple deep breaths. Slowly, he turned around. "Fine. Just try to pretend that you like me. It'll help the next three weeks to go better."

It took some doing, but Rosalina nodded her head. "I think I can pretend."

She received an exasperated look before Marco clenched his jaw and returned to her side.

Another block of silence passed and Rosalina was about to go crazy. She liked to talk. But what could they possibly talk about. It seemed whenever they tried to converse it ended up in an argument. Too bad they weren't college debate partners or something.

"So," she had to break the silence. "We're going to tell your parents we met at Ricardo's *Restaurante*?"

"Gotta keep our story consistent."

He had a point. And it wasn't a lie. That is where they met for the first time—two days ago. Which led to another question, "How long ago?"

Marco's head ticked from side to side in almost perfect tandem with their steps. "I don't know. We need a happy medium. If it's too soon they might not take us seriously. If we claim we've known each other for too long, my mother might wonder why we don't know more about each other than we do. Because I'm sure she's going to ask questions that will have us grasping at straws. She's a first-rate interrogator."

That didn't settle well in Rosalina's middle. "Plus, you've had a crush on Mrs. Harrison's daughter, so it's extra tricky to pin down a date."

"Ugh. I never should have opened my dumb mouth and got into this mess."

"No, you shouldn't have."

He glowered at her.

"It's the truth."

"Must you be so blunt?"

She shrugged one shoulder. "You'll have to get used to it, but I'll try to soften up a bit."

"How about we say we met two weeks ago. That's enough time for a couple to think they might be interested in each other. Don't you think?"

"Whoa, now. I'm not the one to ask." Rosalina pressed a hand to her chest. "I don't know the first thing about dating and couples and attraction."

"Really?" His furrowed brow told her he didn't believe her.

"I've never been on an actual date." And she wasn't about to claim Friday night's as a real one either.

"Great." He said it slowly. Pensively. "And I've only always hung around with Lillian. I guess we'll make this up as we go."

Had anything ever sounded so horrible? Rosalina longed to slap herself in the forehead. "Two weeks is good, like you said. And we met at Ricardo's. Um, what else do we need to know?"

"Depends on how many questions Mom has up her sleeve."

Rosalina let out a puff of air. "Okay, this is too stressful. Let's forget the pre-planning and wing it."

"Isn't that what I said?"

"*Sí.*" She hated to admit it. Hated this was the way it was going to be. Still hated she agreed to it. She supposed she could bow out right now. They hadn't made it to their destination yet—

"Well, we're here."

Rosalina choked on her own saliva and a coughing attack seized her as she fought to clear her airway.

"You okay?" The obvious concern in Marco's eyes was anything but fake, which was nice for a change—amongst all the pretending.

All Rosalina could do was nod as she continued to cough.

"Need me to pound on your back?"

Rosalina opened wide her tear-filled eyes. "No," she managed to eke out. She had a feeling he might not be able to monitor how much force he used with his strong arms and broad shoulders. Did roofing build such muscle mass? José didn't sport the same impressive biceps.

Impressive biceps?

Lord, help her silly thoughts.

What was she even thinking?

With one final throat clearing, Rosalina felt confident she could speak again. "All better." Her voice was still crackly, but good enough.

"Good. You know, I'm beginning to think you have a choking problem."

"Oh, brother." Rosalina rolled her eyes. "Let's get this over with."

Marco snickered and proceeded up the walkway to the house. Rosalina steeled herself against the opening door. How would this show go down?

"Mom, I brought someone for you to meet." Marco was already inside the door, and he beckoned for Rosalina to join him.

With a gulp, she stepped up and in and took notice of all the reds, oranges, teals, and golds in the living room décor. She was right at home.

A tiny dog came soaring from around a corner, barking its head off as it charged Rosalina.

"You have a dog? You didn't say anything about it." Rosalina could only smile at the adorable short-haired Chihuahua.

Queenie started barking then, which took the Chihuahua's attention away from Rosalina. The two dogs began checking each other out.

"Yes, we have a dog. That's Luigi."

"Luigi." She chuckled. "Cute name for a little thing. But I'm sure he's mighty."

"Loud too."

"And is he an ankle biter?" She pursed her lips, daring him to admit it. Chihuahua's were known as the biggest biters.

"Well, Luigi might nip friendly at Mom's ankles when he's hungry, but he's never attempted to bite company." He waggled his head at her, a *take that* expression on his face.

Rosaline put her mouth in an overbite position and crossed her arms. "I have no idea what came over Queenie. That was not at all like her."

"Eh, let's move beyond that. Want to have a seat?" He motioned toward the gold and red checkered couch. I'm not sure where Mom is. She should be here. I'll go see if I can round her up."

"She might not be here." And Rosalina wouldn't mind. She could collect her dog and return home.

"No, Dad said they'd be here all afternoon. I told them I might bring a friend over."

"A friend? That's it?"

"I didn't want to open the door for Mom's questions too early."

"Fair enough."

Rosalina folded her hands in her lap and waited for Marco's return, meanwhile roaming her eyes over the living room—especially all the family photos on the wall in front of her. Marco looked like his mother, she noticed.

And she had no time to even blink once more before the woman herself surfaced with Marco on her heels, his cheeks darker tan than a moment ago.

Chapter Nine

Marco held his breath as they entered the living room.

His Mom's arms went wide as she neared Rosalina. "My, my. And you must be Marco's friend. Marco, you didn't tell me your friend was a woman."

"I told you I had a surprise."

"A delightful one." Mom wiggled her fingers at Rosalina. "Come here, come here. Let me give you a hug. I'm Maria, Marco's mother. And you are?"

Rosalina stood and awkwardly accepted the embrace, leading Marco to believe she didn't care much for hugs.

"Mom, this is Rosalina Torres."

"A pleasure to meet you, Rosalina. What a lovely name for a beautiful girl."

Rosalina ducked her head. "Thank you. It's nice to meet you, Mrs. Mendez."

"Oh, I'll have none of that. Call me Maria. So, is this serious...?" She turned to Marco, but still had one arm around Rosalina in a friendly side embrace.

Marco longed to cover his eyes. "Uh, well."

"Yes, it is," Rosalina answered, rendering Marco speechless.

"Oh!" Mom's expression was brighter than the summer sunshine. "Well, this a wonderful surprise. Marco, why on earth have you kept this a secret?"

"Well...I—"

"You see," Rosalina butted in. "He wanted me to meet you sooner, but I wanted to be sure things were really serious. You know, it's a big thing meeting your boyfriend's family."

Marco didn't know if he should be horrified or grateful she was taking charge. But of one thing he knew for certain: Rosalina was engaging in a ruthless game of turnabout is fair play. He didn't doubt for one minute she was enjoying this.

All he could do was fight the head shakes and glares he wanted to send her, and he realized then that's likely how Rosalina had felt the other night.

Talk about getting a taste of his own medicine.

He didn't like it.

But, the answers seemed to appease his mother, so he supposed that was all that mattered.

Mom finally released Rosalina and backed up to the couch. "Come, let's sit and talk. I want to hear all about this."

"Um, I think I'll go see Dad." Marco thrust his thumb in the direction of the garage door, as he could hear the sound of a saw running.

"Absolutely not. He'll come in soon enough. Sit down and fill my ears with how you met."

Marco swallowed and lowered on the chair adjacent to the couch. "Well, José is actually who set us up."

"Ah, José."

"He's my cousin," Rosalina added.

"You don't say?" Mom stacked her hands over her chest.

Rosalina nodded. "And we met two weeks ago at Ricardo's Mexican *Restaurante.*"

Marco gave a slight bob of his head in agreement when both women's eyes landed on him. "And we knew right then we wanted to get to know each other better."

Rosalina's pleasant smile, which he knew was only in place for Mom's sake, faltered for a moment, but then it turned frighteningly sugary. "That's so true. Why, when your son entered the restaurant—late, might I add—he took my breath away."

Marco was certain his mother was going to swoon. "My heart! I always knew he was a catch. I've been praying for the right woman to realize it." Then she turned a more pointed look at Marco. "And, you, running late for a date. *Tsk, tsk.* I hope that's not been a common occurrence."

"No, Mom."

"Do not fear, Maria. He's learning. I'm teaching him how to be the perfect gentleman. Isn't that right, Mars?"

If she called him Mars one more time...

Marco nailed Rosalina with the strongest face he dared pull off for fear of his mom looking over and catching him. He hoped Rosalina read the *how dare you* he was spelling with his quavering lips as he fought a retort.

Two people could play that game. "Yes, Lina. You are teaching me much."

Like how little patience he had.

How much he regretted running his mouth.

He noticed the twitch under Rosalina's right eye, and he knew he was only being spared one of her fiery glares because of his mom's presence.

Speaking of fiery, Marco pulled at the collar of his shirt. The room temperature had to have risen by twenty degrees since they arrived.

Where are you, Dad?

Couldn't he need a drink right about now? Or a bathroom break? Anything?

"...but I must. You will simply love them."

Marco missed the beginning of his mom's sentence, but with that ending, he had one suspicion...and it wasn't good. "What are you doing, Mom?" He pressed a hand into the armrest of the chair, ready to rise and...and do something.

"Why, I'm going to show Rosalina my picture albums of you."

"Now, Mom, there really isn't time for that. Rosalina needs to be—"

"It's not a problem. I have no plans. I'd love to see Marco's baby pictures, Maria." Rosalina sent him an overly large smile that frosted Marco's veins.

He sagged in his chair and ran both hands down his face as his mom left the room to get the picture albums.

Once she had made a complete exit, Marco leaned forward and spoke through gritted teeth. "What. Are. You. Doing?"

"Whatever your mom wants. I need to make a good impression on her. If a woman is really interested in you, she would want to get close to your mom too. Don't you think?"

Marco grumbled. "I don't like it."

"They're just pictures."

"Humph." Rosalina had no idea what kinds of pictures his mom liked to take and save...and, sadly, show as if they were her prized possessions. True, it showed how much his mom loved him, but really? Rosalina wasn't even his real girlfriend, and now she was going to be seeing personal pictures, and he knew Mom would be telling stories to go along with them.

The minute his mom returned to the room, Marco clapped his hands down on his knees and surged to his feet. "I'm going to go check on Dad."

"Stay with us, dear." Mom laid a hand on his arm in passing on her way back to the couch.

"Do stay, Mars." Rosalina fluttered her eyelashes.

Marco clenched his jaw. "I would like Dad to meet Rosalina, and so I think I should go let him know we have company."

"Oh, dear." Mom covered her mouth with one hand. "I did forget about your dad, didn't I? I was so excited about meeting your friend." She winked at him then turned to Rosalina. "But you must meet Guadalupe before leaving. In fact, how about you stay for supper?"

Since his mom wasn't looking his way, Marco began shaking his head and mouthing no.

Figures Rosalina would develop a Cheshire grin, and while locking gazes with him, replied, "I would love that, Maria."

This time Marco did slap himself in the face, then made a bee line for the garage door. He needed to get away from the women. They were going to be the death of him.

He missed Lillian. She never caused him trouble.

Regret was a bitter pill to swallow. He wished the lingering taste would finally go away.

Would it ever?

Oh, he couldn't wait to get to work Monday morning and start scraping away shingles. There was nothing like good, hard manual labor.

The sound of a saw running grew louder the closer Marco got to the garage and he steeled himself for the assault on his ears when he opened the door.

He waited patiently in a spot within easy viewing of his dad, so he didn't scare him with a touch or holler while the dangerous blade was running.

When his dad noticed him, he powered down the saw and pulled off his ear protection. "You look like you ate a bagful of sour green apples."

Marco let out a mirthless laugh. "Not quite. Mom's showing my girlfriend the picture albums."

"Ah. She does love her pictures."

Unfortunately.

"Girlfriend, you say?" One of Dad's brows rose and interest lit his gaze.

Marco took his discomfort out on his ear. "It's a pretty new development."

"I'll say. Can't wait to meet her." Dad clamped a hand on Marco's back.

"Well, she's staying for supper."

"Great. So, in the meantime, wanna help me with this project? I'm sure you're trying to avoid re-entering the house until the albums are put away." Dad understood so well.

"I'd be glad to help." Marco grabbed a pair of ear muffs and safety glasses, more than happy to get covered in saw dust rather than sit in the living room getting embarrassed by the women.

□□□

Going back in the house was inevitable—no matter how much Marco wished they could finish building all of Mom's new kitchen cabinets in one afternoon. Not that such a feat was possible, but anything to avoid some more of Rosalina's...whatever she was pulling off today.

Mom's holler from the door leading into the house, though, came in that moment, telling them supper was ready.

Oh boy.

Marco turned to his dad. "Ready to meet Rosalina?"

"Ooo, pretty name."

He only nodded, but Dad laid a hand on the back of his neck, gave a squeeze and a wink, and, together, they stepped up into the house.

Rosalina was at the sink washing a dish, and she turned a saucy smile at him, which Marco returned with an equally cheesy one, letting her know how he felt about her earlier display with his mom. He was surprised when she didn't jerk her head away with an upturned nose, but he supposed there were too many watchful eyes to do that right now.

Marco walked straight up to her, and when she finished drying her hands, he placed a hand at the small of her back and directed her a step closer to his dad.

"Dad, my girlfriend. Rosalina."

"Nice to meet you." Dad stuck out his callused hand and the two shook. "I'm Guadalupe."

"I'm pleased to make your acquaintance." And Rosalina did sound genuinely pleased.

Mom came bustling in-between them all, waving her hands toward the table. "The food will get cold. Sit down. Sit down."

Marco and his dad made quick work of washing their hands and taking a place at the table. Of course, Marco sat next to Rosalina on one side of the table, with his parents on either end. Antonio's chair sat blessedly empty. He wasn't ready for his brother to know about his new "relationship."

The meal went better than Marco expected. Simple conversation flowed easily without any ridiculously fake sweetness coming from Rosalina's mouth, or entirely too probing questions from his mom.

However, when they sat back in their chairs as Mom went to the counter and filled plates with what he considered her blue ribbon worthy flan, fingers reached out for his hand that dangled beside his chair.

He jumped at the unexpected touch and seared Rosalina with a look.

She gave him a mock innocent smile and proceeded to try and hold his hand.

All of a sudden, Marco wished he would have thought to set a few ground rules when this whole charade began. Number one on that list would be: NO TOUCHING.

He pulled his hand away, but she sought it as determinedly as a roofer does a roof leak, and when she tried once again to weave her fingers through his, he wiggled his to protest the intimate touch. But Rosalina wasn't giving up. They continued to engage in a game of—well, it probably looked like footsie, but these weren't feet, so—"handsie," and Marco could feel his face heating up at the frustration of her obvious disregard to his refusal.

And confound it all, when his mom at that moment had to come bearing plates of flan, expertly balancing them on her pudgy arms.

Lest it be found out by his overly-perceptive Mom that he balked at the thought of holding hands with his girlfriend, Marco admitted defeat and let Rosalina clasp her hand around his. For several moments he kept his lax, until Rosalina gave it a tight squeeze. The vexing woman...

He reluctantly closed his fingers around her smaller hand and his breath hitched—for no reason he could figure. The temperature rose a good twenty to thirty degrees more inside and Marco longed to rip off his shirt. But that would never do. The last thing he wanted was for Rosalina to see him half naked. And something told him she would enjoy the sight of his bare chest far too much. Or at least *pretend* to for the sake of their audience.

But then, thank the good Lord, his mom set his plate of dessert before him—and he needed his right hand to eat—so he broke free from Rosalina's hold and snatched up his fork.

His appetite wasn't near what it'd been when his mom had announced she'd made something special for dessert, but he stuffed a big bite in his mouth and chewed more aggressively than necessary for the wobbly, jelly-like treat.

When he chanced a look at Rosalina, instead of finding the searing brown eyes he expected, she wore a sickening self-satisfied smile and had a victorious lift to her chin.

He could only ask himself one thing.

What is she up to?

Chapter Ten

"You've got to be kidding me." Marco held his nail gun in a lax hand as he stared at José, who was working a few feet away, closer to the peak of the roof. So much for a refreshing Monday.

"Nope." José shook his head and repositioned his hat. "I got the reminder invitation in the mail Saturday. Yours will probably be sitting in the mailbox waiting for you when you get off work today."

"Heritage Days. Really?" Marco groaned. "I thought with the soon-coming Harrison-Bishop wedding they would have canceled the event."

José shrugged. "One might think, but you know how important that is to the Harrisons."

Marco sighed. "True."

Heritage Days was an annual event that Lillian and her parents had been putting on for the past seven or so years. Marco hadn't missed a single year yet. He enjoyed the event. It was fun to get to meet people of different ethnicities and backgrounds, taste the variety of foods (some good and some, well, not so good), and watch the dances and hear about all the (sometimes strange) traditions.

As hard as it would be to see Lillian there with Clint, Marco had to admit he would miss Heritage Days if he didn't go.

But since he had to run his big mouth to Mrs. Harrison, there was no question that he would have to bring Rosalina, and that was sure to open another whole box of nails of questions that he had no desire to be answering. Especially if Rosalina took to answering them.

She was a feisty one. She'd proven that yesterday with the way she handled things with his mom. Marco couldn't say he didn't deserve it. But he could hope they were even now, and any future "dates" would be easier to get through.

"So, are you going?" José once again asked the question that had had Marco thinking the man was kidding.

He rubbed the back of his sweaty neck. "Probably. I always do."

"Yeah, you do. But I didn't know if you would this year with the whole, you know...issue." He put air quotation marks around "issue."

"I have to accept the fact I'm the loser and get over her." By her, he meant Lillian, but José already knew that, so Marco saved himself the heartache of speaking her name.

"Are you going to take Rosalina then?"

"I likely have to. If she'll go."

"You better not wait too long to ask her. It's this weekend."

Marco returned to nailing shingles, needing to work to continue this conversation. "I'll get to that tonight."

"Don't forget."

"I won't."

"Want me to send you a reminder?"

"Would you stop? You're nagging."

"Okay, okay." José raised his hands in surrender. "I just want to be sure you treat my cousin right. No girl likes to find out about plans last minute."

"Rosalina did fine with my last minute invitation Sunday to have her meet my parents."

"Whoa! You had her meet your parents and I'm just now hearing about it? How'd that go?"

"As well as could be expected with two sassy women."

José arched a brow. "What's that supposed to mean?"

"Well, let's just say Rosalina thought I needed a reminder of how our first dinner date went."

"I'm not going to ask you to elaborate on that one."

"Good. But, she did stay and share supper with us, and that went fine. I'm just glad Antonio wasn't home."

"So your brother doesn't know about Rosalina yet?" José's nail gun rang out in several quick successions.

"No, I haven't told him. I will soon. Although, Mom has probably already said something to him."

"How is your brother? Is he going steady with a girl yet? He's what, nineteen?"

Marco coughed out a laugh. "He's not that young of a pup. He's twenty-one. And, no, he doesn't have a girl yet. Not that I know of anyway. He is going to be moving out this fall when he transfers colleges, though. He's going to be the big shot of the family going for schooling to be a nurse anesthetist."

"Ah, wow. Guess he didn't want to follow in your dad's footsteps in construction."

"Ha, no. Antonio hates the smell of asphalt."

José laughed. "Roofing isn't a bad job either. Didn't want to come to Torres Quality Roofing?"

"To be honest, my brother doesn't like getting sweaty. He's more of an inside kind of guy. But, yeah," Marco shrugged one shoulder. "We're pretty proud of him. I don't think Mom is too happy with him moving several hours away, though."

"But of course. He's the baby of the family. Moms take that hard."

"I suppose. But I'll never forget how much she cried when Isabella married."

"Don't tell me that. I'm the first—and only—child to get married in my family. I don't want to think of my mom balling her eyes out like a baby at my and Regina's wedding."

"Maybe she won't."

"Hmm, she has handled all the planning fine."

"Don't let that fool you, *amigo*. The emotions don't kick in until the night before. I thought Mom was going to spend the night in Isabella's room."

José choked on a laugh. "That does sound like your mom."

Marco clucked his tongue. "And then I'm the especially blessed middle child who gets nagged about girlfriends, marriage, and grandchildren."

"Blessed, indeed. It's the way she shows her love for you. Remember that." José shook his finger at him, a lazy smile in place.

He let out an exasperated sigh. "It's a strange sort of love. José, she showed Rosalina my baby pictures. All the photo albums, actually."

"She didn't!" José guffawed.

Marco slanted a whipped pup expression at him in response, which made José laugh harder.

"Sure makes me wish I could get moved into my new house sooner rather than later. You just had to go and kick me out."

"Hey, sorry. But I was not about to bring my new wife home to a house with two other guys. Not happening."

Marco chuckled. "No, I don't suppose so."

Conversation fell silent then while they worked for a few minutes, until José shattered the work groove once again.

"So, when are you going to ask Rosalina about Heritage Days?"

"Would you cut it out?!" Marco ripped his sun hat off and tossed it at José, who deflected it with his forearm, then threw it back.

Marco promptly replaced it. "I'll send to her at lunch break. Will that satisfy the cousin police?"

"I should think so."

"Fine. Now, excuse me while I go have a coconut water break. I need to de-stress."

José's self-satisfied laughter was the sound Marco left behind.

Not wanting to forget to ask Rosalina about Heritage Days, Marco typed up a text and scheduled it to send at noon. Then he wouldn't have to think about it again. Not until Rosalina's response, that is.

After slipping his phone back in his pocket, Marco twisted the lid off his carton of coconut water and chugged the refreshing beverage. Before returning to the roof, he splashed some of the water from the Igloo thermos on the back of the truck on his sweaty face and let out a satisfied sigh at the cooling effect.

A dog and its owner walked by then and Marco waved at them. The dog was small and white, reminding him of Queenie...which led to thoughts of Rosalina.

So much for not thinking about her until she replied to his text. The woman was frustrating. He was going to be in danger of developing ulcers or losing his hair if this was what his next three weeks or so was going to be like. Couldn't she be nice? Be like Lillian?

He turned and saw his reflection in the finish of the truck. He smiled and studied himself.

"Rosalina thinks my smile is fake."

Sure, sometimes he forced a less than sincere smile. But he'd thought for sure the one he'd greeted Rosalina with on Sunday had been real.

He tried different adjustments to his smile, hoping none of his coworkers were watching him. They'd probably think he'd lost his mind and was making faces at himself.

"This is madness."

He gave his head a hard shake and allowed himself one more glance at the man looking back at himself.

"My smile is not fake. Rosalina is impossible."

Marco huffed and squeezed the back of his neck. He only had himself to blame for this situation.

If only he wouldn't have dragged his feet where Lillian was concerned.

If only he wouldn't have run his big mouth and pulled Rosalina into a ruse without her prior consent.

He'd always been a pro at getting himself into trouble, but this one took the cake.

"God, if you could make something good come from this mess, I'd be grateful."

Who was he kidding? Asking God to bless a lie? Was he insane or something?

"And I promise I'll not lie again after this is over," he added for conscience sake.

And may God grant him the grace to keep that promise.

Chapter Eleven

Rosalina hadn't been this nervous since her college days. She'd always suffered from test anxiety. How she ever survived college, she would never know, but she thanked God for helping her get through with passing scores.

Now she prayed he would help her in her meeting with Truman Scott. Her checkbook and envelopes containing recent letters from her landlord shook in her hands as she walked up to the little deli's door, where they agreed to meet.

Rosalina had no intentions of eating. Her stomach was too knotted up to consider putting anything in it. Her business. Her dreams. Everything was at stake. All her hard work could go kaput if Truman Scott decided she was beyond mercy.

She couldn't see how they could already be at that point. She'd always been a good renter. Took care of the building as if it were her own. Always asked Mr. Scott's permission before making any changes. Surely all those good points would add up in her favor.

Surely?

Her only negative was that she'd not been able to make her full payment last month. She couldn't have helped it.

But, unfortunately, she was more behind than she'd calculated, since Twisted Truman and his twisted schemes started charging her interest too. Rosalina knew that wasn't normal, and she could bring that to someone's attention. But if she could settle this peaceably and without possible further expenses of an attorney, that would be preferred.

The bell above the restaurant's door dinged when Rosalina entered the building, and sitting at the first table her eyes landed on was none other than Snaky Scott himself.

Rosalina wasn't having fond thoughts of him. If she could find a new building to rent, she would in a heartbeat. Even with knowing how much work it would take to move everything out of her current place and set it up again. It would be worth it to get away from the tyrant.

Who did he think he was? A king? He'd crossed a line, and Rosalina was ready to fight.

Bolstering her courage with a deep breath and squaring of her shoulders, Rosalina marched over to the table and plopped her stack of papers and checkbook on the table. It made a satisfying *swack* that brought Truman Scott's eyebrows up a half inch.

He had to finish chewing before he could say anything. What a toad to not wait for her to arrive to order. Not that she cared, because, again, she had no plans of eating.

Truman dabbed at the corners of his lips. "Well, I see you've made it on time. Unlike you have with your payment."

Rosalina sat in the chair across from him with deliberate movements. "I made my payment on time. Just not the full amount, Mr. Scott."

"Which is a problem, Miss Torres. I have bills to pay same as you, and we all need to do our part for things to run smoothly."

As if she didn't know that. "But, sometimes, things come up. Things we do not plan for."

"That's why you should always have an emergency fund."

Rosalina's ire rose, but she counted to ten before responding. "I'm a new business owner, Mr. Scott. I sunk all my savings into The Pampered Poochie's Parlor."

"That's not my problem, Miss." He pointed at her with his fountain pop.

Rosalina looked away and huffed as quietly as she could, when all she wanted to do was blow the man off his chair and give him a what-for for being so callused.

Was it because she was a woman? So young? Was he prejudiced? She couldn't know. For all she knew, he might treat all his renters like this. If so, she felt sorry for every one of them.

She took the time to straighten the stack of papers in front of her. "Mr. Scott, I re-read the contract I signed from you when I rented your building. It stated in there that you would not charge late fees. Now, I understand you have a legal right by law to do so within a certain range, but you promised in this contract that you wouldn't. And I also noticed you are charging me interest on top of the late fee. I have every right to take you to court over that, but I'm hoping we can settle this between the two of us."

Her landlord's eyes widened and his mouth slightly parted. Rosalina noticed his lips twitching, and she felt like a victor for rendering him speechless. Her scouring through the contract with a fine tooth comb had paid off.

His face started to turn red, but then he straightened his shirt and sat more upright, and schooled his face in his normal passive yet condescending expression. "Miss Torres, I'll have you know—"

"I'll have you know, Mr. Scott," she butted in and raised her voice. "I do not intend to be walked over and manipulated into paying you one cent more than what I legally owe you as outlined in our contract." She searched through her stack and slapped the stapled contract in front of him at a safe distance from his plate and drink. She didn't want anything happening to her proof. "You are not keeping your side of the bargain."

A threatening, dark cloud pulled over his eyes, but blew away as quickly. "You have until August fifth to catch up with your payments." His words were clipped. He was clearly unhappy with her, but Rosalina didn't care.

"Without the extra fees." She would be firm. She held Mr. Scott's gaze.

His cheek twitched and red crept up his neck. "August fifth. That's when your lease is up. If you fail to come up with the full payment by then, I will not renew the lease and you will have thirty days to vacate the property."

As impossible as it sounded, Rosalina knew she'd received all the mercy she would get from Tyrant Truman. So she gave him a curt nod, handed him the check she'd made out before leaving her house this morning of the highest amount she could afford right now, and left the small deli, mentally shaking the dust off her as she went.

Of all people she could have rented a building from, why did it have to be Truman Scott?

With a sigh, Rosalina plopped in her Ford Fiesta, taking a moment to release the tension from her shoulders. She ran a hand through her hair and untangled a knot.

"Thank you, Jesus. That went better than I thought it would."

Perhaps, Truman Scott wasn't all bad, as she'd had him painted in her mind. She'd been renting from him for almost two years now and never had a problem. In fact, she'd thought she had a good landlord, as far as those go. She'd heard plenty of horror stories.

She couldn't help but wonder what had changed. Maybe he got hungry for money. Greedy. It happened to even the best of people. Well, if he was going to keep playing games like this, she would find a way to get a new building. Mayhap, a building all her own, so she didn't have to deal with a landlord.

But then there would be other problems. Even more responsibilities.

"Ugh."

Adults weren't joking when they said to enjoy being kids for as long as possible.

Rosalina's eyes drifted to the clock. Only a quarter after twelve. She'd gotten done a lot quicker than she thought she would. She grabbed her phone to turn the sound back on, as she had turned it off before leaving her salon.

Her lips formed an O when she saw a text from Marco. It still felt strange to see his name on her screen.

Was this going to become a common occurrence? She wasn't altogether sure if she wanted it to or not. It wouldn't be so bad to add a friend to her small list. Could they be friends after this? Or would this whole ruse turn them into enemies?

Not that they were particularly friendly at the present time.

She sighed. If only things could have started out differently. There was a reason why the Apostle James said the tongue could not be tamed by man and was an unruly evil, full of deadly poison. Rosalina was feeling the effects of an untamed tongue.

Who was she to cast blame? Her tongue was just as unruly.

Seriously. Why had she said that about Marco's smile? That had been unkind. For some reason the man brought out the worst in her.

Curious as to what Marco might want this time, she opened the text rather than waiting until she got back to work—which, since she was going to arrive earlier than expected, she'd get to enjoy a few minutes of playtime with Queenie.

Marco: Do you have plans this Saturday?
Rosalina: Why do you ask?

She wasn't going to answer that question until she knew what she would be getting into. It could be anything with that man. He probably wanted her to meet his grandparents next.

Not knowing how long he would take to respond, Rosalina threw the car in reverse and headed back to work. Her phone pinged halfway there, and it took every bit of self control not to read it while driving, but she knew better than to take her eyes off the road.

A petty text wasn't worth a human life.

Once she was parked and had entered the parlor, Rosalina opened the message.

Marco: Would you like to go to an event with me? It's called Heritage Days. It's all about celebrating heritage.
Rosalina: Sounds interesting. I would like more information. Call me when you have a chance.

She was surprised when her phone began ringing in her hand. Then again, it was likely lunch break for Marco, so maybe she shouldn't be shocked.

"Hello." She used the nicest tone she'd ever used around him.

"Oh, hi. Having a good day?" His voice sounded much different on the phone. Deeper than in person. Rosalina could almost be fooled into believing Marco had passed the phone off to someone else.

"I guess you could say that." Considering how her meeting with the landlord had gone, yes, she did consider it to be good.

"Well, great. Anyway, Heritage Days is an event where people of all different ethnicities come together and we get to learn more about each other and the traditions and culture, eat regional dishes. Stuff like that."

"It does sound like fun. What time is it?"

"From one to four, but people are welcome to stay as long as they like."

"Hmm." She'd be missing out on a couple hours of dog walking, or babysitting if someone would request that of her. She needed the money. But... "I assume you *need* me to go, or would strongly like me to, but you're being nice enough to ask."

The nervous laugh was undoubtedly Marco. Rosalina could picture him twisting his finger in the ear his phone wasn't wedged up against. "It would be ideal if you came. I promise it'll be fun. We won't be biting each others' heads off."

They would have to see about that. "Where is this event at?"

"Uh, well, it's at Lillian's parents' lavender farm. They are the ones who put it on."

"Oh." Just what Rosalina wanted to do. Go to his former crush's place and have a celebration. But, hadn't she been thinking about being kinder to Marco. Happily tagging along on this would fall in that category. "I will go."

"You will?"

"Mm-hmm."

"Wow. Um, thanks."

"Certainly."

"I guess I'll let you go now. I need to get back to work." There was beginning to be more background noise, leading Rosalina to believe his coworkers had already gone back to work.

"I do too. We'll talk later."

"Uh...yeah. Bye." He sounded shocked. Was it because she was being nice?

The phone connection ended and an old saying popped into Rosalina's mind.

Kill with kindness.

Rosalina didn't want to kill anyone, or anything. But if being kind to Marco could rearrange his landscape a little from all he'd assumed about her, that could be fun. She could render him quite confused.

Fun, indeed.

Oh, she was ready for Saturday.

Ack, why wait for Saturday?

She would start now.

Chapter Twelve

Marco found himself with free time Wednesday afternoon. The job today was a small one and they finished early. Juan Torres, owner of the business, always told them if that happened on a Wednesday, they were to pack up, head home, and attend midweek services if they were churchgoers, or enjoy an evening with family.

Seeing as how he was "dating" right now, Marco decided the right thing to do would be to see his girl.

Rosalina—my girl?

My, but that had a funny sound to it in his mind. Rosalina Torres might be many things, but his girl was not one of them. Not in the truest sense of the meaning anyway.

But they could be friendly toward each other, and Marco would do good to put in some effort to get to know Rosalina before Saturday. He knew there would be enough questions asked at Heritage Days to re-shingle a roof with.

If there was one thing he knew about Rosalina, it was that she was a hard worker and loved her job. And while he didn't know what the working hours of her place of business were, he was almost one hundred percent certain he would find her at work.

Surprisingly, he was able to recall the name of the pet parlor, and Marco did a web search to get the address. But before heading there, he swung by home to pick up Luigi. While the dog might be short-hair, surely there was some service Rosalina could provide.

A nail trimming?

A bath?

Something sensible.

Hopefully, she had walk-ins for friends. This was supposed to be a surprise, and he didn't want to ruin it by phoning ahead to see if there were any openings.

But, seriously. A doggie salon. How busy could it be? It wasn't as if dogs had spa days, did they?

□□□

Marco was not prepared for the sight before him. Upon entering The Pampered Poochie's Parlor, he was welcomed by a place that sported hundreds of painted dog bones with blue and yellow bows on the walls, a front desk shaped like a bone, and dog paw print decals on the tile flooring.

This was no regular dog groomer like Marco had envisioned. This was a pet palace, with all things dog glorified to the next level.

He leaned back on his heel to do an about-face and "flea" this place (pun intended), when a voice called out to him.

"Welcome to TPPP. Can I help you?"

Marco righted his stance and gave a wobbly smile. "Yeah, um, this is where Rosalina Torres works, right?"

"Mm-hm. It's her name on the front door."

Right. He'd seen that.

I'm such a dunce.

Why did everything having to do with Rosalina tie his tongue in knots and steal his brains?

It was ridiculous and it needed to stop. He'd never suffered such issues where Lillian was concerned.

"Right." He flicked a finger toward the woman. "And you are?"

"I'm Haven, Rosalina's receptionist and right-hand gal. I see you brought a furry pal. Can we offer you any services today?"

"This is Luigi." Marco tugged on the leash and the Chihuahua left off sniffing the potted plant near the entrance door and walked over to him. Marco picked the dog up and rubbed behind its ears.

"What an adorable name. It suits him." Haven's eyes looked like they could be replaced with hearts as she reached out for Luigi to sniff her hand.

Good dog that Luigi was, *he* didn't try to nip at the woman's hand like some other beast he knew.

"So, what all do you do here? I have no idea what to ask for. I mean, as you can see, Luigi doesn't need a haircut. He's short-haired. His nails are getting long, if you trim those."

Haven returned her attention to him. "Is that all you think we do here?"

Marco shrugged. "I figure you probably give baths too."

"Absolutely. We have several different options. I recommend the Deluxe Pampering Package for the truest pet lovers. Your dog will get extra massage time, a double lather, which includes a blueberry facial. We'll clean ears, blow dry—which we do for all baths—and they'll leave with either a bandana if it's a boy, or bows in the hair if it's a girl. Oh, and they get a treat."

Marco could only stare. "I...see."

Dogs did have spa days, apparently.

"Or there is the Squeaky Clean Package, which is one lather, ear cleaning, blow drying, and a treat. Most people do that one. For those who need the cheapest option, we also offer the Happy and Clean Package, which is simply a single lather with blow drying and a treat. No ear cleaning provided with that one."

Marco shook his head. "I can bathe my own dog."

Wait. Did he say that out loud?

Ugh. That was so not the thing to say in here.

Haven laughed. That was good at least. "I'm sure you're capable, but it can be extra exciting for the dog to have the pampering experience we make even the cheapest bath option to be.

"Okay. Let's go with the cheapest. And a nail trimming, if you do that."

"Certainly." Haven began clicking away at the computer. "It happens we have an opening right now. We usually leave Wednesday afternoons open for dog parties, but we didn't have one scheduled today."

"Dog parties?" Just when he thought he'd heard it all.

"Oh, of course! That's our favorite thing. So fun."

"What else goes on at this place?"

"Ah." Haven raised a finger and a sparkle appeared in her eyes as she prepared to expound upon his question, but then another voice rang out. A familiar voice.

"Haven, have you seen—" Rosalina's words froze when her eyes met his. "Marco. And Luigi. What brings you two here?" She walked over and offered her hand to Luigi to sniff, which the dog did...without biting.

Goes to show who had the better, nicer dog.

"Well, I scheduled Luigi for a bath for right now."

"Splendid. I can take him."

Marco handed the dog over and Rosalina started giving Luigi a chin rub.

"Do I have time to leave and come back?" One quick sweep around the room told him he'd be bored out of his mind to have to spend much time here.

"Which package did you buy?"

"The cheapest."

"Since Luigi has such short hair, it'll probably only be about twenty minutes. Thirty at the longest. But if you don't want to leave, down the hallway we have a small gift shop where you can buy Luigi a toy if you'd like."

Seriously?

If this was the kind of treatment Queenie received every day, no wonder she was mean and stuck-up. Spoiled rotten thing.

"Well, I'm going to go start his bath now." And with that Rosalina headed in the direction from which she'd come, gratefully sparing Marco from having to come up with a response.

While he loved his family's dog in a simple owner-pet kind of way, everything he'd heard inside The Pampered Poochie's Parlor had Marco feeling as if Luigi had been woefully deprived of canine luxuries.

He turned around and rolled his eyes. He would not fall prey to such spoiling measures. A person could go broke in this place...over a pet.

Feeling a little guilty about his thoughts, though, Marco moseyed down the hallway and into the gift shop. It wouldn't hurt to get Luigi a small toy.

A tiny room it might be, but it put every dog toy department Marco had been in to shame. Floor to ceiling shelves were loaded with colorful squeaky toys, balls galore, what seemed like hundreds of plushies, and more chew toys than he'd ever thought possible to be in one place.

How was he supposed to decide what Luigi would like with so many options?

He eventually settled on a rubber squeaky sombrero, and by then fifteen minutes had passed. Marco returned to the counter, where Haven had the little devil—er, Queenie—sitting on her lap. He was pretty sure it sneered at him.

Marco gave the dog a hard look before relaxing his face in a more pleasant expression, in time for Haven to look up at him. "Find something?"

"Yes. And I need to pay for the bath and nail trimming."

"Yep. I've got you taken care of." She took the toy he'd set on the counter and removed the price tag. Then named his overall total.

For it being the cheapest bath package, Marco wasn't excepting he'd need to pay with his credit card. He *almost* regretted coming as he pulled his wallet from his pocket to make the payment, but he told himself he was doing this to help out with the relationship—or lack of—with Rosalina. At least this showed he liked her...as a friend.

Besides, supporting her business was the least he could do after putting her in such an unwanted position. If only things could have turned out differently during their dinner date. He could have asked her if she'd be okay with the idea. But, Lillian's parents *had* to have a date that night too. At the same restaurant. How ironic.

The entrance door behind him whooshed open at that point and a deep bark sounded. Marco spun around to see a bear of a dog entering, followed by a dwarf of an old woman.

The pair made for a comical sight, but Marco wasn't laughing. As much as he liked little dogs, he feared big ones more and all he could think was how on earth the woman could possibly manage the dog.

He got that question answered. She didn't.

In one instant the monstrous pet was the very image of a well behaved animal, but in the next it had turned possessed and came running toward Marco.

By reflex, he tossed his wallet in the air and made for a quick break around the desk, but the dog jumped on him, tackling him to the ground. Marco screamed.

"Get away! Get away! Get. Him. Off."

The dog barked, and Marco prepared to have his nose bit clean off his face, but instead the monster's large tongue left a slobbery wet trail from chin to forehead.

Marco growled. "Get. Him. Off. Me!" He didn't care if he sounded borderline irrational.

"What is going on out here?"

Marco recognized Rosalina's voice, and it was followed by Luigi's barking. He could picture the Chihuahua now. Eyes bulging out of its head, and backing up farther and farther with each bark.

Oh, yeah, doing a real good job of protecting his owner by retreating.

"I'm sorry. Ladybug pulled the leash right out of my hand and took the poor man to the ground." A frail voice replied, which Marco knew belonged to the old woman who had no business owning a dog three times her size. It could eat the lady if he or she so had the mind to.

Wait a minute...

Ladybug?

Surely he hadn't heard right. How could a bear-like dog be named Ladybug?

Another swipe of Ladybug's tongue went across Marco's face, this time from ear to ear, managing to slide right over his lips.

"Disgusting!" He roared through his tight lungs. It was hard to breath with who knew how many pounds—ninety plus, maybe?—on him.

"Come on, Ladybug. Let's get off Marco, okay?" This in Rosalina's voice again.

Coaxing? He wanted the dog ripped off him. Not coaxed, as if letting Ladybug decide when and if she wanted to move.

At last, Marco was set free when the bear-dog hopped off him. He let out a whoosh of air and sucked in a deep breath now that his lungs could fully expand.

He pushed up from the floor, upset with the trembling of his arms. Shaking a finger at the old woman, he said, "Keep that dog away from me."

The old woman's lips formed an O as her eyes rounded, and she laid a protective hand on Ladybug's head. The big dog leaned into her mistress and licked the hand currently administering chin rubs.

"Luigi, come on." Marco snapped his fingers.

Luigi obediently came to his side and Rosalina handed Marco the leash.

"He's all clean," she said with the pleasantest of smiles, as if a possible murder scene hadn't almost taken place.

Okay, so maybe that was exaggerating.

But when you've been scarred as an eight-year-old boy with a dog attack that resulted in an emergency room visit and dozens of stitches, a dog scenario was easily exaggerated in the mind.

To his further aggravation, Marco could tell Rosalina was fighting laughter.

With a grumble, he picked his wallet up from the floor and accepted his credit card back from Haven. Then he ducked his head at Rosalina. "Thanks for Luigi's bath."

"You're welcome. I'm sorry about your being tackled."

"Me too." Marco brushed off his clothes and straightened his orange work shirt. "Can't promise I'll be back."

Rosalina muttered something. Marco didn't catch every word, but what he could put together was that she basically said something along the lines that he screams like a girl and is a scaredy-cat...in Spanish.

Just wait until he made it known to her that he could speak Spanish too. Her secrets were not safe from him. But now wasn't the time or place.

He proceeded toward the door, but Rosalina stopped him as she hurried across the floor and laid a hand on his arm. "Let me make it up to you."

Marco waved a hand. "That's not necessary."

"No, please. How about I treat you to supper?"

"You don't have to."

"How about a picnic?"

Marco considered it. A picnic did sound nice. And it would provide a good opportunity to learn more about her. Because now they were two for two.

She knew that he didn't like to read and was scared of dogs.

He knew that she had a mean pet and loved dogs beyond what's reasonable.

They had a lot more to learn. Hopefully, they could get to some facts that would prove helpful come Saturday's likely questions.

Marco gave one quick nod. "A picnic would be fine."

She gave him a smile. "Tomorrow night?"

"Sure." That would give him time to build his confidence back up. Going hysterical over a teddy bear of a dog wasn't exactly a score to his manliness. Fear could fell the strongest of men, though. Plus, it didn't seem like a good idea to skip out on church after some of the thoughts he'd had considering Ladybug and her owner. Might be wise to pay a visit to the altar tonight.

"Great. Do you mind if it's in the backyard at my place? My *tía* and *tío* have an amazing patio and a peaceful yard."

Marco shrugged and wound Luigi's leash around his wrist. "Sounds fine to me."

"Okay. What time works best for you? I know you sometimes work late hours."

Marco took a moment to think of what tomorrow's job had looked like when he'd checked the company app schedule. It was a big one. "Is seven too late?"

"No. That is perfect."

"Very well. I'll be at your place by seven."

To his surprise, Rosalina's smile only got bigger.

Since when did she have ready smiles in his presence?

Where was her sass?

Maybe it was because she was trying too hard not to laugh she couldn't remember she didn't like him.

Yeah, that's it.

He could only wonder how tomorrow's meal would go. It couldn't go any worse than their dinner at Ricardo's had. So long as no big dogs showed up. But if he remembered right, the Torres' had a sturdy privacy fence.

As Marco settled in his truck and drove home, with Luigi standing on his lap staring out the window, he had to wonder if Rosalina had some kind of scheme cooked up if she were still mad at him over the whole fake dating thing.

Then again, she had been nice this afternoon. Maybe she'd needed time to warm up to the idea...and him.

"I guess I'll find out tomorrow."

Chapter Thirteen

As Rosalina bustled about the kitchen Thursday after work, she began to question what had come over her to offer cooking for Marco and inviting him on a picnic.

As his girlfriend, she had every right. True. But that wasn't why she'd offered.

No. It'd been the raw fear in his eyes underneath the barely controlled anger he'd portrayed toward Ladybug. The stocky, tough looking guy with the silly smile was scared of dogs.

Well, not every dog. His family had one, after all. But, apparently, he was terrified of big dogs. She'd noticed the tremor in his hands as he pocketed his wallet and had taken Luigi's leash from her.

That kind of fear didn't come from lack of interaction with the large animals. If she had to guess, she'd say Marco had some kind of traumatic encounter with a dog sometime in his past.

Now she could agree there were certain breeds that deserved more cautious respect than others. But the worst thing a person could do was demonstrate fear around a dog bent toward doing harm.

Being the dog-lover she was, Rosalina felt compassion for Marco and wondered if she could help him overcome his fear somehow. Just because a dog was big didn't mean it was vicious and dangerous.

Like Ladybug, for instance. There wasn't a sweeter dog than her. A big teddy bear, is what she really was. But, a hundred pound beast was hard for a seventy-six year old woman who maybe weighed eighty pounds soaking wet to manage.

And so here she was nervously sweating, fearing Marco would dislike her food even more than he did her, yet cooking for him all the same because she wanted to help him.

"He probably doesn't even want to be helped."

If he did, he likely wouldn't appreciate it coming from her.

□□□

Her good intentions were replaced with complaints and a bit of anger when fifteen minutes after seven, Rosalina found herself, yet again, waiting on Marco for a date.

The meal was ready. She had the table set with cute strawberry patterned paper plates, red and white checkered napkins, and matching red plastic silverware. She'd been pleased with herself making it look summery and laid back; she sure didn't want to decorate in a way that could be misconstrued as romantic.

But here she was wondering if the man of the hour was going to show up. Rosalina huffed and dropped onto the couch.

"Not even a text." She let her phone slip from her hand onto her lap.

Rosalina was beginning to understand how Lillian Harrison wound up engaged to another man than Marco. If their dating life had been anything like the few days she had known him...

She was curious of what this Lillian was like. And the man she was engaged to. She would look forward to meeting them on Saturday. How would Marco handle that introduction?

Speaking of Marco, her phone pinged and, wouldn't you know it, she finally had a message from him.

Marco: Sorry. Running late. Be there in ten.
Rosalina: K.

Short and sweet. Oh, but inside she was feeling anything but sweet. He'd better have a good reason for being late this time.

Rosalina would find it easy to believe Marco's one talent was being late.

With another huff, she stood and began carrying the food out to the patio table. Thankfully, it stayed bright out until almost nine o'clock this time of year but, still, Rosalina turned on the Edison bulbs draped on the pergola.

She smiled at the sight and hoped the evening would go well. She wasn't asking for a romance, a relationship, or anything that could remotely lead to marriage. But it would be nice to have a friend. And with Marco sharing in her heritage, he could make a fun friend.

Rosalina chuckled. She doubted Marco would complain about all her seasonings like Haven. The poor girl about choked to death the first time Rosalina shared a home-cooked meal with her coworker. Now they only ate out together.

"It's safer this way," Haven had said.

Rosalina would never understand people who liked such bland food. Give it some kick. Not to mention, spices and seasonings had many health benefits too. It was a win-win.

Knock, knock.

"Oh!" Rosalina sped through the sliding glass door that she'd left open while transferring food from kitchen to patio, and rushed to the front door. Before answering it, she took a moment to smooth her hair. Queenie came running from down the hall where Rosalina knew *Tía* Carmen was taking a moment to ice her sore back while she waited for *Tío* Juan to come home so they could eat together inside. Rosalina had made extra so her *tía* wouldn't have to do any cooking tonight. If only she could do something for the back ache. Take the pain away.

Knock, knock.

"Oops!" Rosalina reached to unlock the door, but stopped.

Why be in a hurry?

Why should she be concerned about making Marco wait?

She rested her hand on the handle and waited, her forehead leaned against the door. She found herself holding her breath as she awaited the next knock. When she expected it to come but it didn't, Rosalina gasped.

"No!" She thrust the door open and saw Marco's retreating back. "Marco, wait!"

He slowly turned around, shrugged his shoulders up to his ears, and held his hands out and up at waist level. "Thought nobody was home."

The smile she'd criticized was stretching from ear to ear on that bubbly face of his, and Rosalina felt her heart do a silly flutter. *What?*

She took a steadying breath and smoothed her hands down her front. "Sorry. I was transferring food out to the patio."

"Ah." He started walking back up to the house, his eyes never leaving hers. They coaxed the truth from her...against her will.

Rosalina ducked her head. "That isn't true. I mean, I had been. But I heard your knocks. I just...well—"

"Thought you'd make me wait since you had to wait on me?"

She looked up and nodded. It didn't feel as fun as it had sounded. Now she felt guilty. He was easy to pick on. But her "picking" was probably coming across as unkind. "Sorry."

"You don't have anything to apologize for." He stepped up. Close. Their shoulders bumped.

Rosalina sucked in a breath.

Marco went one step beyond her, then leaned back until their shoulders were touching again, and he whispered in her ear. "I'm the one who is sorry."

The little hairs in Rosalina's ears took up break dancing as a cold tingling sensation frolicked through her veins.

Whoa. What is going on?

"You were late." She managed through a dry throat, then twisted around in tiny increments until they were facing each other.

So close. His face, his nose was mere inches—maybe even centimeters—away.

"The job took longer than I thought it would, and then we had to clean up. Your uncle is strict about us leaving a jobsite spick and span."

She could smell him. He smelled like sweat and the pungent odor of tar shingles. She was familiar with the scent as it was practically a part of her *tío* and cousin's DNA. "You may have cleaned the jobsite, but you clearly didn't wash yourself up."

"Didn't have time. You'd still be waiting if I swung by home to take a shower."

"Could have at least changed your clothes." She sniffed in disapproval as she walked past him and through the front door.

He followed her in and closed the door behind them. "I could have, but something tells me you don't like to be kept waiting."

"Humph. I have good reason to be ticked off. This is only our second date. And the first one, if you remember, you were running late too. I was beginning to think I'd been stood up."

"Hey, it's not my fault José didn't get my messages right when I sent them, nor could I have done anything about the accident. And I can't help it that I had a job that had to be done that kept me over tonight. At least I sent you a message. I didn't leave you hanging."

"I do thank you for that."

"Wow. Gratitude. You *can* be nice."

Rosalina tossed him a dirty look over her shoulder. That whole being friendly thing wasn't working out. She didn't respond.

"You know, I expected you to make some kind of remark. Now I know you don't like my smile and you think I stink. Want me to leave and we forget this picnic? I'd hate to ruin your appetite with my presence."

They were in the dining room now, standing before the still-open sliding glass doors. Queenie was outside sniffing the petunias around the edge of the concrete pavers.

Rosalina sighed. "You're harder on yourself than I am. I didn't mean any of the things I said the way you took them."

Marco raised a brow, his face disbelieving.

"I-I don't know what it is. I guess you're an easy target to tease."

"Doesn't seem like teasing."

"Hmm." As she'd thought. "I don't suppose it does. I have a tendency to be blunt and speak whatever first comes to mind. I need to do a better job of filtering my thoughts."

Marco twisted his finger in his ear. "Not sure I want to know what your unfiltered thoughts are of me." His face registered mock pain.

Rosalina raised her eyes to the ceiling. Exasperating man. "Can we change the subject?"

"Fine by me."

"Let's eat. Everything is ready and getting cold while we spat."

They sat in chairs opposite each other at the small square-shaped patio table.

Marco ran his hand over the tablecloth. "Nice spread."

"I had to make sure it was picnic-y."

"I'd say you pulled it off."

Rosalina rubbed her hands on the chair's armrests. She was getting clammy all of a sudden. "Do you want to pray?"

"Sure." He pulled a pair of sunglasses off the top of his head and set them on the table. How had she not noticed those up there? They must have blended in with his dark hair.

She found herself staring at the sunglasses, wondering what Marco would look like with them on.

"Dear Lord,"

Oh. Rosalina bowed her head and squeezed her eyes shut, but she couldn't pay attention to a single word he prayed as she worried about whether or not Marco would like her cooking.

She'd made her *tía's* homemade street taco recipe with corn tortillas, chorizo, onions, a squeeze of lime, and seasoned it to perfection with plenty of cilantro.

She hoped he would appreciate her fine taste.

"In Jesus' name. Amen."

Rosalina lifted her head and sent Marco a soft smile across the table. "I hope you brought your appetite."

"I've been working like a horse all day, so you have nothing to worry about. My lunch was used up a long time ago."

"Getting hot doesn't affect your stomach? I can't eat if I get overheated."

Marco shrugged. "The heat doesn't bother me anymore. I'm used to it."

She supposed if one worked outside all day every day through the summer that would be the case. She pulled off the red and white checked cloth napkin she'd used to keep flies away from their food. "Well, eat up."

Marco let out a delighted, "Ahh! Tacos. How did you know they were my favorite?"

"Oh." Rosalina was taken aback. "I didn't know. But this is one of my favorite meals my *tía* makes, so I followed her recipe, although added a little more cilantro to my preference."

Marco rubbed his hands together greedily and scooted forward in his chair. "You've made my day."

She felt her cheeks warm. She hadn't expected that to happen. Perhaps this picnic wasn't a bad idea. Maybe they could get along—despite the rocky beginning.

They each selected a tortilla and began assembling their tacos. While Rosalina figured Marco would be a big eater, she'd been worried she'd give him too much or too little, so had opted to let him make his taco himself.

"So, where's Queenie?" Marco asked as he began folding his taco. "I figured she'd be at the door to greet me."

Rosalina chuckled. "She came to the door with me, but when I waited so long to answer it, she took advantage of the open patio door." She scanned the yard for her dog. "She's over in the back corner there, probably checking to see if the neighbor's dog is out. They like to sniff each other through the cracks in the fence."

Marco followed Rosalina's gaze. "Ah, there's the little devil."

"Queenie is not a devil. She's a dog."

"Same difference."

"*Ummmm,* no. There's a big difference."

"Don't you know every time dog is mentioned in the Bible it doesn't have a good connotation?"

Rosalina lost control of her jaw. The nerve of him. "Would you like me to tell Luigi you said that."

Marco ducked his head but raised it again with that silly smile in place. "You got me there."

"You must believe me. Queenie is an angel. I seriously don't know what came over her that first day she met you. Maybe she was in a mood."

"Could be. She is a girl."

Rosalina glared at him.

He grimaced. "Oops. Sorry."

"Uh-huh." It was the most insincere apology she'd ever heard.

At last, Marco raised the taco to his lips and Rosalina held her breath.

His teeth sunk into the tortilla at the same time as he leaned over his plate. "Mmm." His eyes slid shut and it looked as if he'd died and gone to heaven. "Rosalina, these are perfect."

She didn't care that he spoke with his mouth full, for those words did far more to her than she cared to admit.

He liked her cooking.

He likes my cooking. Eeeeeek!

Now that her nerves were settled by Marco's compliment, Rosalina took a taste of her taco. And she agreed with Marco's assessment. They were perfect.

Queenie came bounding across the yard, a smile on her face. But then she stopped dead in her tracks when her little dark eyes landed on Marco. She growled and showed her teeth.

Marco stiffened and gave Rosalina an *I told you so* look. "That dog is no angel."

Rosalina shook her head. "Give her time to warm up to you. Maybe she's protecting me and her house."

"Yeah, that's it." Marco sent Queenie a dirty look, and Rosalina got the impression he would have stuck his tongue out at the dog if not for her watchful eyes.

"Just you wait and see. Before you know it, you'll be best friends."

He grumbled and picked up a piece of the beef that had fallen onto his plate. "Here, Queenie."

Rosalina didn't normally give Queenie table scraps, but she kept her mouth shut, wanting to see how this turned out.

One wary step after another, the dog drew closer to Marco, keeping a close watch on his hand and face interchangeably. There was certainly a trust issue.

When Queenie, apparently, came as far as she felt safe doing so, she stretched her neck to sniff at the peace offering in Marco's hand.

"Go on. It's all yours," he coaxed and reached his hand out closer to the dog.

Queenie came one step closer, but instead of gently taking the piece of beef, she nipped at Marco's pinched fingers.

He jerked his hand back. "You rotten—"

Queenie growled and darted over to Rosalina, clawing at her thigh to be picked up. Rosalina obliged. Meanwhile, wondering what Marco was going to call her sweet princess.

"I don't know how you think you can call that thing an angel. A fallen angel maybe."

"Marco!"

He studied his fingers.

"They okay?"

"Only a few teeth dents, but, again, she didn't break the skin."

"See? She doesn't mean you any real harm. Queenie is letting you know who is boss."

"I want to show her a thing or two." He shook his finger at Queenie, but the dog looked away.

And so it seemed the perfect opening had presented itself for the subject at the forefront of Rosalina's mind and reason for this picnic. She let Marco enjoy another bite before speaking. Let his mood improve first. Tacos were good for that.

"So," how to word it tactfully? Maybe an apology would be best to begin with. "I'm sorry about what happened yesterday with Ladybug."

Marco shuddered. "Absolutely nothing about that name suits that beast. It certainly wasn't a lady, and definitely no bug. If I saw a bug that big I'd shoot it."

Rosalina laughed. "Come on. No harm was done. She playfully mauled you. Ladybug clearly liked you with all those big licks she showered upon you."

"Ugh, yeah. Sure." He took another bite and chewed faster and harder than before.

Uh oh, touchy subject. As she'd thought.

"Marco..."

"Hmm." He'd already taken another bite.

"Can I ask you something?"

One corner of his lips curved up in an almost smirk. "I haven't known you long, but I think it's been long enough to say I know you're going to ask regardless."

"Not if you say no."

"Really?"

Rosalina lifted one shoulder. "This time."

He stared at her, not moving a single face muscle for a heartbeat. Two. Three. Then he cracked. Literally. Deep in his throat Rosalina heard that choking, crackling cough that erupts when you're trying to not laugh. "Okay, what is it?"

"Why are you scared of dogs?"

The air changed between them. Everything about Marco hardened. "I'm not scared of dogs. We have a dog."

"Oh, yeah. A Chihuahua. Real scary."

Man, if looks could kill...

Rosalina cleared her throat. "I know you have a dog. But I also saw how shook up you were over Ladybug's tackling you. Admit it. You're scared of—if not dogs in general—at least big ones."

A long moment of silence descended. Only the sounds of a distant lawn mower could be heard and a few childish screams from the neighborhood.

Marco set his food down, his shoulders rounded in defeat. "Okay. I admit it. I am sort of scared of dogs."

"Sort of?" She quirked a brow.

He muttered something under his breath that sounded like *frustrating woman.* "All right. Okay. I'm scared." He growled the admission.

"How come?"

"How come?"

"Yes. How come?"

"Does it matter?"

Oh, the man had far more sass in him than Rosalina had originally credited him. Perhaps, that's why they butted heads so much.

Rosalina chose her words carefully. Men didn't like their ego tampered with, and the last thing she wanted to do was offend him. "You don't have to tell me if you'd rather not. I just thought I'd ask. I work with dogs every day. I know a lot about the different breeds, their personalities, et cetera. I might could help..."

Marco took a drink from his iced tea. She hoped he liked sweet tea. She hadn't considered asking him what he might want to drink, but had poured their glasses ahead of time. Sweet tea was a staple in this house. *Tía* Carmen always had a pitcher of it ready-made in the fridge.

He moved to pick his taco back up, but stopped and looked away. If Rosalina followed his focus correctly, he was watching Queenie.

"I was attacked by a dog when I was eight years old."

Rosalina sucked in a breath, glad she hadn't recently taken a bite or drink to have a repeat choking scene like their first date. "Marco..." She covered her lips with one hand.

"My sister and I were playing in the front yard together, enjoying a game of catch. Isabella threw a wild ball and I went to fetch it. When I returned, there was a pit bull that I could tell was getting ready to maul her. To protect Isabella, I hollered at the dog and took off running."

"Oh, Marco, that was..."

"I know. Stupid. You should never run from a dog. But, I was young and I didn't want my sister getting hurt. I was raised to be a protector, taught to respect and care for my sister and women. That's the only distraction I could think of. My speed was no match for the dog, and it quickly overtook me, taking me to the ground."

Rosalina shook her head. No wonder he'd been so shook up after Ladybug tackled him. It must have brought back terrible memories.

"Thankfully, Isabella had run into the house for help the minute I took off, but Dad didn't get there before the beast could cause injury."

Rosalina found herself searching every inch of Marco she could see, checking to see that he had every finger. Looking for scars.

"My face took the brunt of it. Two bites to my left cheek and orbital region. A lot of scratches from my torso up. Some pretty sore bruises too. I'm not sure how Dad managed to get me away from the dog, but somehow he got me inside. Mom was already on the phone with the police. I'll never forget how frantic she was, or how she carried on when she saw me. I'm glad there weren't any mirrors around for me to catch a glimpse."

A shudder overtook Rosalina. She couldn't imagine being in any of their shoes. It would be horrific. "So, did you need stitches?"

Marco let out a snort of a laugh. "Too many. My face looked like an engineering train wreck of railroad tracks."

Rosalina leaned closer and scrutinized his face. "But I don't see any scars."

"Nah. Mom was determined that I wouldn't, seeing as how it was my face. She bought every cream and used every remedy for scar reducing. Made me see a dermatologist. You have to know they're there or look very closely."

"I'm so sorry. If that happened to me, I would be scared of dogs too."

"Probably wouldn't have the job you do."

Rosalina let out a mirthless laugh through her nose. "No."

Marco took another bite and chewed it slowly before talking again. "After that, Dad put up a tall privacy fence and I never played outside it again. I can remember every time I heard a dog barking I'd start shaking and fear would turn me cold. It doesn't affect me quite so much now—except for Ladybug. I guess it was too much of a trigger."

"I can imagine." She pressed a hand to her chest. "Now, how about we talk about something happier?"

"Totally. All for it."

Rosalina chuckled. "Another taco?"

"I can never turn down more tacos." He proceeded in throwing another one together, and then was quick to find a new subject. "What got you interested in the grooming business? Was that something you always wanted to do?"

"Oh my, no. I actually moved here from Mexico to attend college to be an elementary schoolteacher. But in my first semester of college, while I was still homesick and pining for my parents, the school brought in therapy dogs and I happened upon the session. I fell in love with dogs right then and there, and I knew I wanted to do something that would let me be with them every day."

"Definitely not something we have in common. Don't get me wrong. I do like Luigi."

Rosalina fought a laugh. "Well, he is by no means of the threatening type. I could fit him in my purse."

"My parents chose well."

"I'm sure they had you in mind when they picked him."

Marco nodded. "I think that's probably why they got a dog to begin with. To try and help me get over my fear of them."

"How old is Luigi?" If the accident had happened when Marco was eight... There was no way Luigi was old enough to have been gotten shortly after the accident.

"He's almost twelve."

"Oh, wow. I wouldn't have guessed. He still acts like a puppy."

"Yep. Luigi is a spritely little thing. Nothing much slows him down."

"Aww."

Marco didn't seem to know what to do with that response. He shimmied on his chair. "So your parents still live in Mexico?"

"Yes. They are the sole caregiver for my *abuela*, who refuses to leave. I do hope that one day *Ma-má* and *Pa-pá* will be able to come to the States."

"Have you been able to return for a visit since moving here?"

Homesickness twisted in her middle. "I haven't been able to make it possible financially. First with paying my way through college, then starting up a business." She let out an exasperated sigh. "And the continuing expenses involved with being a business owner."

Marco grimaced. "Pretty bad?"

"I won't say it's easy. But there are plenty of perks of being your own boss."

"Ha, I'm sure. I wouldn't know." He smirked. "But I have a good boss."

"You'd better say that. *Tío* Juan is right on the other side of that glass door."

"But you wouldn't dare tattle on me." A twinkle appeared in his eye.

"I wouldn't be so sure." She tapped her index finger on her chin.

They held each others' gaze for a serious moment before they dissolved into laughter.

"This is really nice," Marco said when he recovered.

"What is?" Rosalina wiped at her leaky eyes.

"*This.*" He waved an all-encompassing hand. "The food is phenomenal. The evening is perfect. And, well, we're getting along. We're not arguing."

Rosalina almost choked on her tiny sip of sweet tea. With the utterance of those words, she realized, to her astonishment, she was glad Marco ran his mouth that night at Ricardo's *Restaurante*.

She couldn't remember the last time she'd shared such easy companionship with someone other than her relatives.

A lasting friendship with Marco was looking to be more possible than it had even at the start of this evening.

And that was fine. A friend was all she desired from this arrangement, after all.

In fact, it would please her.

Chapter Fourteen

Marco hadn't expected to stay at the Torres' until after ten, but he'd found it hard to pull himself away.

Had it not been for the fact he had work tomorrow, and Juan kept peeping his head out to give them updates on the time (as if he or Rosalina didn't have a phone that could tell them the time), Marco wasn't sure how long he would have stayed.

He found that quite...peculiar.

But now that he was home and heading down the hallway to his bedroom, Marco was glad he hadn't stayed any longer. He was bushed. Bed never sounded sweeter, and yet he still needed to take a shower.

"Ugh."

There was no way he could skip. He could smell himself. And poor Rosalina had had to suffer through the evening with the stench wafting from him. It wouldn't surprise Marco if there'd been a brown or green cloud around him like Pig Pen from the Peanuts gang.

That made him snicker. Rosalina hadn't minded letting him know he stunk. But if he would have taken the time to shower and then head over for the picnic and been almost an hour late, she would have had plenty to say about that too.

Crazy girl seemed to always have something to complain about.

Well, maybe complain wasn't the right word. Like Rosalina had said, she was blunt. Spoke her mind. He could admire that in a person. In fact, he preferred it. Then he didn't have to wonder what the person was thinking.

Lillian was like that. Perhaps that's why Marco had felt himself relaxing and opening up, having a good time with Rosalina tonight. Maybe she and Lillian had a few more similar characteristics than he'd originally thought.

That would work in his favor. Make it easier to pull off the whole fake relationship thing at the wedding, which was coming up fast. Only two weeks from Saturday.

The big test would be this coming Saturday, two days away, at Heritage Days. If they could persuade everyone they were a serious dating couple, that would be great...at least on the plus-one front for the wedding.

On the flip side, Marco doubted anything was going to help him get through that day. Watching Lillian wed Clint...

It was going to be the worst day of his life since his dog attack sixteen years ago. He doubted there was anything that would help him get through.

He groaned and passed his brother's room, almost to his own bedroom where he'd proceed to take a quick shower, and, finally...blessedly, crawl into bed.

"Marco, that you?"

No... he wanted to whine. But he twisted around and returned to Antonio's doorway, leaned against the threshold because standing was getting to be beyond him. He found his brother at his desk with some big book open, taking copious notes. The boy was always studying something. *Ick.*

Marco tried to get a look at what subject Antonio might be diving deep into this time, but he couldn't see straight any longer. His eyes were too tired. "Yeah, Ant. Whatcha need?"

"Well, you could start by not calling me Ant." Antonio pierced him with a threatening gaze. Might have looked really scary if Marco could see clearly. "Where ya been all evening? You never stay out this late."

To spill all or be vague?

Marco wasn't sure if he was ready to share the truth with Antonio yet, but his brother was bound to find out at Heritage

Days, so he might as well get it out in the air. Although, his mom likely already said something.

He beat a light fist on the doorjamb as he made his final decision. "I was on a date."

"A date? As in, guy and girl go out kind of date?"

"Yep. That's the kind." Marco stepped farther into the room.

"Whoa." Antonio tossed his mechanical pencil down on his book. "That is the last thing I would have expected."

Marco pocketed his hands and raised his shoulders. "Why's that so hard to believe?"

"Well, it's just that...you know. I thought you and Lillian were pretty close. I figured you'd be licking your wounds a long time over her engagement and marriage."

Antonio wasn't wrong, but he wasn't about to admit to it. "Yeah, well, I've been on a couple dates with this girl now."

"Really? Is it serious?" Antonio leaned back in his chair and crossed his arms, looking like the intelligent academic he was.

Marco felt as if he were being studied like an open book. He squirmed. "Could be." Vague answers were all he could offer now. Anything beyond how they met and the extent of their short "relationship" would be grasping for straws, and Marco was too tired to try and fabricate anything and be able to recall it later to repeat. If one was going to lie they had to do it well.

Lie.

Liar.

He'd be glad when the wedding was over and he could be done living a lie. He wanted to set his conscience to rest.

"Wow. I hope it works out. Will I get to meet her soon?"

"Actually, yes. If you're going to Heritage Days. Rosalina is coming with me."

"Rosalina." Antonio turned thoughtful. "Marco and Rosalina. Sounds good together."

Don't go making us a couple, bro. He gave his brother no answer.

"How'd you meet?"

Not that question again. Antonio didn't need the long one. "All thanks to José. They're cousins."

"Ah, that's perfect."

Marco yawned large and loud. "I need to hit the hay, bro."

"Yeah, you get. I'm glad for you. To be honest, I was worried about you. With Lillian, you know. Thought the wedding might be hard for you."

More than you could ever know. "Don't worry about me, Tony."

"It's Antonio," his brother corrected to Marco's retreating back.

He laughed through his nose as he entered his own room. At least Tony was better than Mars.

Marco rolled his eyes.

How had Rosalina come up with that? There wasn't an s in his name. If he had to guess, he'd say she wanted a name that would irk him.

If so, she'd succeeded.

Then he had to wonder. Had she not liked him calling her Lina? She did seem to be one to enjoy some sassy retaliation.

Hmm.

It might be wise to see what her feelings were on the pet name before Heritage Days. He didn't want to say it in front of his mother and have Rosalina vaporize his head off with her eyes.

That would blow the cover for sure.

□□□

Heritage Day.

Marco wasn't sure what to expect, but he hoped for the best. If he and Rosalina could get along as well as they had Thursday night, he'd have nothing to worry about.

Friday had included some friendly texting as well. In fact, Rosalina had invited him to join her as she walked some dogs for commission, but Marco had been far too tired to consider the possibility. He, apparently, wasn't made for dating. At least, not of the late night variety. The five a.m. alarm came way too soon, especially considering by the time he crawled into bed last night the second hand had been bearing down on midnight.

That was a time that should only be seen once a day—accompanied with food.

With a bolstering deep breath, Marco tucked his T-shirt into his pants, slicked a hand over his hair, and sent Rosalina a text to let her know he'd be there shortly to pick her up.

Normally, he would arrive at Heritage Days an hour early. Being a friend of the family, the Harrisons didn't mind. In fact, they welcomed people early if they wanted extra time to talk before the festivities.

This year, however, Marco had no such desire. Extra time to talk meant more opportunity for questions, and he was avoiding them like the plaque.

When he was preparing to leave his room, Antonio showed up in the doorway with an annoying grin as he waggled his eyebrows. "So, today is the big day. I get to meet Rosalina."

Marco grumbled.

"Is she pretty?"

That made him pause. He hadn't considered it before. Was Rosalina pretty? He hadn't studied her in that fashion yet, looked on her with interest. If anything, he'd given her appearance all the attention of a brief encounter with a stranger at a grocery store.

He would have to fix that today. Aside from knowing she had dark hair and skin that reminded him of Lillian was all Marco could say. To be honest, he wasn't completely certain his mind didn't see Lillian when he looked at Rosalina.

It was time to see Rosalina for who she was. Not for whom she reminded him of. He'd do good to stop comparing her to Lillian too.

Since he couldn't give a total educated answer, Marco chose the easy route. "You'll find out soon."

Now it was Antonio's turn to grumble. "I'm heading out now."

"I'm picking Rosalina up and then I'll be there."

Antonio's smile only grew larger. "My brother picking a girl up who isn't Lillian. I need to write this down on the calendar or something. This is momentous."

Marco glared at him.

Antonio raised his arms in surrender. "Ouch. That doesn't look like a man in love. Right now you look like someone stole your last taco."

Accurate description. Someone had "stolen his last taco" in a sense. That Clint Bishop who swooped in and swept Lillian off her feet and placed a ring on her finger.

But, like an eaten taco couldn't be gotten back, neither could Marco get Lillian back. He could only get another taco.

There was one reassuring fact, though. Marco never had to doubt the next taco would be as good, if not better than the one before. A taco was a taco. But every once in a while he got an exceptionally good one.

Like Thursday night's. Made from Rosalina's hands.

Could Marco find something even better in Rosalina?

He almost didn't want to consider it. The friendship, the fascination he'd had with Lillian, had been special.

Then realization struck him like a brick. Even if things had been different, had Lillian not met Clint, he doubted she would have accepted his proposal. Marco saw the truth for the first time. She'd never looked at him like a woman in love. She'd always seen him as a friend. In her eyes, they'd shared nothing more than a brother and sister kind of love.

A conversation from earlier in the year—on Easter, to be exact—resurfaced. He had asked Lillian if she wanted to go bowling, and she'd turned him down due to a prior engagement. Marco would be lying to say he hadn't been disappointed.

He could recall Lillian's next words with perfect clarity: *"One of these days you'll find a girl that'll push me down a slot."*

She'd had no idea she was the only girl he wanted. Marco had simply replied with: *"Perhaps, Lillian, but I am in no hurry. When the right girl comes along, I'll know it; but for now I'm just enjoying the life I've been given."*

With you, he'd added in his mind. Maybe he should have tried speaking his feelings then. But what would it have mattered? Anytime he'd hinted to anything between *them* in vague terms, she always deflected it. Obviously, Lillian had never cared for him in the same way he had for her.

So why was he letting this upcoming wedding affect him so badly? Shouldn't he be able to get back up, brush himself off, and be on his merry way.

Ha. There was nothing merry about the way Marco felt. But fact was fact. He couldn't do a thing about it.

Suck it up, buttercup.

"It is what it is." He rubbed his ear at the distasteful words.

"Huh? What's that supposed to mean?"

Marco had forgotten his brother was standing there. What had he said aloud? "Never mind. I'm still recovering from Thursday's late night."

Antonio looked at him slit-eyed. And if Marco could read minds, he'd say his brother was thinking something smelled fishy.

He needed to be more careful. Couldn't let his mind and tongue have free run. He had a whole ruse depending on his self control.

Chapter Fifteen

Marco tugged uncomfortably at the neck of his orange T-shirt as he took begrudged steps away from his car and toward the group of people gathered for Heritage Days out at the Harrisons' lavender farm—Rosalina beside him. They walked in perfect synchronization, which could only help their ruse, right?

He'd always looked forward to this event, but now he dreaded it. So many people. So many friends. Too many opportunities for questions. Plus, he had to worry about what Rosalina might say.

Then if they got separated, he'd have no idea what she told others and he might say something different. All it would take would be for one person to be on top of things and they'd know something wasn't right.

Marco decided he needed to be sure and keep Rosalina at his side. Not lose sight of her, or get out of earshot. It shouldn't be too hard to do. After all, they were a serious dating couple, on their way to falling helplessly in love.

Not.

"Hey, hey, hey. If it's not my brother and his new girlfriend."

Of course Antonio would be the first to ambush them.

Marco forced a smile. "Hey, brother. Meet Rosalina Torres. Rosalina, this is my *little* brother Antonio Mendez." Had to rub in his seniority.

"A pleasure to meet you, Antonio."

"No, the pleasure is mine." The two shook hands, and Marco watched as his brother looked Rosalina over. Approval lightened his eyes. "So, what about my brother endeared him to you?"

Scheming was what Marco would call the twinkle that appeared in Rosalina's eyes as she looked to him before answering. "Without a doubt, his smile. That was the first to get me."

Marco hoped the cloud of confusion he felt wasn't on display for all to see as he stared at Rosalina. The little liar. His smile had been the first thing she'd insulted.

Antonio turned to him. "And what about Rosalina garnered your attention?"

Marco wanted to slug his brother. Figures he'd be the one to interrogate them so...annoyingly. He was pretty sure "little pests sent to earth to annoy their siblings" would be the definition for younger brothers if he were to look it up in the old *Webster's 1828*.

How had Rosalina fired off her answer so quickly? Marco couldn't stall. That would be an automatic ding in their ruse. What had he noticed about her so far? *Ah-hah.* "Her sass. It's her most endearing quality, for sure. Things are never dull."

That last part was one hundred percent true. The most endearing quality part? He'd made that up. It was her most infuriating quality.

Rosalina was shooting fiery darts at him with her scary eyes, which in an instant changed to doe eyes when Antonio switched his attention back to her.

"Well, I'm glad for the both of you. You make a cute couple. Maybe I can manage to sit at the same table as you two for the meal so I can get to know Rosalina better."

Not if Marco could help it. He would find a table that was already full, save two chairs, with only strangers around it.

Finally, Antonio left and Marco was able to take in a full breath. Then he narrowed his eyes at Rosalina. "My smile? Really?"

"Mm-hm." She wore a disgustingly self-satisfied grin.

Marco grumbled.

"I'm glad to know you like my sass. I do believe you said it was my most endearing quality. I'll have you know I take that compliment straight to the heart."

"I'm sure you do," Marco muttered.

"What's that?" Rosalina leaned close, then gave the most uncalled-for tittering laugh. The kind a woman might make when a man said something sweet.

What is that all about? When he saw the reason his entire body stiffened. Standing before them now was none other than Lillian and Clint.

"Marco, hi!" Lillian sent a playful jab to his biceps. "Who is this lovely woman you have with you?"

Rosalina linked one arm around Marco's and all but snuggled up to his side.

He instantaneously developed brain fog and laryngitis at the same time. The three were ganging up on him.

Lillian for asking questions.

Rosalina for playing the part far too well.

And Clint, well...Clint for being there, with Lillian hanging onto his arm as if they were glued together. The perfect image of two people madly in love.

He'd be lying to say it didn't frost him.

"Ah, yes, Lillian. This is my girlfriend, Rosalina Torres."

"Girlfriend?" Lillian got a greedy glint, clearly desiring more information. "Mom hinted to as much the other night. I have to say I didn't see that coming, but I'm so happy. Rosalina, you got yourself a real keeper in Marco."

Then why didn't you keep me? He wanted to ask.

Rosalina's smile was borderline fake. "We've only been dating about three weeks now and I can already tell what you say is true."

Marco longed to roll his eyes. This was absurd. He should be worried by how well his "girlfriend" could lie. Shamelessly.

"Oooo!" Lillian squealed as she squeezed Clint's arm tighter. "Marco, you've already met Clint. So, Rosalina, meet my fiancé, Clint Bishop."

Clint extended a hand, which, thankfully, forced Rosalina to unlink her arm from his, since her other arm bore a bag, which contained some sort of dish for the potluck (which she didn't trust him to carry, apparently). "I've heard so much about you two. Congratulations on your upcoming wedding." Her radiant face was genuine.

"You must come with me." Lillian wiggled her fingers toward Rosalina. "I'll help you find the perfect spot for your dish, and we can get to know each other better. I must know all about the girl who finally caught Marco's fancy."

Marco knew Lillian. She wouldn't take no for an answer. Lillian detached herself from Clint and linked an arm through Rosalina's. "I'm glad you could come to Heritage Days. It's going to be a blast."

Marco feared what might be said between those two, but he was helpless to do anything about it. He wasn't sure if that was worse, or being left with Clint.

If he wanted to remain friends with Lillian, however, it stood to reason he should become friends with Clint too. So Marco forced every bit of fake interest and kindness to strike up a superficial conversation with the man, all while keeping a close eye on Rosalina and Lillian.

□□□

Marco didn't see Rosalina again until they met up in the food line twenty minutes later. So much for keeping her at his side or within earshot. Who knew how many people she'd told, only God knew what, about their relationship. How could he be sure he kept the story straight now?

At least it was time for the meal and they could sit together and he could get caught up on how far their story had grown. He strongly hoped Rosalina was not the exaggerating kind.

"So, what dish did you bring?" Marco asked Rosalina when they were halfway through the line.

"What do you think I brought?"

As if he would have any idea. "Well, my stomach wishes that you brought those tacos you made the other night, but I don't see them anywhere. So, I don't know." He shrugged, then made a wild guess. "The enchiladas." He pointed at the two of them on his plate.

"Nope."

"Don't you want me to taste your dish?"

"I don't want you to know what it is, get it, and say it's good because it's mine."

Marco snorted. "Believe me, I'd be honest. Seeing as that's how you prefer things to be between us regarding our opinions on each other."

"Humph." Rosalina turned her nose up. "I told you I didn't mean my remarks about your smile as an insult."

107

"Right," he said sarcastically. "Because it's your favorite quality of mine."

Rosalina huffed and proceeded to the dessert table without him.

Marco finished filling his plate in quick fashion with some baked beans and hurried to her side again. He would not let her away from his side for the meal. A dating couple had to eat together. Right?

The dessert table proved to be overwhelming. There were too many mouth-watering options, but Marco settled with a brownie and some sort of green Jell-O dessert. He could never pass up the jiggly treat, *and* it had whipped cream in it too. Even better.

Rosalina sent him an almost too large smile as they left the desserts and grabbed their drinks. "Where do you want to sit?" She leaned close and asked.

The soft brush of her breath along his jaw momentarily robbed Marco of his.

Say what?

What was that all about?

Marco gave himself a hard mental shake and searched the spread of round tables until he found one with two empty chairs. There were two young adults Marco didn't recognize, one of whom appeared to be of Asian descent (probably a relative of Clint's) and, unfortunately, Antonio, and Clint and Lillian were also seated there.

He was going to find a different table option, but Antonio waved him over. Marco considered pretending he hadn't seen, but their eyes connected and there was no way he could claim not noticing his brother's wild waving above his head.

"How about over there." Marco gestured with his hand that held the Styrofoam cup of *unsweetened* iced tea. His teeth still hurt from the tea he'd drank Thursday night on the picnic with Rosalina. He didn't want to know how much sugar had been used to make that sweet drink. If he ever ate at the Torres house again, he'd be sure to bring his own coconut water or something.

"That's great. I'll enjoy talking with Lillian more. She is an easily likable woman."

Don't I know it?

Marco helped Rosalina in her chair like a good boyfriend, then tucked into his food like there was no tomorrow. One-thirty was way too late for lunch, in his stomach's not so humble opinion.

His appetite didn't last for long, though, as he watched Clint and Lillian interact. The way Clint looked at her, and the way Lillian looked at him. The way they seemed to not be able to keep their hands to themselves. The little whispers and silly grins they shared.

No doubt about it. They were in love.

Antonio peppered everyone at the table with questions Marco didn't want to answer or hear answered. His brother should have been an interrogator.

"So are you two going to dance tonight?" Marco thought he heard Lillian ask.

He popped his head up from preparing to take a bite of his baked beans. "Excuse me?"

Lillian was speaking to him and she was serious. "Rosalina has been telling me about her heritage, and she told me about the Mexican Hat Dance."

"The what?" Marco crinkled his eyes and shook his head, feeling only slightly guilty for not knowing more about his own heritage.

"What did you say it was called in Spanish?" Lillian asked of Rosalina.

"*Jarabe tapatío* ."

Marco couldn't help but smile as Rosalina's accent showed up more in speaking her native tongue. He decided he might like to hear her use it more. Maybe he should make her aware that he knew Spanish.

"Doesn't that sound cool?" Lillian's excitement was palpable. It started to rub off on Marco, until she said, "Rosalina tells me this popular dance represents courtship."

Marco choked on his tea. Rosalina rubbed his back as he coughed. As inconspicuously as he could, he raised the hand he'd used to cover his cough to shield most of his face so he could shoot Rosalina a glare.

She returned it with a saucy grin.

Marco cleared his throat. "Uh, yeah, sorry. But that's not happening. I don't even know how to do it."

"Rats. Well, maybe next year. You two will have plenty of time to practice."

Not a chance.

He was only too glad when the table fell quiet while everyone turned their attention to their food for a blessed few minutes. Now Marco would at least enjoy his dessert in peace.

The brownie was melt-in-your-mouth good, but it was the Jell-O dessert he was most looking forward to. Saved the best for last.

He sunk his spoon into the wobbly green substance and shut his eyes as he closed his lips around the utensil. But the minute he pressed his tongue into the Jell-O and whipped cream mixture, Marco's heavenly moment turned into chaos as he started gagging and, without meaning to, spit the disgusting surprise out of his mouth. Thankfully, it ended up in the paper bowl it'd come from.

All eyes were on him as he continued to spit remaining chunks out, longing for something abrasive to scrub his tongue with.

A hand rubbed circles over his back. "Are you choking, honey?" Rosalina sounded genuinely concerned.

Honey?

Marco did choke this time, which made the whole scenario worse.

She continued to rub his back, *almost* distracting him from the assault he'd had to his texture-sensitive tongue.

Strange, that. Lillian had touched him a couple times over the years. A friendly jab in the biceps or an understanding hand on his forearm, but it'd never affected him.

"No, I'm not choking." He pointed at his bowl. "That stuff is disgusting."

Rosalina's mouth fell open and her change of countenance had him wanting to make a hasty escape. "Excuse me." He could tell she wanted to put more volume into her tone.

"There are chunks in it. Curds, or something. That should not be. It's Jell-O and whipped cream. Whoever made this—"

"I. Made. It." Rosalina's lips barely parted as she spoke.

Marco was dead meat.

He'd spit out Rosalina's dessert.

Said it was disgusting.

Insulted her.

"What's wrong with it?" He couldn't think of apologizing right now. Not when he was so grossed out it made his feet shake in his boots. Besides, she had wanted him to be honest.

She must have been lying.

Funny, that.

Not.

"I'll have you know it's one of my family's favorite recipes. And there is nothing wrong with it. It's exactly as it should be. There is cottage cheese in it."

Cottage cheese. It was worse than Marco could have imagined. He feared he'd lose his lunch.

"I hate cottage cheese," was all he forced out with the strong gag reflex in his throat as he pushed away from the table. "Excuse me."

He rushed to the bathroom in the Harrisons' shed, where he splashed cold water on his face, rinsed his mouth out, and leaned over the sink until his stomach settled.

Cottage cheese.

Revolting.

Marco shuddered and another gag threatened him. It was nothing more than curded milk.

And for crying out loud, who put cottage cheese in Jell-O?

Unfortunately, his fake girlfriend.

Boy, he sure knew how to pick them. This was never going to work.

When he no longer felt in danger of bringing up his lunch, Marco stepped out of the bathroom and took a big breath of fresh air, but was startled when Lillian rounded the corner pulling a seven-day cooler.

"You okay?" Her tone was soft, concerned.

Shouldn't Rosalina be the one checking on me? is what he wanted to ask, but Marco swallowed the words. "I'm fine. Is Rosalina okay?"

"A little dent to her pride, I think, but she'll be okay. You'll probably each suffer a few dings as you work this relationship out. Romance isn't all sunshine and roses."

Marco wouldn't know. He'd yet to have a romance, but Lillian clearly spoke from experience.

"Love takes work," Lillian continued. "Humility. Being willing to ask forgiveness. But true love is the best thing in the whole world. I do hope you can find it. Like I have."

All he could do was swallow.

"Rosalina is a lovely woman. She's a treasure."

The last person Marco wanted giving him advice for his love life was Lillian Harrison. He looked out where all the festivities were going on. Antonio had taken his chair and was now talking animatedly to Rosalina. She looked to be enjoying herself. When he turned back to Lillian he afforded her a quick nod.

She smiled. "Now I need to get a refill of water bottles. It's a hot one out there and people are drinking up."

Marco stepped out of the way so Lillian could wheel the cooler by, then he strode back to the table he'd fled, and towered over his little brother. "I do believe that's my spot."

Antonio grinned up at him. "You weren't occupying it. I was keeping it warm for you."

"A warm chair is the last thing I want."

"Want me to dump your iced tea on it instead?"

Marco rolled his head and groaned. "Get out of here." He lifted Antonio by the arm and moved him out of the way before sliding back into his chair. "Brothers." He let out an exasperated sigh.

Rosalina chuckled. "I have a brother."

"Do you?"

"Mm-hmm. He still lives in Mexico too. I miss him. He's a pastor and is doing a good work there. Does a lot with children's ministry."

"Hey, that's awesome."

"*Sí.*" Her countenance brightened, and Marco hoped all was forgotten about the Jell-O mishap.

Then he recalled Lillian's words about humility and asking forgiveness. Their relationship might be fake, but he knew he'd feel better if he apologized. "I'm sorry about the dessert. I didn't mean to—"

"It's fine." Rosalina waved a hand. "I forget not everyone loves cottage cheese. I think it's the best dairy product out there. But my *tío* would agree with you."

"I guess I did say I'd be honest about your dish."

She choked on a laugh. "You kept your word."

"I wish it wouldn't have been quite so insulting."

"I'd say the whole spitting it out of your mouth wasn't the kindest way to share your honest opinion."

"It happened. Textures should not mix like that." Marco still shuddered and wanted to gag.

"Duly noted." Then she lifted her full lips into the most sincere, sweetest smile she'd ever sent his way that had Marco wrinkling his forehead.

Even after the Jell-O debacle they were getting along? He'd thought for sure there would have been at least a small argument. Her response had him curious.

What changed? Or was this part of her playacting? She'd been doing a good job portraying herself as a girlfriend today.

We'll see if it continues.

He doubted it. It wouldn't surprise him that by the time they were shut inside his truck together he'd get an earful.

He deserved it.

Chapter Sixteen

Being kind had about killed her.

Rosalina's blood had wanted to boil over Marco's display at Heritage Days yesterday when he'd spit out her Jell-O dessert.

Spit. It. Out.

Who does that in public?

The man either had no manners or no shame. Rosalina hadn't yet decided which.

But, she'd stuck to her resolve and managed to snuff out the fire burning inside while Marco left for...wherever he'd gone.

It'd surprised her when they were able to continue with civilized conversation. To be honest, she was proud of herself.

The strange thing...she'd found she enjoyed being nice to him instead of arguing. And she much preferred Mellow Marco over Mad Marco.

Maybe she could make this friendship work. Make it last. Marco was a nice guy.

The kind she could see herself falling for.

But she wasn't the falling for type. Not right now anyway. She had too much else on her plate. This whole fake dating thing was already proving to be far more work than she'd expected. How much more would a real relationship require?

Nope, she wasn't in the market for a romance. She'd keep her word and do this thing with Marco through the date of Lillian's wedding, and then they could be simple friends. That would be enough for her.

Only, for some reason her heart cried softly that it wouldn't be enough.

"Ack. The heart is deceitful above all things and desperately wicked." She'd quote scripture to herself.

Queenie let out a yip and yanked at the leash, so Rosalina tightened her grip. Church and Sunday lunch were over, and now she and her dog were enjoying a relaxing afternoon walk.

She let Queenie take the lead upon first setting out, and it was no surprise they ended up at the dog park. Since there was no hurry to be anywhere or do anything today, Rosalina took the leash off and let her furry baby have a play date with all the other little doggies in the fenced in portion for small dogs.

She watched the antics with a smile on her face until, of all things, Luigi came to mind. Although at the age to be considered senior, the still hyper Chihuahua would no doubt enjoy an outing like this. Rosalina began to mentally plan a dog party at The Pampered Poochie's Parlor for little dogs only, with a special invitation to Luigi.

Since she'd be throwing it herself, she couldn't charge for commission, but she could set out a tip jar and, hopefully, be able to raise a bit of money to put toward what she owed Truman Scott. The dog owners who dropped their dogs off usually gave her a handsome amount, considering her to be dog sitting. Some stuck around and interacted with their dogs, but they still tipped her for providing their pets with a fun time.

Apparently, her subconscious was still thinking about Luigi (and one certain family member of his), for on the way home Rosalina looked up to find they were passing Marco's house. She paused.

"We're this close. Might as well pay a visit. Don't you think, Queenie?"

The bichon paid her no mind, but was busy sniffing the mailbox.

"Let's do it." Rosalina tugged on the leash and Queenie fell in step at her heels.

When she raised her hand to press the doorbell, her palms turned sweaty—for no reason Rosalina could determine. Except, it was hot and humid.

Sure, that's it.

Before she could do any more analyzing, Rosalina pushed the button.

Ding-dong.

High-pitched barking ensued, which set Queenie on high alert, making adorable head tilts at the door, which opened to them in quick order.

"Hi." Rosalina needed to give her heart another scripture-filled lecture, for it dropped in disappointment when it was Antonio who greeted them.

"Hey. Come to see me? I'm flattered." Antonio flung a hand to his chest. A hand far paler than Marco's sun baked skin that gave him a rugged advantage over his academic little brother.

Wait a minute?

What was she doing?

There was no call for making comparisons between the two brothers. She could be friends with both of them. Not a problem. Rosalina gave herself a mental shake. "Well, I can't say you were the first on my mind."

"That's the problem with being the brother of the boyfriend. You wouldn't consider transferring your infatuation over to me after yesterday's dessert incident would you?"

"I do believe I said we wouldn't bring that up again." Marco's booming voice entered the conversation and—what on earth?—Rosalina found herself smiling.

But any words she'd planned completely evaporated as her lips parted at the surprising sight of Marco wearing glasses—classy, dark brown, thin wire frames in a rounded rectangular shape. If she'd thought Marco was easy to look at before, nothing prepared herself for this more sophisticated and scholarly image of him. All she could do was stare mutely.

Marco quirked a brow. "You feeling all right there, Lina?"

Lina. Again?

Ugh. That pulled her out of whatever spell he'd cast on her with those glasses. "I-I'm fine. Hello, Marco."

He stepped around Antonio. "Let's have us some privacy and talk out here."

"Hey," Antonio feigned hurt with his decidedly whiny tone.

Marco shut the door behind them, on his brother. He turned a fairly real and pleasant smile to her.

"So, what brings you over? Decided to finally give me a tongue lashing about yesterday."

Rosalina chuckled. "I already told you we were good about that."

"But I still feel bad."

"Don't. But I will say something about you calling me Lina."

"You don't like it?"

She wrinkled her nose. "Not so much. If you insist upon calling me something other than my full name, then I'd appreciate Rose or Rosa. I'm partial to that part of my name."

Marco assumed a thoughtful expression. "You like roses?"

Rosalina smiled, visualizing raindrops on roses, as the song about *"my favorite things"* said. "I do. Very much."

"Okay, then. I'll try and remember that."

"Thank you."

They stood in awkward silence until Marco rubbed his ear and pointed around the corner of the house. "If you want, we have a small concrete pad with a few lawn chairs. Wanna have a seat? Stick around a while?"

"Sure." Since he offered, and she couldn't very well hurry away. She was his girlfriend. She should be seizing every available moment to be with him.

Rosalina followed Marco around the house and she took note of how he waited to sit until she had picked a chair and gotten settled. The man was proving himself to be surprisingly chivalrous.

He'd made sure to open her car door for her on Saturday. He'd helped seat her at Heritage Days. Now this. A woman could do worse than Marco Mendez.

"I see you brought Queenie along." Marco didn't sound happy about it.

"Surely you aren't scared of my little dog. She doesn't even weigh fifteen pounds. Not even soaking wet in the tub."

"Just because something is small, doesn't mean it's not dangerous."

"True. But I can assure you Queenie is not dangerous."

"Tell that to my finger."

Rosalina dropped her jaw, but detected the slightest glint of humor in Marco's eyes...accompanied with a wary distrust as he flicked his gaze to the bichon. "May I remind you Queenie didn't draw blood?"

"Yeah, yeah, yeah. It's not for lack of wanting to."

"Oh, come on!"

"Look at the way she's eyeing me. That little miscreant has evil intentions toward me."

"Perhaps she can sense that you don't trust her."

Marco didn't appear to believe that, but he was going to humor her. "So you think it all boils down to a trust issue?"

"Isn't that usually why there is trouble in any relationship."

He closed one eye as if thinking hard.

"Build trust, Marco. She'll come around."

He looked doubtful, but tugged at his pants before squatting before Queenie. "Hi there, Queenie. Your momma thinks we can get along. I t-trust you."

Rosalina caught the hitch on "trust." Whether he wanted to admit it or not, Marco *was* scared of her twelve pound dog. Poor man. She was still determined to cure him of that fear.

Marco inched his palm out toward the dog. "See? I'm not a threat. Be nice." There was a warning tone to the command.

Queenie barred her teeth and growled deep in her throat. Marco retracted his hand in a blink of an eye and straightened his form. "Now do you believe me?"

Rosalina shook her head. "Well, with that big smile of yours, maybe you should try Davy Crockett's method."

"Huh?"

She choked on a laugh at Marco's clueless expression. "Davy Crockett grinned down a bear. Maybe you could tame Queenie with one of your grins."

"Are you picking on my smile again?"

"Picking? Are you forgetting it was the first thing that attracted me to you?" She batted her eyelashes at the falsehood.

Or...was it false?

Marco groaned, gave up on befriending Queenie, and dropped into the chair across from Rosalina.

The only sounds for several long moments were those of a distant lawn mower and a few robins' laughs. In an effort to start up a conversation of any kind when the silence grew uncomfortable, Rosalina said the one thing that was most prevalent on her mind. "I didn't realize you wore glasses. Is that new?"

"What? Oh." Marco reached up and adjusted the frames on his face. "No. I usually wear contacts because I like to wear my safety sunglasses while working. But I always switch them out for my glasses when I get home in the evenings, and on Sunday afternoons, because I have a tendency to fall asleep if I sit down. I've been known to crash and not rise again until morning, or until someone wakes me up so I can actually get in bed." He laughed through his nose.

"I see. Cause you're not supposed to sleep with contacts in, right?"

"Nope."

"So you're the go-go-go type, who crashes when they finally get a chance to chill."

"That's me in a nutshell." He pulled his glasses off and rubbed at his eyes.

Rosalina noticed he looked tired, and it made her feel bad. "I'm sorry. Did I wake you from a nap?"

"No, you're fine. I hadn't drifted off yet. I'd been staring at my phone screen too long. This is a welcome break."

A welcome break. She shouldn't let that warm her so much. Shouldn't read too far into it. Marco meant nothing by it, she knew. "Are you a gamer in your spare time?"

"Ha, no. I don't have the time nor desire for that. I'm looking for a motorcycle."

"A motorcycle!" There was no reason to feel such a strong desire to tell him he had no business getting a motorcycle. That they were too dangerous. But that's something a real girlfriend would do, and she had no right. But, boy, was it hard to keep her mouth shut.

"I've been saving for a while, but I'm taking my time. Waiting for the best deal. Well, and trying to decide whether I want to go with the motorcycle or save a little longer and get a boat."

A boat. Rosalina shivered as her body went numb. She didn't know how to swim, and the thought of anyone wanting to go out on water had her wanting to panic.

"You okay over there?" She heard Marco's voice through tight hearing.

"Mm-hmm."

"You're gripping the chair awfully hard."

"Oh." Rosalina released the armrests and clasped her hands loosely in her lap. Queenie stretched against her leg and begged to be picked up. Rosalina obliged and it reminded her of why she originally came. "So, um, I actually came to ask you something."

"What's that?" He leaned back in his chair and laced his fingers behind his head, looking oh, so, relaxed and...kind of cute, if Rosalina were being honest.

Especially with those glasses. They were a whole mood. Made her think of cuddling on a couch, watching a movie, and...

Whoa, whoa, whoa. She reined in her thoughts before they could run any wilder. That was completely unacceptable.

She cleared her throat and sat up straighter, forcing herself to look out across the neighborhood instead of at Marco. "I was wondering if Luigi could come to a dog party if I threw one this Wednesday."

"A dog party." His tone said he found it ridiculous. "Your secretary said you did such a thing, but..."

"But nothing. It's a real thing and it is a blast. My favorite part of the week when we have one."

Marco crossed one leg over the other and yawned. He was looking drowsier by the minute, his eyes getting cloudy, and his face more and more relaxed. "You said this Wednesday? What time?"

"I was thinking from two to four."

He yawned again and sunk further in the plastic lawn chair. "Well, I don't doubt Luigi would have a...fine time. But I wouldn't be able to bring him. Can't get away from work in the middle of the day for something like a dog party. Boy, I'd never hear the end of it."

Rosalina chose to ignore the last part—for the sake of kindness. "Can't anyone else bring him?"

"Sure. Antonio doesn't have anything much to do right now. He's preparing to leave for college next month. I'll see if he can. If not, maybe Mom is free."

"Great. Then I'll send out an invitation to all my little dog clients and see what size of a party I can put together. It's going to be so fun." She gave Queenie a squeeze. "Yes, it will. So much fun. Right, doll?" Queenie gave her a wet kiss on the mouth.

Marco grunted. "Some doll. I could think of a few more fitting nicknames."

Rosalina sent him a glare. "You may keep them to yourself."

He gave her a slow, silly smile. The kind a bratty child might make right before doing the exact thing they were told not to do.

Rosalina was familiar with the expression, for she had—key word *had*—babysat a little boy like that.

Burt for some reason the same smile and gleam in Marco's eyes affected her far differently and had her looking away toward off the strange reaction going on inside her middle.

What was wrong with her?

She set Queenie down. "I think it's about time Queenie and I continued on our walk."

"You starting out or heading home?"

Of course he had to ask. "Going home."

"Then what's the rush?" His words were starting to slur into each other, his eyes barely slitted.

"I have some things to get done before tomorrow. You know, stuff there isn't time for during the work week."

"Mmm." His lids were completely shut now.

Rosalina remained still and watched as he drifted asleep, his lips slightly parting and all tension lines fading from his face.

She found the sight far too endearing. And with those glasses...well, she couldn't look away. It was as if she were seeing him for the first time. The real Marco Mendez. Without pretense. She had to admit she liked what she saw. Very much.

"Oh, Marco!" The screen door slammed from around the corner and Maria's voice rang out.

Marco's eyes flew open and he jumped at least two inches out of his chair. He sucked and rolled his lips together a few times. Rosalina had to fight a chuckle. He'd been so out of it he'd started drooling already?

"Marco, are you and that girl of yours out here still?"

He cleared his throat. "Yeah, Mom. We're around here." He pulled his glasses off and rubbed his face. Replaced the spectacles.

"Oh, good. I wanted to be sure and catch you two together before Rosalina left."

Marco pushed up from the chair, and Rosalina noticed how he swayed a tad. Still drowsy. The man fell asleep as fast as a dog, but he didn't wake up as quickly. "Why's that?"

Maria laid a hand on Rosalina's arm. "Honey, do you have plans Thursday night?"

Rosalina thought she heard Marco growl in his throat, but she kept her attention on his mom. "I don't think so. Why?"

"Splendid. I wanted to invite you to our Christmas in July *fiesta*."

"Your what?" Rosalina chuckled.

"Christmas in July," Marco answered. "Mom loves Christmas and can't keep herself from celebrating it twice. Every July twenty-fifth she makes us spend the evening watching Hallmark Christmas movies, drinking hot chocolate, and eating fudge, nuts, and decorated sugar cookies."

"Seriously?!" Rosalina couldn't contain the squeal. Maria was a woman after her own heart. Who didn't love Christmas? The idea was sensational.

Marco gave a derisive laugh. "Sometimes she goes way out and puts out decorations too."

"You sound as if you don't approve." Maria jabbed Marco in the biceps.

"Seems a bit excessive to me."

"Will you come?" Maria's face was hopeful as she looked to Rosalina.

"I'd love to. That is, if you don't mind. I mean, it's probably a family thing."

"Ack. You're part of the family. You're Marco's girl, after all."

Right. Yes. How could I have forgotten?

She waited for Marco to confirm his mom's words. No such affirmation came, and it disappointed Rosalina more than she cared to admit. "Then I will be sure my schedule is clear so I can be here."

"Wonderful! The more the merrier. Now I need to find Antonio a girl. Maybe by December Christmas."

Rosalina laughed outright.

December Christmas.

She's never heard it said like that before, but it was cute. Christmas in July and December Christmas.

"Well, I can tell you are about to go, Rosalina, so I will leave you two to say goodbye." And with that Maria ambled off, but her infectious personality lingered, leaving Rosalina with a smile.

"This will be fun," she said to Marco.

"Yeah, real fun." His words dripped with sarcasm, and there went his finger into his ear again.

Rosalina wondered if he had a wax problem, or if it was a simple act of habit.

"You do realize this means an evening movie night...as boyfriend and girlfriend, don't you?" Marco looked pained.

Rosalina frowned. "I think I can put two and two together."

"I wasn't insulting your intelligence." He growled.

Rosalina hid a smile behind her hand as she reached up to move the hair out of her face that the slight breeze had blown. "I think we can pull it off."

Marco scrutinized her, and it was even more disconcerting with those glasses of his. "You sound a little too happy about it."

"Do I?"

"If I recall, you were the one set against this charade from the beginning."

"I do remember that. You are correct. You also said it could be whatever I wanted it to be. And since we have to do this because of your big mouth and slow brain, I'm choosing to make it enjoyable."

His face turned dark.

Uh-oh. Talk about big mouth and slow brain. She suffered from the same unfortunate malady. And now she'd made him mad.

Where had Mellow Marco gone?

How could she get him back?

Where was the knockout powder when she needed it?

"Weren't you getting ready to leave?"

Rosalina dropped her head and barely squeezed a "yes" from her lips. "Come on, Queenie."

The dog obeyed and took off walking in the direction for home. Rosalina was glad Queenie knew the way, because she was too busy lecturing herself for forgetting to be kind.

She'd let her mouth run faster than her filter could manage. It had only been a few nights ago during their picnic that she'd thought how glad she was Marco had run his mouth.

Truly, she found she enjoyed Marco's presence. Maybe not in a true boyfriend/girlfriend way—yet—but she was warming up to the man who equal parts infuriated her and fascinated her all in one encounter.

What did that mean?

For her? For them?

She wasn't sure. But of one thing she was certain, Marco did not feel the same. Clearly, he was still carrying a torch for a woman he couldn't have. Rosalina wasn't sure she wanted to compete with that. So why did she feel like crying?

Was she developing feelings for Marco beyond that which would lead to the simple friendship she'd hoped for?

"That's absurd."

It didn't feel absurd. This was a special kind of torture she'd never known.

She'd had friends come and go, and it'd never been a big deal. Shed a little tear here and there and moved on.

She'd left her family and country, for crying out loud. And that hadn't felt like this either.

What she'd never experienced before, however, was a relationship. A romance. A real interest in a man.

Was that where this was heading? With a man who only wanted to pretend a relationship?

Maybe, just maybe she could prove to Marco this didn't have to be fake. That it could grow into something real and wonderful.

That sounded better than only being kind.

A slow smile stretched her face until she felt giddy with her decision and started giggling.

It was time to ramp up her game.

No more child's play.

If Marco had thought she'd been doing a good job at their ruse...well, just wait.

Thursday night couldn't get here soon enough.

But, before then, she had money to earn to pay her seemingly insurmountable bill.

If only she had as good of a plan to solve that problem.

□□□

Rosalina's heart skipped a beat when her phone pinged the next day with a message from Marco.

> **Marco:** Sorry about yesterday.
> **Rosalina:** I'm sorry too.
> **Marco:** Can't we get along?
> **Rosalina:** I think we're doing the best we can, but we have some things to iron out yet.
> **Marco:** We don't have to keep bringing up how this all came about...
> **Rosalina:** Agreed. It's in the past.
> **Marco:** Great. My thoughts exactly. Oh, and about Christmas in July. We need to set some ground rules.

Rosalina: What do you mean?

Marco: We should have set some up from the beginning. I did say you could make the rules and boundaries of our "relationship," but you haven't yet.

Rosalina: Oh, right. Because this was supposed to be whatever I wanted it to be. <smug-face emoji>

Marco: Must you keep reminding me? Yes, your in charge. <disgusted emoji>

Rosalina: That should be *you're*. I have no rules or boundaries in mind. I think we're doing fine by winging it.

Marco: I told you I don't like to read. I also stink at grammar. And I disagree. Thursday night is going to be a movie night, and I know Mom is going to try something sneaky at some point.

Rosalina: What do you have in mind?

Marco: At the very least, no touching.

Rosalina: Not happening. It's not practical. Dating couples are going to be touchy.

Marco: We're newly dating. We're not that comfortable with each other.

Rosalina: Aren't we? <blushing emoji>

Marco: <glaring emoji> No unnecessary touching then. Only when we're in viewing of Mom. And ABSOLUTELY no couch cuddling.

Rosalina: *Gasp* But isn't couch cuddling the best part of a movie night while dating?

Marco: You're going to be the death of me.

Rosalina: Can't have that.

Marco: You are being sarcastic, right? Ur looks could have killed me several times over.

Rosalina: Abbreviating now because you don't know which spelling of "your" it should be? Tsk, tsk. ...Looks cannot kill. I promise I'll only send heart eyes your way Thursday.

Marco: Just be normal. You'll make me sick.

Rosalina: No, that will be all the sweets your mom will have. Oh, btw, should I bring a dish or something?

Marco: I guess if you want to, but Mom would probably say just bring yourself. But PLEASE nothing with cottage cheese hidden inside.

Rosalina: How could I forget? <puking emoji>

Marco: I'm shuddering at the memory.

Rosalina: Any other rules I need to know about?

Marco: Not sure at the moment. You aren't bringing Queenie are you.

Rosalina: Should be a question mark (?) after you.

Marco: It's texting for crying out loud! Who cares about punctuation. YOU, I guess. <rolling eyes emoji>

Rosalina: Touchy, touchy. You're such an easy target. Do you not want me to bring Queenie?

Marco: Do you have to ask

Rosalina: Close the sentence, *hombré*.

Marco: Grrrrrr! *?*

Rosalina: <cheesing emoji> I'll ask Queenie if she wants to come or not. She and Luigi might want to snuggle up in a bed together and watch the movie.

Marco: I refuse to picture your meaning behind that. Besides, they will be playing together Wednesday afternoon.

Rosalina: The party is going to be so much fun! Wish you were the one bringing Luigi.

Marco: Maybe next time...

Rosalina: I hope so.

Marco: Gotta get back to work. Lunch break is over.

Rosalina: If not sooner, see you Thursday night.

Marco: <face palming emoji><Thumbs-up emoji>

Rosalina: <winking, blowing kiss emoji>

Marco: <Expressionless emoji>

Chapter Seventeen

The party was a success. The energy high. The barking loud. And the overall experience crazy fun.

To top it all off, Rosalina's tip jar was filled to the brim and it brought tears of gratitude to her eyes. She clutched the jar to her middle and lifted up prayers of thanksgiving. She'd count it later tonight and see how big of a dent she'd made toward her overall sum.

Also, to her delight, Luigi had enjoyed himself to the uttermost. When Antonio collected the dog to take it home, Luigi was still high strung and not at all ready to stop playing. She had no doubt the little guy would crash hard when he got home.

She loved how she had so many pictures of Marco's dog on her phone now too. Because, after all, she had to share them with Marco.

And she had. She'd sent him pictures throughout the entire party, letting him see how much Luigi was enjoying himself and why puppy parties were such a great thing.

Worn out herself, Rosalina made slow work of putting away all the small dog toys, tunnels, ramps, and doggie safe bubbles. She'd also dragged out the water hose and put a little water in a kiddie pool for extra fun, so there was that to clean and dry yet too.

But she wasn't complaining. At least she didn't have to worry about having energy enough for any grooming appointments, as she'd told Haven to leave the entire afternoon open.

No sooner had Rosalina finished drying the kiddie pool than her phone pinged. A smile she couldn't contain lifted her lips when she saw who it was from.

Marco: I'm done with work early today. Would you be interested in going to church with me?

Rosalina: I'd love that. Unfortunately, I have to babysit tonight, though. The baby's father is a wealthy businessman and he has a soiree tonight. That check is too sizable to skip—as much as I hate missing church.

Marco: I have an idea. Want to hear it?

Rosalina: Of course! Why wouldn't I?

Marco: Well, you haven't heard it yet. You know, it's not uncommon for me to have some hare-brained ideas.

Rosalina: I never would have guessed.

Marco: <straight-face emoji> Haha. Very funny.

Rosalina: Spill the beans, *hombré.*

Marco: Ok, ok. Would your client care if I joined you at the job?

Rosalina: You want to help babysit? <O-mouthed emoji>

Marco: We can have a Bible study together. But I'm telling you right now…I'm not changing no diapers."

Rosalina: Not changing *any*

Marco: That's what I said.

Rosalina: Never mind.

Marco: <cheesing emoji> Well? Would that be acceptable?

Rosalina: I don't think the parents will mind. I will check with them to be sure. If it's okay, I'll send you the address.

Marco: Perfect. Make sure you tell me what time.

Rosalina: Why? So you can run late?

Marco: Grrr! You like to throw my faults back in my face, don't you?

Rosalina: As I've said before, you're an easy target.

Marco: I'm going to have to work on that…

Rosalina: I'm an excellent markswoman. <blushing, smiling emoji>

Marco: Oh, are you? That I've got to see.

Rosalina: I mean it metaphorically only. I've never shot anything.

Marco: Good. Hate to think of how dangerous that would be.

Rosalina: You. Are. Rotten. Have I said that before?

Marco: Maybe a time or two. I'm starting to think it's a compliment.

Rosalina: You are incorrigible.

Marco: I don't know what that means. Remember? I don't like to read and I stink at grammar.

Rosalina: I wish there was an emoji for how I'm feeling right now.

Marco: I'm glad there isn't.

Rosalina: I could take a selfie and send it.

Marco: Please, no. It'd probably melt my phone screen.

Rosalina: You are on a roll today.

Marco: <smirking emoji>

Rosalina: I'm ready to drive home now. Talk to you later.

Marco: <thumbs-up emoji>

Rosalina couldn't explain why she felt such a giddy happiness inside with all the texting she and Marco had been engaging in this week. After the way they'd parted Sunday afternoon, she'd thought for sure it'd be silent for a few days. Never would she have guessed these fun digital interactions would take place.

She had to admit she liked it. Very much.

They got along this way. The banter was friendly. They didn't lose their tempers. If only this was all a digital relationship instead of needing to be acted out for the public to see.

Because when they were in person...man, they fought like cats and dogs. And Rosalina was at a loss as to explain why.

She liked the guy. He was an easily likable sort. Funny. Thoughtful. Had manners. Treated his family and her with respect. So why the verbal sparring? Even when she tried her hardest to be kind?

Maybe things would be better moving ahead. After calling that truce, per se, in text. The past would remain buried in the past. They were in this "mess" and they were going to get along and make the most of it.

Well, Rosalina planned on making the most of it, regardless of what Marco's thoughts were on the matter. Dare she hope the playacting could turn into something more? Did she want it to turn into something more?

With each day that passed, she found she did. A real relationship was sounding better and better. She could see it being a possibility, provided Marco mirrored her growing feelings. She had no idea, though. He was hard to read.

Regardless, she found herself anticipating tonight with Marco. But she looked forward to tomorrow night's Christmas in July party even more.

□□□

Rosalina was pleasantly surprised when Marco showed up to the Brinkmans' million dollar home with his street glasses on. To be honest, she hoped to see him in them during the winter—with a pair of dark denim jeans, a Christmassy button-up, and a sweater vest...or a knitted sweater would work fine too. Oh, he'd be a showstopper for sure.

At the very least, a heart stopper for her.

Marco wore a big smile as he passed through the arched doorway into the mansion. "I brought goodies." Dangling from one arm was a bag from Casey's General Store. Tucked safely between his other arm and body, Rosalina could make out a black leather spine. His Bible.

Marco Mendez in glasses, wearing a dark orange button-up (instead of his usual bright T-shirt), and a pair of denim pants, carrying a Bible was enough to make Rosalina swoon. She was discovering new facets of Marco that she found were downright endearing.

"What do you have? I never asked you to bring snacks." Rosalina adjusted the eight-month-old on her hip.

"No, you didn't. But I thought babysitting called for snacks." Marco looked down at his feet. "Do I need to take my shoes off? This place looks snazzy."

"They do appreciate that. But...babysitting *and* a Bible study. We don't need snacks for that. We don't eat in church."

Marco set the bag and Bible on the floor, dropped to one knee, and began untying his work boots. Rosalina was beginning to think he didn't own a pair of tennis shoes. "Okay. If you don't want a Starbuck's iced coffee and a giant chocolate chip muffin with salt crystals on top—"

"On second thought, snacks, babysitting, and a Bible study sound like the perfect trio."

"That's what I thought." Marco gave her a cheeky grin, which little Calvin found infectious, for when Marco turned his attention to the boy, Calvin lit up like a Christmas tree. "Hello there, little man. Do you like chocolate chip muffins?" He tickled the boy's tummy, making the child laugh.

Rosalina found the interaction adorable. And with those glasses on, Marco looked every bit like dad material.

Dear me!

She could not, should not, WOULD not, let her thoughts go there?

What is wrong with me?

"So, do I get a grand tour of this place? Hard to believe a person could afford such a home." He took in the entrance hall with wonderment in his eyes.

"This is nothing. Wait until you see the rest of the house."

"So I do get a tour?"

"Not a full one. Only the rooms I've been given license to enter."

"Let me guess, only the kitchen, bathroom, nursery, and whatever the playroom is."

"Pretty much." Rosalina shrugged the shoulder that didn't currently have a slobbery mouth sucking on it. "Let's go to the kitchen and I'll see what I can find for a snack for Calvin too."

"I bet the kitchen is the size of my parents' whole house."

"Not quite, but close."

"I'm confused as to why Mr. Brinkman—that is the name you typed in the text, right?"

"*Sí.*"

"Why doesn't he hold the soiree here? It's big enough."

Rosalina settled Calvin in his highchair and Marco set the plastic bag with the goods, as well as his Bible, on the granite-topped island.

"He does at Christmas, but I think he rented a banquet room downtown, or something. I'm not made aware of all the details. I'm just the babysitter when called upon."

"Is that often?" Marco was making her uneasy as he made himself at home, looking at everything in the kitchen.

"I'd say close to every other week. I've been Calvin's sitter since the time he was six weeks old. I think we have the closest bond of any of my kiddos."

"And dogs?" Marco turned to her with an easy smile and one brow raised.

Rosalina ducked her head. "*Welllll*...dogs are a different kind of bond.

Marco chuckled. "So, what's the plan for tonight?" He planted his forearms on the island and leaned toward her.

Rosalina did likewise...until there were only mere inches separating them. She searched his face. Thought she may have detected the smallest hint of one of his scars from the dog attack. "Well, I think God should always come first. Don't you?"

"Agreed. Although, you did choose to babysit over going to church. A little hypocritical, don't you think? You do know the love of money is the root of all evil?"

She planted a fist on her hip. "I don't love money. Life would be a whole lot easier without it. But I have bills to pay, plus I've been the most faithful of babysitters for the Brinkmans."

Laughter creased the corners of Marco's eyes. "I'm toying with you. I understand. But you keep saying that about the pay you'll receive, and having bills. Are things not well financially?"

She was not going there with him. Maybe if they were truly boyfriend/girlfriend. Well, maybe not even then. Unless they were close to tying the knot and sharing every little detail with each other. "It's not easy being a business owner, but I'm doing okay."

Lie.

She wasn't doing okay. She could be kicked out of her building next month. But it was none of Marco's concerns.

"Okay, well, so Bible study is first. Over our coffee *and* muffins?"

The earnestness of his request was adorable and Rosalina found herself chuckling. "Very well. That does sound..." *Intimate.* She refused to let the word slip past her lips. That was not what should be on her mind in conjunction with studying Scripture. So she finished lamely with, "...nice."

"Okay." Marco sat on one of the barstools along the breakfast bar side of the island and produced the iced coffee bottles and giant muffins from the plastic bag.

Rosalina's mouth took to watering. And to think she'd said they didn't need snacks.

She said her thanks when he slid one of each over to her, after having broken the seal on the coffee for her. Talk about a thoughtful, chivalrous...and sweet gesture. Or maybe she read too deeply into it.

Could be.

Marco grabbed a napkin from the basket on the counter and removed the paper from his muffin. Rosalina wasn't sure why she was mesmerized by his every move. Only more so when he closed his eyes upon his first bite.

She forced herself to look away before he could notice her staring, and she pinched off a taste of the muffin.

By then she heard the rustling of pages and Rosalina feasted her eyes on the sight of Marco—with his glasses on—slightly hunched over, his tongue in cheek, as he paged through the Bible.

This is ridiculous.

There was no call for her to be infatuated with the man. Wasn't it this weekend they'd been arguing again? For some reason she found that she could no longer stay mad at the man.

Far from it.

She had to admit. She was having feelings for the man. Strong feelings. And they seemed to grow with each time she saw him. Each time they texted.

It struck her as preposterous. After all, they'd only known each other for—well, it would be two full weeks on Friday. Could a person develop feelings that quickly?

An impatient squeal from Calvin pulled Rosalina out of her thoughts and reminded her the poor boy was probably jealous of her and Marco's muffin. "Oops, I totally forgot, Cal." She fetched him a jar of his favorite baby food and made haste to give him his first bite, which resulted in a big baby smile.

Marco looked up from his Bible. "Good stuff. Huh, little guy?"

Calvin kicked his legs and laughed.

"You're a happy kid, aren't you? Food makes me happy too. Yeah, it does. You're going to be a good eater. A good eater." Marco poked the boy in his chubby little tummy, inciting a giggle.

Okay, there wasn't much else cuter than Marco employing baby talk. It was almost comical, yet sweet, to hear it coming from his usually deep voice.

Now Marco turned serious. "Shall we begin?"

"I'm ready if you are?"

"I figured we'd read a portion of Scripture and then we can talk about it. Bring up any questions and work through them together."

"Sounds good to me."

"All right."

But Rosalina didn't soak in a single word Marco read, as a pang of intense homesickness constricted her middle. Seeing Marco with his Bible, hearing but not *hearing* his voice read the verses reminded her of her brother, parents, Mexico, and home.

She sniffed and Marco looked up in time to see her wipe away a tear.

"Hey, you okay?" The tenderness in his tone made more tears come to the surface.

"I'm sorry. A little homesick all of a sudden."

"Oh." His forehead crinkled. "Is it the portion of text I chose? I can read somewhere else."

She shook her head. Not that she knew where he was reading. "Please, continue. I'm fine."

"If you're sure."

She could only nod past the tight wad of emotion in her throat, and the confounded disappointment that Marco didn't reach out and rub her hand in a comforting gesture like a real boyfriend would do.

Marco began reading, but it was a few moments before her mind calmed to listen in this time. She recognized the text being from Colossians chapter three.

"'...Lie not one to another, seeing that ye have put off the old man with his deeds...'" He read slowly, almost as if he was struggling, but the words still sunk in deep. Hard.

Rosalina's hand froze in its progress to give Calvin another bite. Of all the verses her ears would pick up on...

Marco quit reading. She met his gaze. Her own conviction was mirrored in his eyes. She swallowed.

Was this where he was going to stop reading and they begin discussing? She wouldn't mind if he continued on a few more verses. Would prefer it.

But he didn't. She watched his Adam's apple bob, then he twisted his finger in his ear and adjusted his glasses. "Kind of getting a little warm in here, isn't it?"

"I d-do believe conviction can increase body temperature." As could Marco's eyes fixated on her.

"You feeling it?"

Rosalina nodded. "I've been uncomfortable long before your reading that verse." And that's why she was determined to not live the lie of this any longer.

Was she calling off things with Marco? No.

Was she going to be truthful? With herself—yes.

She liked Marco. She wanted to be with Marco. Wanted to be his girlfriend. Desired to be his plus-one. From this time forward, it would no longer be playacting for others. It was going to be the real deal, from the bottom of her heart, with honorable intentions.

And she'd hope and pray Marco felt the same...

He squeezed the back of his neck. "It's only for a little over a week longer. The wedding is next Saturday. Then we can lay this ruse to rest."

Her heart sank to the bottom of her dangling toes on the tall stool.

Marco did not reciprocate her feelings.

It made her want to cry all over again.

But she wouldn't.

Fine, if he wanted to continue lying and living a falsehood. Fine, if he could ignore his conscience. But she wasn't going to make it easy on him.

Not one bit.

Because, after this was all said and done, she didn't plan on walking away as if nothing ever happened. Her heart had gotten too involved—despite her resolve to not let it.

And truth always trumps lies, so she was confident she'd come out the winner...

Her trophy being Marco Mendez's heart and love.

Chapter Eighteen

Unfortunately, Marco got done with work at a decent time on the day of the Christmas in July *fiesta*. He would have preferred working until dark, sneaking in the back door, and locking himself in his room until his mom's party, and dreaded movies, were over.

Of course, he couldn't be so fortunate.

So now he was dressed in a pair of tan pants and a red T-shirt—because Mom had ordered him to wear something festive.

Well, this was as close as it was going to get. He'd rather be in pajamas. It was a movie night, right? He almost—*almost*—put on his PJs after his refreshing shower, but all he had to do was remember Rosalina was coming, and that had him doing his mom's bidding.

He did *not* want Rosalina seeing him in his nightclothes.

Her comment about couch cuddling had him working saliva into his dry mouth. Surely, she wouldn't. Would she? This thing between them was fake. For show only. But they didn't have to perform a Hallmark-worthy show.

Besides, he comforted himself with the fact Rosalina didn't seem like the kind to appreciate signs of affection. She'd been stiff as a board when his mom had given her a hug that first day he introduced them.

With that in mind, Marco was able to breathe easier.

That is...until the doorbell rang and he answered it—and the sight of Rosalina stole his breath away.

For the first time he *saw* her—and understood the look of pleasure in Antonio's eyes when he'd first met Rosalina.

Now he felt woefully underdressed. Good thing he'd not gone the ultimate comfort route. Rosalina wore a red, what he would guess was velvet, dress that made her look like royalty. It was sleeveless, but for a little cap of a ruffle covering her shoulders. The style accentuated a beautiful form he'd not noticed before. Her lips were glossy, her cheeks rosy, and her eyes sparkling and mesmerizing. And with her long black hair, the only thing she was missing was a tiara.

Speaking of royalty, he looked down. It didn't come as any surprise to see Queenie herself standing there regally by her owner, sending warning glances his way.

"Rosalina..." was all he could croak out of his dry throat and empty lungs.

"*Feliz Navidad*, Marco."

"Yeah...that too. C-come in." He stepped away from the open doorway, giving Queenie a wide berth. He needed to get his wits about him. Quick. "Uh, I see you decided to ignore my request that you not bring your dog." He couldn't let Rosalina know how much she affected him tonight. This was fake.

Fake.

Too bad it wasn't working to tell himself the heat inside him was fake. Whatever reaction she was eliciting in him was real. Undeniable. And he had no idea what to do about it.

Rosalina let out a huff of a laugh. "Oh, but should I pull up the conversation? You didn't request that I not bring her. Your words were, and I quote 'You aren't bringing Queenie, are you?' And I said I'd ask her if she wanted to come. Naturally, she always wants to go where I go."

"Naturally." Marco spoke sarcastically.

Rosalina gave him a pointed look as she bent to remove the leash from the dog and give it free run. "Luigi had a great time yesterday."

"That's what Antonio said. And I could tell by the pictures you sent."

"That dog of yours kept up with the young pups as if he wasn't a day older than them."

"That's our Luigi."

Rosalina smiled, then said, "So, I hope your mom doesn't mind, but I did bring my one weakness." She held out a plastic plate covered in cling wrap, both of which matched her dress.

"No cottage cheese, right?" Marco hesitantly took it, and prepared to take it straight to the trash if it contained the dairy product that should be outlawed.

"I already told you I wouldn't. They are Oreo balls."

"Mmm." Marco groaned. "The best. Mom will only make them once a year at Christmas because they are so addicting."

"It's the cream cheese," Rosalina said with a laugh. "The stuff is dangerous. And, of course, Oreos are America's favorite cookie for a reason."

Marco laughed. "I think you mean milk's favorite cookie."

"What?"

"The package on Oreos says it's milk's favorite cookie. Not America's."

"Oh, well..." She acted flustered at her mistake and it made him smile.

"I hope you don't plan on taking any leftovers of these home."

"If you eat that whole plate, Marco Mendez, you will be sick. And it won't be because of my heart eyes and couch cuddling." She cocked one hip and plopped her hand down on it.

Marco was fairly certain his mom had turned the heat up to make it feel like there was a cozy fire in here to add to the Christmas element.

Cozy?

No, no no. Why did his mind have to go and think of *that* word...and on the heels of Rosalina talking about heart eyes and cuddling?

Marco hardened his gaze. "Both of which you *are not* going to do." She obviously needed reminding.

"But aren't I?"

Marco growled. "You aren't."

The sassy girl went and batted her lashes at him with the lovesick-est eyes he ever did see. He turned away and feigned a gag—although he felt anything but gaggy right now—which earned him a slap on the back of his head.

"You are rotten...Mars."

Marco sent her a big grin (because he knew she loved them— NOT) and pointed a finger at her. "You weren't supposed to see that. And don't call me Mars."

"I won't, so long as you behave." Her singsong voice was playful but nauseating.

"You won't. Period."

"Behave and you won't have to hear it."

"Very well then...*Lina.*"

Oh, he hit a nerve. Marco waited to see if he'd succumb to those death-threatening eyes.

Was there a word stronger than sassy? Feisty?

Rosalina was every synonym.

"Marco, I heard the doorbell. Was that— Oh, it was. Rosalina! I'm so glad you could come." His mom came bustling out of the kitchen, arms wide open, as she swallowed Rosalina in a hug.

Rosalina appeared to be more comfortable with the embrace this time. "I wouldn't miss it, Maria. Thank you for including me. And I hope you don't mind, but I brought some Oreo balls."

Mom's expression read *you shouldn't have.* "Those things are so good they should be illegal."

"I know it. My favorite."

"Marco, she's a keeper," his mom said as she took the festive covered plate from his hands.

His laugh sounded far too breathy to his own ears, but he could hope Mom didn't pick up on it.

"I have a few more things to do before we're ready to sit down for the first movie." Mom started toward the kitchen again.

"Can I help with anything?" Rosalina offered.

Yes. Give her something to do...in the kitchen, Mom. He needed some space so he could get his blood down to the cool temperature he was used to.

By the scheming gleam in his mom's eyes, however, Marco knew the request would have fallen on deaf ears had he said it out loud.

"I can handle the kitchen work. However, I did get an extra festive spark in my heart this year and decided to drag out some decorations. I already set up a small tabletop tree in the basement. Nothing more romantic than watching a movie with the soft lights of a Christmas tree."

Romantic? Marco rolled his eyes and pulled at the neck of his shirt. That's the last thing they needed.

Mom continued, "But if you and Marco would like to set out the nativity, that would be wonderful. I thought we could put it on the table where all the candy and beverages will go."

Please, no. He did not want to get the heirloom nativity out, which had been in the family for one hundred years, and share it with Rosalina. That was too personal a thing to share with a fake girlfriend.

"How positively lovely." Rosalina clutched her hands under her chin and her eyes sparkled more than enough to make up for not having the earlier-mentioned tiara atop her head. "Let's go, Marco."

Oh joy. Marco gave what must have looked like a forced smile, which earned him a *don't be like that* expression from Rosalina.

"Now, off with you two." His mom made a shooing motion with her laded hands. Marco wanted to warn her to be extra careful with Rosalina's Oreo balls, but as much as Mom loved them, he didn't think he had cause to worry.

"Ready, L—" he caught himself before accidentally calling her Lina. "—ready?"

She narrowed her eyes, every bit of the sass he knew she possessed filling her radiant face. Christmas in July looked good on her.

Marco thrust his finger in his ear. Since when did he notice how Rosalina looked?

Since today.

He wasn't sure if he was ready to admit it or not, but something had changed. Whether it'd started last night at the Brinkman Mansion, today upon opening the door to Rosalina, or if it'd been germinating over the last two weeks, he didn't know.

He also wasn't sure if it was a good thing or a bad thing.

Does it matter?

This "thing" between them was fake—no matter how real the heat inside had been a few minutes ago—and it would be over in less than two weeks time.

He should be relieved. It'd be great to be able to lie down at night without his conscience niggling him in the stillness of his room. The only thing that saved him was that he conked out within seconds of his head hitting the pillow, thanks to his long days in the heat.

If he should be relieved...why did his stomach do a downward whirl?

Nothing made sense.

Except...setting up a nativity made sense, and they now stood in the large room of the basement where their home theater was set up—Mom's tabletop tree fluffed and festooned to perfection in the back corner.

"I can't believe we get to decorate for Christmas in July." Rosalina sounded giddy as the girls Marco remembered from his grade and middle school years. Somehow, it didn't annoy him coming from Rosalina as it had back then.

Perhaps, it was because she was a grown woman and knew how to control her giddiness. His female classmates had always gone too far and too long with it.

Ugh...

"Earth to Marco."

Marco snapped out of his strange recollection. His thoughts were as crazy as a squirrel stuck on a roof.

He gave himself a mental shake. "Sorry. Here." He lifted the box that held the nativity off the floor and set it on the refreshment table his mom wanted it displayed on. "How about I unwrap the pieces and you can arrange them?"

"Love it."

"Now, this isn't any old nativity. It might look weird and laughable to you."

Rosalina shook a finger at him. "Marco Mendez, that is no way to talk about a *nacimiento*. They are precious family heirlooms"

He raised his hands in surrender. "Don't say I didn't warn you." He closed his hand around a wrapped figurine and began removing the tissue paper.

Rosalina fairly jittered with impatience.

At last he produced the first figure. An angel. He handed it to Rosalina.

"Aww. This brings back memories of our display back home. Hand painted. Made of clay. It doesn't get more special than homemade."

"Yes." This nativity was priceless. Passed down through the generations and added to by each owner. Tenderly set out, accompanied with storytelling of past Christmases.

A muffled throat clearing came from the front of the room. "What's going on in here?" It was Antonio. As Marco had expected, already claiming his spot on the long sofa.

His eyes roamed over the available remaining seating and he swallowed. The two recliners along the opposite wall of the long couch were also claimed. The one held Mom's neck pillow and favorite blanket (which she used no matter how warm outside), and the other contained Dad's lap pillow and the TV remote.

That left only one piece of furniture left. The small—*ahem*—love seat, which faced the TV straight on and was set back a little from the others...with the *romantic* Christmas tree only a few feet away. He'd been right about his mom scheming.

How am I going to survive this evening?

"Ah, the company has arrived." Antonio sat up from his prostrate position on the couch with ruffled hair and groggy face and eyes.

"Yes, Rosalina is here. Aren't Isabella and Oscar and their brood coming?"

Antonio stood, stretched, and yawned largely. "No, they had prior plans. I guess when you no longer live under the same roof as Mom you're not obligated to sit through her disgusting movies."

All the more reason Marco needed his house offer to go through...quick. The only good thing about tonight would be stuffing his face full of Oreo balls.

Marco continued unwrapping figurines and handing them to Rosalina, who made detailed work of where she put everything.

"What on earth?" She laughed outright when he handed her the next piece. A rooster that was three times bigger than everything else he'd given her so far. "Roosters aren't part of the nativity story."

Marco shrugged. "Who knows. If Jesus was, indeed, born in a stable, there probably was a rooster."

"Fair enough. But...it's bigger than the angel!"

Antonio slipped up beside Rosalina. "Setting out the nativity, eh? It's been passed down through our family for one hundred years. The pieces are mismatched because each ancestor who had it added to it, and since they are handmade, no two figurines are the same."

"Yes, I am aware of the tradition." She used a tone that said Antonio should know that. Then she turned wide, sparkling eyes on Marco. "One hundred years. So many memories. I'm sure there are precious stories wrapped up in this heirloom."

He nodded, unable to do anything more than look into Rosalina's deep gaze—something going on between them as they stared. He cleared his throat, which broke the spell, and they finished setting out the nativity.

Rosalina had a comment about each piece, touched each one reverently, and exclaimed over the crocheted clothes on the baby Jesus. "It's lovely." She stepped back to look at it when finished.

"Isn't it?" Mom arrived, and in her next breath belted out, "Okay, let the *fiesta* begin!" It was then he noticed she now sported a red T-shirt that had the image of a Scottish terrier with a Christmas wreath around its neck. His mom also wore a felt headband that had candy canes sticking up, with jangling bells hanging from the candy's ends.

Marco slapped his forehead and felt the heat crank up again—this time for a totally different reason. Did his mom have to embarrass him in front of Rosalina?

"Oh, Maria, I love your shirt! And that headband...ahh-dorable." Rosalina then hurried to relieve his mom's full load by taking the tray bearing all the sugary Christmas candy for the night, leaving Mom with a breakfast tray loaded with mugs of hot chocolate.

Dad was close behind Mom, carefully transporting three large bowls of popcorn in his arms. Marco was glad to see his dad was "normal" in his standard comfy house clothes he changed into after work, although he had been wise to choose the dark green pocket tee from that wardrobe to, no doubt, appease Mom. He was surprised Mom hadn't managed to weasel Dad into wearing antlers or a red nose, or something.

Mom began taking charge. "Antonio, turn the lights off."

He went to do her bidding.

"Marco, plug in the Christmas tree." He got right on it.

"Rosalina, you're the guest of honor. There are paper plates and bowls. Get all the candy and popcorn you want. Don't forget to grab a hot chocolate too."

Rosalina chuckled. "I'm going to have to avoid sugar for a whole month after this."

Mom gave Rosalina's cheek a soft pat. "Christmas in July only comes once a year. Calories and sugar don't count"

And with that the evening proceeded, with everyone settling in the exact places Marco had figured.

He hesitantly took his place on the love seat, while Rosalina settled far too anxiously. Marco pulled at his shirt collar and adjusted his shoulders.

Luigi and Queenie got the memo and joined them in the room, Luigi claiming Marco's lap, and Queenie demanding to settle next to Rosalina's leg and the armrest, which forced Rosalina to sit closer to him.

Marco almost swallowed his Oreo ball whole when their legs connected. He feigned a cough to cover up his, no doubt, obvious reaction.

Rosalina sent him a smile as the first movie started. "This is fun," she whispered.

"This is torture." Is that what Marco heard? Torture?

She couldn't have said fun, could she?

It's going to be a long night.

By the time the second movie began, Marco had had his fill of sweets and he folded his arms over his chest, relaxing into the couch. Maybe he could fall asleep for the rest of the evening.

As the movie continued to play, his eyes grew heavy and dreamland wasn't far off, but then every hair on his right arm took to dancing when he felt a warm pressure. Fully alert now, Marco looked over to see Rosalina's head resting on his shoulder.

He shimmied, hoping she'd get the message this was not part of "no touching when mom's not looking." And it was a direct disobedience to the whole "no couch cuddling" rule.

Keeping her head in contact with his shoulder, she looked up at him and smiled. Then she looped her left arm around his and reached out her right arm and settled her hand on his chest.

Marco's body heated up again.

It's fake. It's fake. It's fake.

It was the high intake of sugar making him so hot.

It's fake. It's fake. It's fake.

Rosalina smelled like chocolate, vanilla, and clean laundry. A few strands of her hair tickled his neck, making him shiver.

How could he be hot and shiver at the same time?

He reassured himself once more that it was all fake. These feelings. Rosalina's cuddling. It meant nothing. Shouldn't affect him at all.

But they did.

Strongly.

Rosalina should have been an actress. She could put any one of the leading ladies on the screen tonight out of a job.

He craned his neck to look at her again. As if she'd been expecting it, Rosalina looked up at him again. Her eyes were unfocused, her lids heavy.

Marco's mouth went dry.

It was too much—these feelings he'd never experienced before. He wanted to claim a necessary bathroom break so he could get away and lie on the tile floor to cool off.

Maybe, he'd developed diabetes all of a sudden and was experiencing a diabetic attack. Could he get his hands on some insulin? It might help.

He didn't know what the symptoms of a diabetic attack were, but there was something going on inside him that *was not* normal.

When the third movie began playing, Marco decided the bathroom idea sounded more and more appealing as Rosalina grew heavier on his arm—making her all but impossible to ignore. He shook his shoulder to get her attention. She didn't budge.

Stubborn woman.

She knew he'd not wanted any couch cuddling.

He shook his arm again with no response.

Marco huffed and when he turned his head to give her a glare, he found her eyes were shut, mouth parted ever so slightly with little puffs of breath escaping and making a gentle wind sound. Her face looked so soft that he couldn't help but reach over with the arm Rosalina didn't still hold captive and run a finger down her cheek.

It is soft.

Another shiver ran through him.

Then light exploded in the room and Marco sucked in air to the point of choking. He squinted his eyes against the blinding brightness. "What was that for?"

"I think it's late enough to call it a night," his mom answered from behind him at the light switch. "Three movies are plenty for one sitting."

How had he not noticed his mom get up?

A cute moan escaped Rosalina and she rubbed her cheek on his shirt. A slight dampness passed through to his skin, and Marco realized she'd used his shirt to wipe her drool.

Gross.

Her head slid to his chest, her hand lowering to his stomach. She was out cold.

Marco needed her to move. Now. Before he did something crazy. Like kiss her hair. Or twirl a piece of her long black glory around his finger.

Not happening.

That's something a *real* boyfriend would do in a *real* dating relationship.

As mad as Rosalina had been about agreeing to fake dating, he could only imagine what cruel fate she would issue him if he called off the ruse and told her he might actually have true feelings for her.

Not that he was saying he did.

He needed time to first evaluate the way his body had reacted to her tonight.

So he did the sensible thing and began lightly tapping Rosalina's cheek.

She stirred only slightly, another moan passing from her lips.

"Time to wake up, Lina. Party's over."

"Mmm. *Fiesta?*"

"Yes. It's over."

She mumbled something in Spanish and Marco worked to decipher it. Hoped he'd translated wrong, or else she'd said he was very comfortable and she wanted to stay all night.

That did not help his current problem.

He worked some saliva into his mouth so he could talk. More firmly this time. "Rosalina, it's time to go home. Wake up." He tapped her cheek a tad harder and gently untangled their arms so he could maneuver her to an upright position.

Her eyes slowly opened and then squeezed back shut. "It's bright."

"You slept through the last movie. Christmas in July has come to a close."

"Oh... Oh!" She looked at him through one eye, the other shut against the overhead lights. "I guess I did fall asleep, didn't I? Oops. Was the last movie a good one?"

Marco was not the person to ask that question, so he avoided it. "Ready to go home?"

She yawned. "Ready for bed."

Marco did not like how the simple comment reminded him of her Spanish mumbling mere moments ago.

"Let me help you up." He stood and held out a hand, which Rosalina took without hesitation. Good thing, for she wobbled at first. He eyed her curiously.

She giggled. "I'm good now. I think I was out long enough to fall into a deep sleep pattern."

I would say so. If her dead weight and increased body temperature against his arm for the last twenty to thirty tortuous minutes of the evening were any indication.

A different kind of torture than he'd initially expected.

Everyone pitched in for the cleanup and by thirty minutes later they were marching up the stairs. Marco saw Rosalina to the door.

"You're not too sleepy to drive, are you?" He should have picked her up, but she'd insisted upon driving herself...in case he ran late.

Humph.

"I'm plenty awake now after moving around."

"Okay. Well, good night."

"Ooooh. Oh, oh oh!"

Rosalina's face mirrored Marco's confusion at his mom's exuberant outburst.

His stomach twisted and it had nothing to do with all the junk he'd eaten tonight. It told him his mom had one last scheme up her sleeve.

"Mom...?"

"There's a mistletoe above you two."

"What?!" Marco snapped his head back and, sure enough, the blasted parasitic plant hung from the threshold. He hadn't noticed it up there earlier this evening when Rosalina had arrived.

Rosalina chuckled in what sounded like a nervous way to him. "There is. Isn't there?"

"You know what that means..." Mom crossed over to them and backhanded Marco in the biceps. "Kiss her, Marco."

"Kiss her?!" A real boyfriend wouldn't make it sound so preposterous.

"Yes!" Mom waved her hand.

Marco looked to Rosalina, expecting to see a death threat in her eyes should he consider it, but, rather, she watched with mirthful expectancy.

Did she want him to kiss her?

Again, she was far too good an actor.

To humor his mom, and for the sole purpose of their cover, Marco took a step closer to Rosalina. Leaned in. Barely made contact with his lips on one corner of her mouth.

That would surely be enough to appease his mom.

But as Marco started to back away, Rosalina's hands gripped his shirt and she pulled him to her, claiming his lips with hers.

Kissing him right on the mouth.

The roof of sanity collapsed on him, and at that moment Marco had no idea what was real and what was lie.

But one thing was true.

This was a real kiss.

Chapter Nineteen

Rosalina doubted she'd ever sleep again.

Not with how alive she felt right now. It was as if her body and blood were electrified and she was running on a high she wasn't accustomed to.

That kiss.

So that was why people dated and got married.

Now she understood.

She'd been won over to the side of romance.

Who had she been kidding saying she didn't want a relationship?

It wasn't any old relationship she desired, though. It was Marco she wanted. No other would do.

No, not after her lips had been on his and she'd tasted of him. He'd tasted of butter popcorn, hot chocolate, Oreo balls, and...well, something decidedly Marco.

Rosalina stared at herself in the mirror of her bathroom, after having washed her face and changed into pajamas, and she touched her fingertips to her lips.

Surely—*surely*—Marco knew she wasn't dating him for fake now. Not after she kissed him like *that*.

Whatever had possessed her?

She'd never even kissed before.

And yet, when his lips had barely brushed the skin next to her mouth, something inside of her had yearned for more.

He must think she was some sort of wanton woman. There wasn't anything further from the truth.

"Oh..." Rosalina covered her face with her hands. "How embarrassing!"

She could well imagine how stilted things would be between them now.

Marco had been so kind and fun tonight. Mellow. Now she'd probably resurrected Mad Marco again.

"What have I done?"

Since she wasn't tired anymore, Rosalina decided a couple hours in God's Word was in order. Flipping the light switch off to the bathroom, she padded over to her bed, and cozied up with her Bible.

Proverbs seemed like the perfect place to read. Where she could soak up some wisdom. And learn all about—*ahem*—silly women and how not to act versus the priceless virtuous woman Rosalina strove to be.

Apparently, she needed a reminder.

Then again, didn't God create love and romance? The attraction between a man and woman? There was nothing wrong about that.

Now if she let the fire inside take her too far, then there would be trouble. She knew where the line was drawn that if she crossed over would land her in sin. By God's grace, though, she would not cross it.

Didn't want to cross it.

Of that she was resolved.

Rosalina grabbed the notebook she always kept on her nightstand and decided she would make a list of dating do's and don'ts that she would glean from her study of Proverbs.

Then she would know how to proceed and conduct herself as this dating—definitely, no longer charade—proceeded.

If the way Marco had responded was any indication, Rosalina had an inkling he would agree. She shivered at the memory of his hands on her waist. The way he first tried to push her away, then gave in and kissed her back, seeming to explore and make sense of what was going on between them.

She wondered what his thoughts were tonight. Was she on his mind? Or had he fallen asleep before his head hit the pillow? It seemed impossible to leave a kiss like that unaffected.

But how would she know? She was a woman. Maybe men didn't have such reactions.

If that was the case, maybe they'd still be back at ground zero. She trying to win the heart of and prove her love to a man who was in love with another woman.

But she had to wonder...was he in love with Lillian, or the memory of their friendship?

Perhaps, the ties that held Marco Mendez bound weren't as strong as she once thought.

◻◻◻

Over the noon hour the next day, Rosalina's phone pinged, and when she saw Marco's name on the screen a searing heat rose into her face and brought with it a delightful memory of last night's kiss.

Not at all interested in her small lunch fare of pita chips and guacamole, Rosalina grabbed the device and opened the message.

Marco: Lunch time. Have a minute to text?

Rosalina: Yup.

Marco: Do you have plans Saturday evening?

Rosalina: I'm open. Why?

Marco: Well…after that uh kiss last night Mom spilled the beans to my sister and now Isabella is adamant about meeting you. They think we're really serious.

Rosalina: Talk about a run on sentence there. Have you forgotten where punctuation goes? …I would love to meet your sister.

Marco: I'm going to have to stop texting you if you can't leave off with the criticism. I dont care about accuracy.

Rosalina: Obviously — *Don't*

Marco: <angry face emoji> Back to the topic. Wanna go bowling?

Rosalina: Sounds like fun! I've never gone bowling.

Marco: Are you for real?

Rosalina: <one shoulder shrug emoji>

Marco: Bowling it is. At 6. I will teach you how. Is there an emoji for rubbing one's fist?
Rosalina: That sounds kind of evil. Maybe I don't want you teaching me.
Marco: It will be fun.
Rosalina: Promise?
Marco: Promise.

Rosalina paused with her fingers poised over the keyboard. She wasn't ready for the conversation to be over, but she found herself at a loss for words.

What could she say?

She had so much she wanted to ask him. But that one line—*they think we're really serious*—had Rosalina wanting to cry. Marco thought nothing of that kiss last night.

She hung her head.

Enough time passed for her phone to go dark on its own and then ping with another text. Like a lovesick dog, Rosalina jerked her head up and swiped the screen. The message, however, killed her spirits.

Marco: I'm sorry about the mistletoe deal. That wasn't supposed to happen.
Rosalina: It's fine.

It broke her heart in two to type those words. She felt anything but fine with the major letdown incited by Marco's apology.

Apology!

For sharing such a toe-curling kiss?

They think we're really serious.

"We are!" She screamed at her phone, wishing it were Marco's face.

She dropped her volume and her phone. "At least, *I'm* serious."

Three dancing dots appeared on the screen letting her know Marco was typing again.

Marco: Not sure how kissing never came up in our ground rules for fake dating. Never would have thought it'd be an issue.
Rosalina: You made the rules. Not me.

Marco: Yeah, and you broke every one of them.

Rosalina: <cheesing emoji> I apologize for nothing.

Marco: What was that big word you called me the other day that started with an i.

Rosalina: You forgot the (?) again.

Marco: You're annoying.

Rosalina: The word was incorrigible.

Marco: Does that work in this instance? Are you incorrigible?

Rosalina: NEVER. It's not in my DNA to be.

Marco: <expressionless emoji> I'm going to consult with the dictionary and decide for myself.

Rosalina: You should probably get more acquainted with it.

Marco: <rolling eyes emoji>

Rosalina: What?! You mean to tell me you weren't one of those kids who read the dictionary?

Marco: No. Remember, I don't like to read. What kind of twisted kid would read the dictionary?

Rosalina: I'm insulted.

Marco: YOU DID!?!? Sorry. Didn't mean you personally.

Rosalina: I'm not convinced.

Marco: How can I make it better?

Rosalina: How about another kiss like last night...?

Marco:

Rosalina: ?? Do you know you sent a blank message?

Marco: Time to get back to work.

Rosalina: Ttyl.

Rosalina sighed and pressed her phone in the dip of her chin. The man was...

"Incorrigible."

And annoying. And frustrating. And oh, so, worth every battle she was going to have to fight to win him.

She was going to hold to faith that it wasn't a losing battle.

"Could you maybe fight this battle for me, Lord? Or at least help me?"

That is...if this is a battle I'm supposed to fight.

Maybe she needed to get her heart out of the equation and move on when this whole thing was done.

She wanted to have a good cry at the mere thought of walking away from Marco.

Crazy to think how fast he'd grown on her.

"Here's the mail." Haven plopped a stack of envelopes, fliers, and brochures on the table with a loud *thunk*.

"Thanks, Haven. Anything interesting?"

"I didn't look." Haven went to the small dorm room size fridge they kept there in the back room and grabbed a Capri Sun. "It's a hot one outside."

Rosalina turned her eyes to the window. It even looked stifling out. She could see heat waves radiating up from the roofs of the surrounding buildings. "Ugh. You know what they say about August."

"The dog days of summer. And we're almost there. Can you believe there are only five days left in July. I wish we could skip ahead to October. I hate the heat."

Rosalina chuckled. That was a fact about Haven. And she would hear about it every day for the next several weeks.

Her chuckling turned to a frown when she thought of Marco working in the heat, baking on the roofs. She hoped he was being careful to avoid heat stroke.

Of course, he was used to it. It's not like he was new to the job or the heat. Still, she couldn't help but worry about him.

Because she cared. She wanted him to be okay. Safe.

She thought of the heights. Steep roofs. Ladders. Slippery slopes.

She had to squint her eyes against a wave of—was it fear?—that spiraled through her body, making her stomach feel hollow, her legs weak, and her head a little dizzy.

Good thing she was sitting.

"You okay? Heat affecting you?" Haven sounded genuinely concerned.

Rosalina shook away the feeling. "Sorry. Just had an unsettling thought."

"Oh."

Speaking of unsettling, Rosalina's vision picked up on the top envelope and her stomach tightened.

Truman Scott's address taunted her.

Why would he have needed to send her anything? They'd settled everything at their meeting. She had until August fifth to make up her payment, or else her lease would not be renewed.

There was no reason for any other conversing between them in the interim. Not until her time was up and she had to see him face to face again.

A sight *and* encounter she was looking forward to about as much as being peed on by an overly excited dog.

Actually, she'd rather wear dog urine every day than have to deal with the likes of Scott the Snake.

Forgive me, Jesus, for my less than Christian thoughts.

She would have to work on loving those who despitefully used her. She made a note to study Matthew five tonight. She could make another list titled: How I Should Conduct Myself with My Fellow Man.

Her hands shaking with dread, Rosalina broke the seal and slid out the piece of stationary.

She wanted to crumple it in her fist when she read the quick summary of their meeting from the fifteenth. He was outlining the terms of their agreement, reminding her she had until August fifth to come up with the sum.

Of course, he used fancy legal jargon, but that was the gist.

Rosalina needed to check and see where she stood. She had a week and a half yet to raise the funds. She would have to balance her checkbook tonight and see how she was doing.

And see if she could pick up a few more dogs to walk on Saturday. Before time to go bowling with Marco.

Rosalina pressed her hand to her forehead and gave her head a shake. She should have told him how bad of an athlete she was.

I'm going to humiliate myself. I know it.

□□□

Rosalina was a sweaty mess by the time she finished her last walk Saturday. She'd put the miles on her shoes today.

It was already four-thirty by the time she got back home, so a quick shower, a brief snack, and some electrolyte water was all she was able to make time for.

The rush was a good thing. It kept her mind off of how much she did not wish to go bowling tonight. But it meant spending time with Marco, and she wanted that.

Now wasn't that a mark of a true girlfriend? Doing something she wouldn't normally do so she could be with her man.

She'd also be meeting Marco's sister, and that was another plus. As long as Isabella didn't bring up Thursday night's kiss.

"Ugh. There is so much that can go wrong."

Ding-dong.

Woof, woof, woof.

Queenie's loud bark from beside her startled Rosalina more than the doorbell.

She pressed her hands to her cheeks. "He's here..." She smoothed a hand over her hair and checked her reflection. It hadn't gone unnoticed by her how Marco had reacted to her Thursday. At last, he'd *seen* her.

For the first time, a man *noticed* her.

And Marco hadn't in a lustful way, but with approval.

It had made her feel...well, good.

Kind of helped the bruised confidence that had taken so many hits over the years from being the only girl never asked out during high school and college.

Knock, knock, knock.

Bark, bark, bark.

This time Queenie took off running out to the living room where the front door was.

Rosalina couldn't leave Marco waiting again. She hurried from her room and opened the front door before he could have a chance to knock or ring again, and something surprised her.

Marco's smile.

No, it hadn't changed. It was the same silly, little-too-close-to-fake grin that drove her bonkers.

But something inside her had changed. Her reaction to it. The same smile she'd "insulted" was now the smile she looked forward to seeing. The one she thought of in her mind.

It was Marco.

Fake or real, she liked that grin...a lot.

Because, she liked Marco.

Amazing how small things like that can change when perspectives are altered.

"Ready to go bowling?" Marco asked.

"Yes. If you'll teach me."

"I'll try to. Not sure what kind of a student you are."

"The overachieving kind." She batted her eyelashes.

"Then I expect a strike from you tonight."

"If I do, you'll blame it on beginner's luck, won't you?"

"No way. I'd take all the credit. For being such a good teacher, you know." He flashed an extra toothy grin.

"Well, that's to be determined."

"Humph." He shoved his hands in his pockets.

Rosalina laughed, then turned around to say goodbye to Queenie. "You be a good girl now. Momma will be back later."

"Hey, Queenie." Marco's voice was right behind her and Rosalina twisted her neck to find him leaning over her, looking at the dog.

"Look who is here, Queenie. Your friend."

"Ha." Marco let out a snort. "I'm pretty sure my name isn't on that list. But, maybe...that can change."

Rosalina furrowed her brows and twisted on her feet so she could squat against the door and see what Marco had up his sleeve.

Rather...in his pocket.

Marco produced a small dog biscuit.

"Here you go, Queenie. Peace offering?" He held the treat out with uncertainty.

The dog sniffed the biscuit curiously. Gave it a lick. Another lick. Gently, Queenie took the offering and hurried to her pillow bed in front of the sliding glass door.

Marco wore a pleased expression. "She took it."

"She sure did! And she didn't try to bite you." Rosalina was proud of Marco for doing it. For taking a step toward overcoming his fear. She was proud of her dog too.

"Not like when I offered her the bit of beef."

"Queenie knows better than to accept table scraps."

"Oh, well...you could have told me that." He stood to his full height, and Rosalina was once again reminded of how much she enjoyed the fact that he was only a few inches taller than her.

"I could have. But I thought it was worth trying." She shrugged.

"Enough about that. Let's go."

"Sounds good." Rosalina said bye to Queenie one more time, but the dog was still working on her biscuit and couldn't be bothered.

As Rosalina walked with Marco to his truck, she wished she had a biscuit to keep her busy in the corner of a room so she didn't have to go embarrass herself. She was certain she would.

She'd be more surprised if she didn't.

Chapter Twenty

Isabella was even more welcoming of Rosalina than Marco's mom had been their first meeting—and that's really saying something.

Within three minutes after the introduction, any onlookers would think the two women were sisters. Marco was relieved—especially that no mention of Thursday night's kiss had been brought up.

Now, he couldn't say for sure what had been said while he and Oscar shared small talk during the girls' gushing. How did women make something as simple as an introduction so mushy?

Or, maybe that wasn't common. He just had to be stuck with a sister and a fake girlfriend who were emotionally expressive.

Yay.

He had to say he preferred Rosalina's sass than the giddiness Isabella incited. And with the giggling going on right now he had to wonder what Isabella was telling her. Probably something about him.

He hoped Rosalina stuck to their story and didn't go making things difficult. They only had one more week until the wedding. One more week to keep their story straight, fabricate a break-up, and go on their merry way.

Only...Marco didn't feel merry thinking about it. Even if it was how they'd planned it to end.

It doesn't have to end that way.

But Rosalina didn't care for him like that. This was fake. He'd roped her into it, she'd proven to him how much she disliked the idea, and, no doubt, she'd be thrilled to be freed from this "contract" as soon as possible.

"What's with the big frown, little brother?" Isabella backhanded him in the stomach.

Marco rubbed his abdomen and turned his lips in a one-eighty. "I'm not frowning."

"Liar."

More than you know.

Isabella didn't have to know that.

On the other hand, Rosalina's expression read: *That's right. And what are you going to do about it?*

He'd take care of it soon.

For now, "Let me give you your crash course in bowling, Rosalina."

She smiled and left Isabella's side to stand with him. The way she looked up at him, he almost thought he saw adoration in her eyes. He told himself it was all for show.

Fake.

It's fake.

Rosalina Torres wouldn't adore him. She insulted his smile. He made her mad. Those weren't building blocks for adoration.

Swallowing, Marco adjusted his shoulders and assumed a teacher's voice. He demonstrated how to hold a bowling ball and couldn't keep the mirth from showing on his face as he watched Rosalina attempt it.

"This feels weird. And I had no idea a bowling ball would be so *heavy!*"

Marco chuckled. "Well, there has to be some weight to carry the thing clear down the lane and knock down the pins."

Rosalina nodded thoughtfully. "I suppose. I bet professional bowlers have a lot of shoulder issues."

"No doubt." Marco proceeded to show her how to throw the ball and she watched his every move like an eager student.

An overachieving student is what she'd called herself. Well, they'd see about that. He was still counting on her to make a strike tonight.

"Okay. I think I got this." She smiled at him.

"Do you want to try a practice throw first? We'll let you." Marco offered, but looked at the others to be sure they were in agreement.

"Nah. You make it look easy. It can't be hard. So long as my arm can hold up under the weight. I might not be able to play a full game."

"Once you get to having fun, you won't notice anything."

"I hope so. Although, I don't find these shoes very comfortable either. I want my cushy sandals back. Why can't we wear our own shoes, anyway?"

"To protect the lanes," Oscar answered. "See how pretty the flooring is? If they let us wear our street shoes they wouldn't be clean and shiny, but covered with dirt and scratches and yuck."

"Ah." Rosalina was soaking it all in like a good pupil. She'd ace the final exam if Marco were to give her one.

"You'll do great." Isabella reassured her. "We'll go easy on you."

"Don't go easy. Have fun and be yourselves. I'll hold my own."

Marco leaned close to Rosalina until their shoulders bumped. "Are you competitive?" He waggled his brows.

She got a mischievous grin. "But of course."

"Then show me what'cha got, beginner."

A light sparked in her eye. "You better believe I will."

"Who's going first?" Oscar was getting impatient. No surprise. His brother-in-law wasn't noted for that virtue.

"Rosalina should." Isabella pointed to her, excitement making her look less weary than normal. Having two littles under the age of two kept her on her toes. She was probably relieved Mom was watching the kids and giving her and Oscar a night out.

Marco was glad too. So far it was going good, and he was certain they were going to have a blast.

Rosalina shook her head emphatically. "Oh no. I want to watch first."

"Very well. I'll go first." Of course, it was Oscar.

Everyone waved Oscar on, and he grabbed his ball. Marco watched as Rosalina calculated his every move.

She jumped when the ball crashed into the pins, but she cheered and clapped when they went crashing to the ground, only two pins remaining standing.

Marco loved the way her cheeks flushed and her smile reached new dimensions he'd not witnessed before. The way her brown eyes twinkled and reflected the shiny floor.

She turned and caught him staring, which added some pink to her cheeks. Knowing he'd not done anything wrong—a boyfriend was entitled to study his girlfriend—Marco slowly looked away (not quickly jerk like he felt compelled to do), letting a slow smile play his lips.

Ah, but he felt a little flirty tonight.

Good. It'd help validate their charade for Isabella's watchful, documenting eyes. Marco knew she'd give Mom a full re-telling of the evening, not missing a single detail on the new "couple."

Isabella went next, but not before receiving some friendly ribbing from Oscar. It wouldn't be a night of bowling with his sister and brother-in-law if they didn't engage in some heated competition.

He and Lillian had always added to the heat, and they'd had a jolly good time.

That caused his brows to furrow. He missed bowling with Lillian. Missed their friendship. He wished that could remain the same; didn't have to change with marriage. But he knew that wasn't how it worked.

If he put himself in Clint's shoes, he wouldn't want another man—no matter how good of a friend he was—spending friendly time with his fiancée/wife/girlfriend, whatever the case.

But, today was a new day. As Lillian started her new chapter in life, he could work on starting a new one. This was a chance to make new memories. With Rosalina. Even if it was for a short time, a person couldn't have too many good memories.

Unless they proved painful. Like the ones he had with Lillian. Surely with time they wouldn't be painful any longer.

"You're next!"

Marco jumped at the barked words from his sister, accompanied by a slap to his back. "Man, you should learn to keep your hands to yourself."

"Pfft." Isabella threw her nose in the air.

So much like Rosalina.

He grabbed his bowling ball, made meticulous work of positioning his hold for Rosalina's sake, and zeroed his attention in on the pins. Putting every ounce of precision and the right amount of strength he'd learned was necessary to get the ball down the lane, Marco used a few steps to gain momentum, then let the ball fly.

He loved the sound of it releasing from his hand and gliding across the floor. He watched with bated breath as it rolled and rolled and rolled.

CRASH!

"Strike!" Marco made a double fist pump and spun around to his opponents. "Yeah, baby! Woohoo!"

Isabella rolled her eyes. "He's so humble."

Rosalina laughed.

Oscar looked to be calculating, likely planning on how he could still manage to cream Marco, despite his early lead.

He'd have to consult the score to see how Isabella's first turn had gone—since he'd completely missed it with his roaming mind.

He slid his gaze to Rosalina. "You ready, rookie."

She let out a nervous breath. "Kind of hard to beat that."

He let out a gloating laugh and puffed out his chest, which she playfully slapped.

It wasn't annoying like when Isabella slapped him.

It wasn't un-noteworthy like when Lillian jabbed him.

No, this was charged, baby. Charged. And if Marco could run on that energy the rest of the night, he'd get a strike every turn.

Rosalina eyed him strangely, and it made him wonder what his face revealed. He cleared his throat, stepped aside, and bid her take position. "Show me what you got. Make your teacher proud."

"I'm starting to regret telling you guys not to take it easy."

"Don't be nervous." Isabella piped in. "All you have to do is throw the ball and knock down the pins. You can't do it wrong. None of us are professionals."

Rosalina snorted. "You sure about that?" Her eyes were on Marco.

He grinned. "I've been playing awhile."

She let out a sigh and focused all her attention on obtaining the proper hold on her ball. "Like this, right?"

"Very good." She was making him proud already.

She went through the motion of a throw, but didn't release the ball. "Just practicing," she said with a wink.

Marco could only smile as he crossed his arms and settled into his stance, anticipating her first throw.

Rosalina gave a nod. "Okay. This time for real."

"You can do it." Every good teacher was also a cheerleader.

Rosalina's nervous face relaxed slightly and she smiled, then proceeded to repeat the process of a great beginner's throw.

Only...when it came time for the release, her fingers didn't let go. Marco doubted what he was seeing, but he knew he was awake and his eyes open. Rosalina *somehow* went right along with the ball, sliding a little over halfway down the lane, shrieking all the way.

What was she trying to do? Make a strike with her whole body?

Was that how she planned to win the game? Use herself as a giant bowling ball?

Didn't seem smart to him.

Isabella gasped.

Oscar stood.

Marco jogged down the lane. "You forgot to let go of the ball!" He couldn't keep the laughter out of his voice. "Are you hurt?" He was concerned, but, something like that...well, that's not something you see often. If ever. Although, he'd heard of it happening. His stomach started to shake with the deep laughter that wanted to erupt.

He could hear snickers and whispers from a group of teenage bowlers. A few young children out with their parents were outright laughing.

He was trying—oh, he was trying—to hold it in. He knew Rosalina's personality enough to know she'd blow her top if he laughed at her.

But...

Rosalina lifted her head and her long hair draped in a curtain over her face. Even with the obscured view, Marco could see her mortification. "I'm n-not hurt. Only my...pride." She looked around and her face flushed an even deeper red with all the attention on her.

Marco heard a little boy "whisper" to his sibling about the woman who didn't know how to bowl, when even his young self could.

"You sure?" His words wobbled with humor, despite his desire to sound genuinely worried about her.

"You're laughing at me."

That was the wrong accusation, for it made the laughs choke through his throat and spurt out his tightly clamped lips. "I—"

"You can't deny it. I can see it. Hear it."

"I'm sorry. You're sure you're okay?"

"I'm fine. Help me up."

Marco gave her a hand up and he assessed her movements. Everything appeared to be working correctly. That was reassuring.

She huffed and brushed off her clothes. "I knew this wasn't a good idea."

"How could you forget to release the ball?"

He asked it loud enough that the little boys started guffawing and poking fun again.

"I didn't forget! My fingers got stuck in the ball." She flexed her hand into a fist and wiggled her fingers. "I think they got swollen while waiting for my turn. Nerves and sweating, you know."

Marco fought the chuckles, but to no avail. "Man, if only I had that on video. That's like *America's Funniest Home Videos* worthy."

"Excuse me!" Rosalina glared at him.

Uh-oh. He shouldn't have let that thought pass his lips. Making a joke? He was no different than the little mockers a few feet away.

"Um..." How could he redeem himself? He'd gone and let his big mouth move faster than his slow brain. Why couldn't he remember to think before he spoke? All the time. Not some of the time. Would have come in handy this time, for sure.

"I could have been seriously hurt, Marco!" She speared him with her fiery eyes. Hands on hips.

"I know. I was concer—"

"Is everything a joke to you?" She stamped her foot and leaned in toward his face—definitely not because of flirting this time.

"What—?"

"Don't you take anything seriously?"

Marco all of a sudden had a feeling they were talking about way more than the incident. He found himself unable to speak.

"Well, let me tell you something, *Marco*. I'm done with it." With a huff and exaggerated steps, she left her ball and him, giving him one last indignant snort as she stormed away—with Isabella and Oscar looking on, as if they were watching some interesting movie.

Marco's gaze alternated between the two and Rosalina, who was now changing her shoes—he glaring at one, confused at the other.

"Lover's spat?" Isabella questioned.

Marco sent her a look of disgust and trotted after Rosalina, who already had her hand on the exit door. "Finish the game yourself," he hollered over his shoulder before he got any farther away.

The sticky air assaulted Marco the minute he stepped out of the highly air-conditioned bowling alley, but it wasn't nearly as searing as Rosalina's eyes had been. He looked toward his truck first, expecting to see her leaning against the side, but she wasn't there.

He twisted his head from left to right, scanning the area. He spotted her stomping down the sidewalk in the direction that would take her back home.

Marco took off jogging toward her. "Rosalina, stop. What are you doing?" He reached her side and fell in step next to her.

She ignored him.

No surprise there.

"I asked, what are you doing?"

She spun to him. "I know what you asked."

He was pretty sure he felt spittle land on his upper lip.

I will not wipe it away. I will not wipe it away.

His lip twitched knowing it was there. But it was the least he deserved. Remembering Lillian's words once more about asking for forgiveness, he decided to try another apology. "I'm sorry I laughed at you."

"From someone who lies so much and takes nothing seriously, you think I'm going to believe that's sincere."

She liked insults. Marco rolled his eyes and threw his arms up. "Where are you going?"

"Home." She expelled as little breath as possible with the clipped word.

"You can't walk home. It's not a safe area."

"Any person I could come in contact with along this walk would be preferred company to riding in your truck with you."

She'd rather come face-to-face with a mugger?

Ouch.

"What's the real problem, Rosalina?"

"What's the real problem?" She stopped. Marco did too. "Do you have to ask? What is real, Marco? Who are you? I'm tired of this lie. How am I supposed to know what is real and what isn't?" She gave him a little shove with both hands to his chest.

"I'm sorry you feel that way."

"You're sorry I— Well!" She resumed her stomping.

"Don't you think you're acting a little childish?"

She ignored him again, but her lips twitched, clearly having a hard time keeping a comeback in.

Marco had a feeling they would be at the Torres house before they resolved anything. Good thing the bowling alley wasn't too far away.

Bowling alley...

Marco looked down and grumbled. He still had his bowling shoes on.

Great. Just great. Bet I'll have to pay some kind of fee for this.

They walked in silence for several blocks, Marco trying to figure out what he could say, Rosalina puffing with her exaggerated display of walking—although temper tantrum would be a better word for it.

They left run-down businesses behind and nice houses started appearing on either side of the street.

Rosalina found her voice again. "You can forget about this fake dating thing. I'm not putting up with it any longer."

"But the wedding is next Saturday."

"And you can go alone." There was not an ounce of sympathy in her tone.

"How am I supposed to explain that? We were pretty persuasive—"

"You'll have to find a way to clean up this mess. It's of your own making."

He grumbled.

She glared at him from the corner of her eye.

Marco said nothing. Why dig a deeper hole for himself? He'd give Rosalina some time. Once she cooled off she'd be reasonable. This was her temper speaking.

He hoped.

Then again, she hadn't wanted to be his fake girlfriend to begin with. He'd basically forced her into it. Perhaps this was the last straw. They'd had one too many arguments, and this one was the big one to end it all.

He was going to have to think of a monumental apology if he didn't want to eat a semi truck load full of crow come the wedding.

Maybe he should be glad Isabella and Oscar had witnessed their argument. Because even if he couldn't get Rosalina to come with him to the wedding, he could use their spat as an excuse. Then a week or two later he could say they couldn't resolve their differences and had broken up.

Everything would be fine. Just fine.

But he didn't feel fine.

At all.

"Well, I guess this is it." Rosalina's voice lacked any warmth.

Marco looked up, surprised to find they were standing outside of her aunt and uncle's place. "Have you decided to forgive me yet?"

She crossed her arms and tossed her nose in the air with a sniff. "For what exactly?"

Her attitude was getting annoying. "For making a joke at your expense. For laughing at you. For everything. You do realize every relationship has a fight or two? But they usually work through it."

"We aren't in a real relationship. And there is nothing to work through. It's over, Marco."

She still wasn't changing her tune. How long of a walk did it take for her to "walk off her steam."

Marco looked away lest Rosalina see his exasperation. "Fine. I'll give you some time and space."

"I don't need time and space. I—"

Marco raised a brow when she didn't finish. "What...?"

She shook her head and made a mad dash into the house, slamming the door behind her.

Marco sunk his finger in his ear. "Stink!"

What did I do?

Once again, all because of his stupid mouth.

Well...and laughing hadn't helped him any. But how does a person stop such a powerful emotion?

"Stupid, stupid, stupid."

He slammed his foot down on the concrete, the tread scuffing along the surface. Only then did he remember they weren't his work boots.

He lifted one foot, then the other, and looked at the soles. They had taken a beating.

"Stupid!"

He'd be paying a fee for sure.

Grrr!

All because of...

"One crazy girl."

With a growl, Marco spun around and, this time, he stomped all the way back to the bowling alley, where another apology was going to be in order. If only he would have changed his shoes.

Why couldn't his brain work when he was around Rosalina?

The girl had a strange effect on him, and he wasn't sure if he liked it or not. It caused more trouble than anything.

Chapter Twenty-One

Rosalina let out a pent up growl of frustration the minute the door slammed shut behind her.

That infuriating man.

He'd laughed at her.

Laughed. At. Her.

She could have broken any number of limbs, and he'd laughed.

"Ohhhhh." She shook raised fists in front of her chest.

When she opened her eyes after the display, *Tía* Carmen was sitting on the couch, eyes wide, mouth in an O, staring at her.

Rosalina swallowed and composed herself. "Hello, *Tía.*"

"Is everything okay, dear? That was quite the...fit."

Rosalina frowned. Fit made it sound as if she were a five-year-old having clothing issues.

"Don't you think you're acting a little childish?"

Marco's words echoed in her mind.

Had she acted childish?

Rosalina pressed her hands to her cheeks as she thought about what it must have looked like to onlookers...the way she stomped all the way home.

How embarrassing.

She dropped into the rocking chair across from her *tía.* "I think I lost myself there for a little bit."

"Want to talk about it?" *Tía* Carmen set aside her crocheting. It looked like she was making another bandana for TPPP.

Rosalina shook her head. "I got angry."

"It's easy to do things we later regret when we get angry."

She ducked her head and traced the grain in the armrest of the rocker with her finger. "I can't say I regret everything. I meant what I said. I just don't like the way I acted."

"I heard some raised voices out there. Who were you with?"

Rosalina looked away and mumbled her answer. "Marco."

"Ah. Lover's quarrel?"

She angled a look of annoyance at her *tía*. "I'm not sure if I'd call it that."

Tía Carmen took on a faraway look. "My, your *tío* and I had a few tiffs when we were dating. Still have an occasional spat too, you know. You are two separate human beings, Rosalina, with different personalities and family backgrounds trying to understand each other and learn how you can mesh. Don't get discouraged."

If only that were the case, then, maybe, Rosalina wouldn't feel so...well, *discouraged*.

Was it too much to ask for things to actually work between her and Marco?

She couldn't stand to think about it right now, though. It only made her even madder at him.

He'd laughed at her and she wouldn't be able to easily forget it.

True, other people in the bowling alley had laughed too. But the humiliation had built up inside her and then when Marco joined in with their laughter, she'd taken it all out on him. Whether he'd deserved it or not.

Queenie came running down the hall, apparently having finally heard Rosalina's voice. The dog went nuts jumping at the rocker, wanting up, and demanding attention.

Rosalina lifted her furry friend to her lap and welcomed the facial licks.

"It's so good to be home, doll. I missed you. Were you a good doggy for, *Tía*? But of course you were. You're the best. The best." She rubbed her face into Queenie's neck.

Tía Carmen rose, but before leaving the room said, "Whatever the disagreement, don't stay mad at him, honey. The Bible does say to not let the sun go down upon your wrath. It's a wise piece of advice. I live by that verse in my marriage."

"*Sí, Tía.*" She didn't mean for it to sound exasperated, but Rosalina wasn't ready to stop being mad at Marco. Didn't want any advice at the moment.

From the doorway *Tía* Carmen added, "You know, you're quick to forgive that dog of yours when she does something wrong. Don't you think you could offer the same kind of grace to your fellow man?" And with that she left the room, but her words made a direct hit in Rosalina's heart and conscience.

She lowered her chin. "Why are things so hard with Marco? Huh, Queenie? Why?"

Queenie looked up at her with those soulful black eyes of hers, and it made Rosalina smile softly, despite the low feeling inside as she replayed her *tía*'s words. Debating on whether or not she would take them to heart and act upon them.

Maybe.

She knew she should.

But not yet.

□□□

Rosalina felt crummy the next day. Her whole body ached from yesterday's unfortunate accident, and sitting in the pew at church this morning hadn't helped any.

Her brain hurt with all the thinking she'd been doing on how she'd reacted, her *tía*'s words, what she could have done differently, and what she should do now. The little pricking she received with the morning's sermon added to her discomfort.

And now her heart was about to shatter as she rubbed her temples and stared at the numbers on her computer screen with her online banking pulled up.

Despite all the walks she did yesterday and the dog party on Wednesday, she still had more to raise to be able to pay Truman Scott and ensure her lease would be renewed. She was getting closer. But time was running out, and she was losing hope.

She wasn't ready to give up, though.

No siree.

She'd fight until the last day. Last hour. Last minute. As long as she could work, she would. And she'd keep praying that Truman would have a change of heart.

Rosalina rolled her neck and proceeded to dig her fingers into a knot in her shoulder. A chiropractor appointment or a massage sounded like what the doctor ordered, but she couldn't afford it right now.

Every available penny was going toward Operation Save My Business. Her body would calm down in a few days. She'd pop an Advil or two and call it good. And maybe an icepack would be smart as well.

Rosalina stood to get one when her phone went off. She froze, debating whether to look at the screen. She had a feeling it might be Marco.

She couldn't resist. Her eyes traveled to the device and, sure enough, it was from Marco. She sighed.

"Do I bother reading it?"

She wasn't sure if she wanted to know what he had to say. To be honest, she was disappointed about, well...everything. She'd thought this might have been the Sunday they went to church together—since Marco had asked about it Wednesday. But then that whole *incident* had to take place yesterday.

As much as Rosalina wanted to blame Marco for everything, she was as much at fault. If not more. So she was pretty much mad at everything and everyone today.

Her eyes wouldn't stray from the phone. "Fine. I'll read it." She snatched the cell up and swiped the screen.

Marco: Do you forgive me yet?

She wasn't ready to answer that question, so she set the phone back down without typing a response.

When she returned from getting the icepack another text came in.

Marco: You didn't really mean what you said about not coming to the wedding Saturday did you?

It was almost more than Rosalina could bear to not type back and tell him he needed a comma between "Saturday" and "did," but she managed to stand her ground.

Maybe if she made him suffer a little, he'd understand she had meant a lot of what she'd said.

A third message arrived.

Marco: Are you ignoring me?

Marco: Am I going to have to beg you to talk to me again?
Marco: What if I told you I miss you?

Rosalina was getting annoyed with the quick succession of his messages, but when she read the last one, her traitorous heart almost sent her fingers to tapping out a reply.

Does he miss me?

Could she believe that was real? Or was he talking fake boyfriend language?

Grrrr.

How she wished she could know for sure.

Now she understood why God hated lying so much. It made everything messier.

She held the phone, her fingers hovering above the keyboard. The decision had her split down the middle.

In the end, she left his questions unanswered. Because she didn't want to reply until she knew for certain that she would still go as his plus-one to Lillian and Clint's wedding.

Until then, Marco could chew his fingernails and wonder.

□□□

Rosalina didn't feel much better come Monday, and her heart wasn't in her work...although she did make it through the day as any responsible business owner with debts would.

By Tuesday she felt worse. And while she'd always heard the third day after a fall was the worst, she decided the problem wasn't because of sore muscles from the beating her body had taken. Rather, it was the weight of guilt upon her shoulders and heart.

She was ashamed of the way she'd been acting.

"It's time to apologize."

She wouldn't feel better until she did.

As she went about afternoon doggie baths, Rosalina considered meaningful ways to show Marco she was sorry for blowing up, and she'd be sure to let him know she'd go to the wedding with him.

She'd at least be happy to have his friendship back. The silence the last two days had been almost more than she could bear.

Strange how the infuriating man with the silly smile could take up so much space in her heart already.

But he had.

So now it was time to set aside her pride and fight, once again, for Marco's heart.

And pray she hadn't ruined any hope of that happening.

Chapter Twenty-Two

It was a Tuesday that seemed like a Monday, made him wish it was a Friday, and feel like he was working a Saturday.

Simply put, Marco was mad, and the last thing he wanted to do was work. He wanted to sulk. Stay on the couch all day. Watch stupid TV shows. Eat bags of chips and boxes of Cosmic brownies. And he'd even out the junk intake a tad by drinking himself drunk on pineapple flavored coconut water.

"If you don't gentle your touch, *amigo*, you're going to puncture the roof."

Marco ignored José's warning and kept scraping away at old shingles.

Why won't Rosalina respond?
Why did I laugh?
Why do I have to be so stupid?

He'd thought they were going to have a blast during their bowling night. Boy, had he been wrong. It'd been about as much fun as digging out an ingrown toenail.

Scrape, scrape, scrape.

Why had Rosalina said she knew it wasn't a good idea to come?

Scrape, scrape, scrape.

How could he clean up this latest mess?

He had to. The wedding was only four days away. They had to come to some kind of resolution before then.

Scrape, scrape, scrape. Whhhish, thunk, thunk, thunk, thunk. CLANG!

"Stupid!" Marco ripped his sunhat off and slapped it against his knee.

"Did you just throw your roofing shovel?" José's question was laced with mirth.

Marco glared at him and snapped, "Not on purpose!"

"I think you better take some time to cool off. And I don't mean because it feels like a hundred seventy degrees up here."

Marco grumbled.

"Off with you." José smacked him in the arm with his hat.

A break did sound nice. Maybe he'd try typing another plea to Rosalina for forgiveness. The woman knew how to make a man eat a lifetime's supply of humble pie.

He muttered the whole way down the ladder.

Marco went straight for the truck and dug into his lunchbox. Since Cosmic brownies had been on his mind, he grabbed the closest thing he had in his lunch—vanilla Oreos.

They would have to do.

But they made him think of Oreo balls and Christmas in July...and cuddling with Rosalina on the couch. And kissing under the mistletoe.

Stop it.

Couldn't he think about milk instead, and how delicious it would be to dunk the cookie in it?

Not nearly as delicious as Rosalina's lips.

What was wrong with him?

Marco stuffed the whole Oreo in his mouth and chomped down on it, then grabbed a carton of mango and peach flavored coconut water and guzzled down the whole thing.

"Ahhhh, refreshing."

If only there was a refresh button where this "friendship" with Rosalina was concerned.

Maybe he should give up. She clearly wasn't his true one. So why pretend? Why bother? True love wouldn't be so difficult.

He doubted Lillian and Clint had encountered any such difficulties in their romance journey. Not with the way they were so lovey-dovey. It'd probably been true love at first sight and easy as pie.

Marco doubted that kind of love existed for him.

Bachelorhood was starting to sound appealing again. Love and marriage was proving to be too much work, stress, and frustration. It was bad for a man's health.

He'd barely slept the last several nights. His thoughts were too annoying to let him sleep.

His appetite had been out of whack too. Oh, he'd still been eating, sure. But he'd been taking in an awfully lot of junk. Not good.

All-in-all, his life was a mess. He was a mess. And he was getting really tired of messiness.

He popped another Oreo in his mouth, pulled his phone out of his pocket, and typed another text to Rosalina.

> **Marco:** Are you ready to forgive me yet? What will it take? Do I need to invite you to church tomorrow night and confess everything before the whole church before you take me seriously? I promise my apology is sincere.

"Please don't make me eat that much humble pie, Rosalina." Although, if it helped him sleep at night, maybe it'd be worth it.

To his shock, three little dots started dancing on his screen. Marco choked on the Oreo and coughed until all the little jagged pieces made it where they belonged in his stomach.

Sweat of a different kind than he'd produced all morning beaded upon his forehead as he anticipated what Rosalina might say.

The dots disappeared, and it was pure torture. Marco took to walking around, too agitated to stand and wait.

The dancing started up again.

What was Rosalina typing? Was it a long message? Or was she taking a lot of time to think about her words?

When the text delivered, he briefly closed his eyes—not sure if he wanted to read it or not.

He cracked one eye open and saw a lengthy message. Slowly, he opened the other eye and started reading every word as a single unit, rather than speeding through the sentences.

> **Rosalina:** I do forgive you. But you must forgive me. You were right. I was being childish. And, no, you do not have to

get up and confess before the whole church. I would never require that. I believe a person's sin is before them and God…and the person they wronged. Yes, confession is good for the soul, but God is our High Priest and he is the one to whom confessions should be made. Believe me when I say He is hearing plenty from me. As for church, I have to babysit Calvin again. Want to do a babysitting Bible study again?

Marco was certain he had a goofy grin on his face as he finished up reading the message. Things were good between them again—as friends, that is. He was forgiven for his tactless comment and laughing. And she'd invited him to join her for another Wednesday night Bible study.

"Hot dog." He made a fist pump and raised his knee.

Unfortunately, she'd not answered about coming to Lillian's wedding or not, but he could ask her tomorrow night.

"Marco, watch out!" José's shout of alarm sounded from on the roof.

Of course, Marco did the natural but stupid thing and looked up…to have the claws of a hammer connect with his face.

"Aaaagghh!" He threw his phone, raised his hands to cover his face, and fell to his knees, curling in upon the pain until his forehead touched the grass.

"Marco, are you okay? I'm coming down."

Marco had always held to the thought that grown men didn't cry. But that changed today.

Except, as much as he wanted to give into some absolutely pitiful "Ow, this hurts worse than the dickens" kind of crying, he couldn't produce the sound. The pain exploding through his head and face stole his breath away until he rolled to his side, pressed his hands into his face as hard as he could, willing the compression to ease the agony.

"Marco! Marco! Are you all right? I'm so sorry. I dropped my hammer." José's hands seemed to search his body, but Marco wasn't paying the touch any mind.

It seemed like every nerve ending and sense of feeling was zeroed in on and enhancing that of the assault to his face. He didn't want to know how bad it looked.

"¿Amigo? You are conscious, right?"

Marco groaned for an affirmative answer, although he wished he weren't.

Time slowed to the point he felt like an hour of misery had passed, but in reality it'd probably only been a minute and a half. Would the pain ever stop throbbing? He couldn't even determine where the hammer had made contact with his face, as his entire head hurt.

José gripped his arms. "Let me see how bad it is."

Marco fought against his coworker's hold, a strange kind of fear gripping him at the thought of releasing the pressure.

"Here's the first aid." Marco recognized Santiago's voice.

"Thanks, man." This from José.

José nudged him in the biceps. "Come on. Don't be a sissy. Let me look at the damage."

Damage seemed like the perfect word. For all the trouble and money his mom had spent to be sure he didn't bear any scars after the dog attack, he felt like this, for sure, had damaged his face beyond repair. He could see it now. A walking creep with two big holes in his face.

Nightmarish.

Yeah, maybe that was it. It was all a nightmare.

Any chance of that dissipated when José yanked his hands away from his face. Marco cried out. He strained to return them to his face, but other hands clamped around his arms.

Santiago, he would assume. Mean *hombré.*

Marco chanced opening his eyes, and found the action almost numb. He blinked up at José and gave him a glare.

The look on José's face was not reassuring.

"Well?" Marco regretted speaking the moment he moved his lips, for two reasons.

One, the pain.

Two, the liquid that ran in his mouth. A liquid he knew to be red and did not belong in a person's mouth and GI tract.

Nausea turned Marco's stomach upside down and he retched.

"Ah, *amigo.* Yuck." José scurried backward, still in a squatted position.

Marco moaned like a pitiful baby, but turned his face toward the sauna-hot sun again, so José could clean him up to prevent that from happening again.

He barely slitted his eyes, but it was enough to see José come around to his other side, gagging. "Here. Take these towels and hold them on your face. I'm driving you to the ER."

Marco grimaced.

Ouch. Stupid.

Since he was so good at pretending, he needed to pretend his face was paralyzed and quit moving his mouth.

"I think you're beyond my stomach and meager first aid abilities. Let me help you up."

Marco wanted to shake his head no. Standing, he knew, was going to be a near death experience. José had no mercy, but gripped him by one arm and hefted him to his feet.

Marco growled and pressed the towel harder into his face as he swayed.

"I've got ya, *amigo*."

Marco only groaned, and somehow placed one foot in front of the other, trusting José to get him where he needed to go. He was beyond coherent ability. He was in a world of pain. Nothing else existed. Nothing else mattered.

Not even the fact he'd not had a chance to respond to Rosalina—let alone grab his phone. He hoped someone had gotten it.

Just when his day had started to get better, it went and got worse.

Chapter Twenty-Three

Rosalina waited and waited and waited for a reply from Marco, but it never came.

Her gaze strayed to the clock for what felt like the thousandth time. Five hours had passed since she sent that message.

While she understood Marco had a job to perform, she knew he always took a lunch break. At least, he had ever since she'd met him. They texted often during the noon hour.

Today, he'd been silent. She'd held out, thinking the job might have worked out better to eat later than usual, but it was three o'clock now and still nothing from Marco.

The dog she was soaping up—a fluffy Pomeranian that comically turned into almost nothing when wet—let out a nasally whimper, bringing Rosalina's attention to the fact she might be scrubbing too hard with her frustration.

"Why isn't he sending, Millie? Why?"

The dog looked up at her and licked.

Rosalina sighed. "I hope everything is okay."

She started rinsing the soap out and giving the dog a relaxing massage as she did, which helped to soothe Rosalina and turn her mind to some simple explanations.

"His phone might have gone dead."

It was possible, and Rosalina pinned her guess on that one. It was the only option that didn't make her want to give in to a pinch of worry.

She and Marco might argue a lot, but she did like the guy. More than like. And she didn't want any harm coming to him.

Rosalina turned the water off and lifted Millie from the tub. "Let's get you fluffed up again, so you can look like the walking cloud you are." She booped the dog on the nose, towel dried it for a quick minute, then turned on her hair blower, and hummed as she worked.

By the time Millie had been returned to her owner and Rosalina had given another dog a Premium Package bath, and done two Clean and Happy baths, she still hadn't heard from Marco, and it was really starting to bother her.

With a sigh of longing to hear *anything,* she pulled her phone from her pocket and checked for messages. In case her sound had not gone off for some reason.

Nope. Nothing.

She frowned and tapped her chin as she sighed her way into a chair, her feet screaming from being on them all afternoon.

"This is ridiculous."

Text messages were two-way. She could send to Marco and see what was up. Maybe he hadn't received her reply.

Rosalina couldn't type fast enough, and because of that made many mistakes, which had her grumbling as she had to spend time fixing several words. At last, she had a simple inquiry sent, asking if he'd received her text and how work was going.

Now she could...wait some more.

Ugh.

Not two minutes later her phone went off, and although it was Marco's name that pulled up on the screen, the preview of the message read This is Antonio.

That brought no comfort.

Wrinkling her forehead, Rosalina swiped to open the texting app, and gasped when the screen contained a picture of Marco with a horribly swollen and bruised right eye and cheek and several bandages. The caption read:

Marco (Antonio): Had an accident at work. He's okay. Finally out of ER and at home.

"Poor Marco!"

Rosalina wondered what on earth happened to make him look like he'd stumbled into the midst of a violent street gang and walked away within an inch of his life.

Okay, maybe that was exaggerating, but Rosalina hated to see anyone or anything in pain. And the picture of Marco had misery written all over his face. It made her feel terrible. She'd spent the last several days mad at him—exactly what *Tía* Carmen had warned against—and now Marco had been hurt. Not that it was her fault he had an accident, but it still made her feel bad.

She hurriedly typed up a response, hungry for more information.

> **Rosalina:** What happened? Is he truly okay? Does he feel up to company? I'm closing the parlor soon.
> **Marco (Antonio):** He's not in the best of moods, but I think he'd be okay with a visit from his girl. <winking emoji>
> **Rosalina:** I will bring some Jell-O. It's what the doctor ordered.
> **Marco (Antonio):** Wow, you know him so well already.
> **Rosalina:** <blushing emoji surrounded by hearts> What happened? You didn't answer.
> **Marco (Antonio):** I don't like to text. Will tell you everything when you get here.
> **Rosalina:** Fine. Ttyl.

Rosalina bolted to her feet and pocketed her phone.

"Haven! Let's close up early." They didn't have any more appointments scheduled, and thirty minutes early wasn't going to hurt anything. She usually closed at five on Tuesdays, her latest night of the week.

Haven came from the front desk, looking a little lost. "Close early?"

"*Sí*. I have somewhere I need to be."

"Oh. Okay. Sure."

They ran through the usual routine of closing up the parlor. Leaving Haven to turn on the alarm system, Rosalina called for Queenie, and the two of them headed for home, where Rosalina followed the quick-set instructions on a box of orange Jell-O (since Marco always wore orange).

While it set in the freezer, Rosalina changed into something other than the pet-friendly scrubs she wore for work and freshened up, meanwhile debating on whether she should take Queenie or not.

Considering Marco was a suffering patient, she decided against it. Patient's comfort was always priority.

Once she no longer smelled like wet dog and was satisfied with her now-smoothed-back hair, Rosalina checked on the progress of the Jell-O.

"Looks good enough." She cradled the bowl between her arm and body, grabbed her keys and purse, blew a kiss at Queenie, and hurried out the door.

"I'm coming, Marco."

She hoped Antonio hadn't been downplaying the extent of the injuries for her sake. She wouldn't be able to relax until she knew for herself.

Halfway into the short drive of a couple blocks, Rosalina sucked in a gasp. "Surely it hadn't been a dog attack."

That would make a face look like Marco's.

"Please, no."

That would be terrible...and when Marco was starting to make some progress with Queenie. The last thing he needed was a setback.

Never had five blocks felt like so far away.

□□□

Rosalina knocked like a madwoman when she reached the front door at the Mendez home.

Maria opened to her. "Ah, come in, come in."

Rosalina didn't have to be coaxed. She burst through the open door and scanned the living room until she made a whiny sound of sympathy at the sight of Marco sitting on the couch.

His poor, poor face.

"Marco, dear." The endearment slipped out without her thinking—which meant...it must be from the heart, right?

"Let me take that for you." Maria relieved her of the bowl of Jell-O and Rosalina hurried over to the couch, sitting at an angle to fuss over Marco.

He groaned. "Rosalina." Her name came out sounding kind of funny, like someone trying to talk after dental work.

"What happened? You look terrible."

"Humph." Then he winced. "Ow."

Rosalina frowned. "Does it hurt badly?"

"Yeah."

Someone entered the room and she looked up to see Antonio, who was carrying an icepack. "Here you go. Another ten minutes on."

"Thanks." There was no gratitude in Marco's voice, but it was plenty tight with pain.

"Antonio, are you sure he's okay?" She had to ask.

"He'll be fine. Just being a big baby."

Rosalina glared at Marco's brother. "How dare you?"

She heard a little snicker from Marco, followed by a pitiful grunt. "Nice to know your girl will stick up for you." It sounded like too much work for him to talk.

She couldn't help herself and gently trailed a finger down the uninjured side of his face. "What or who did this to you, Marco?"

He gingerly brought the icepack to his face and covered the assaulted sites from her view. She'd counted three Band-Aids, two Steri-Strips, and two raw-flesh streaks that looked like wide claw marks. She didn't bother tallying bruises, for the whole right side of his face was angry red, black, and blue, and, oh, so swollen.

"A hammer," was the simple response she received.

"A hammer?" Rosalina furrowed her brows. "Did someone beat you with a hammer?"

Marco's body bounced with restrained laughter. "No, Lina." She didn't let the name slip bother her. "José dropped his hammer from up on the roof. I happened to be down below and in the line of 'fire.' Unfortunately, I looked up instead of watched out."

"You poor thing. How far did the hammer fall?"

"It was a three story house. High enough to gain some momentum."

"Ouch. I'm so sorry. I'll have a talk with that cousin of mine to be more careful." She planted a fist in the couch.

Marco waved a hand. "It was an accident, and he feels plenty bad about it already. Don't make it any worse. There was no major damage done."

"No major damage! Your face..." Her eyes locked on the icepack as her mind conjured up what his face looked like underneath it.

"Nothing that won't heal. They stitched me up as good as new in the ER. Numbed me up too." He grimaced at that, then winced and moaned.

"Numbing is a blessing and a curse."

He made a sound of agreement only.

"That's the most talking he's done since he got home." This from Antonio. "You're good medicine for him, Rosalina."

"That's what girlfriends are for." Rosalina smiled at Marco, willed him to understand she meant it. And know she wasn't mad at him anymore.

Any remaining thoughts of madness had fled with the first peek of the picture Antonio sent over. The panic of then was now replaced with overwhelming relief to know he was, indeed, fine...and would be okay.

Marco removed the ice. "For being numb, this sure gets to feeling like Antarctica."

Rosalina winced at seeing his face again. "How many stitches did you need?"

"I didn't ask, but I felt like they were cleaning and sewing me up forever."

"Might end up with some scars now."

"Not if Mom has her way. She's already said she plans on keeping me well stocked on anti-scar creams again."

Rosalina chuckled. "Well, your face is always on display."

"Yep, that along with my signature smile." He pulled a lopsided grin. "The first thing you noticed about me." He winked his left eye.

If you only knew how much I dream about your grin now. She laid a hand on his biceps. "That's right. Your shining quality."

Antonio let out a big sigh from where he sat in the recliner that was across the room and in the corner. "I feel like no one knows I'm in here. Guess I'll go to my room."

"Hold on, little bro. Don't you need to take this icepack to the freezer soon?"

Antonio checked his phone. "You have another four minutes."

"I think you can be social for that much longer."

"Social?" He snorted and rose. "I'm not getting a whole lot of socializing in with you two." He gave an exasperated roll of his head.

Rosalina turned to him. "Sorry, Antonio. I had to be sure Marco was okay first. Now that my worries have been laid to rest... When do you leave for college?"

Antonio sunk his bottom in the recliner once again. "Two weeks from tomorrow."

"And you're going for what?"

"I'm going to be a nurse anesthetist."

"Really?" Rosalina never would have guessed. Marco's brother looked more like a college professor than someone who would be dressed up in scrubs and a hair net.

"Yeah, so you better be sure and stay on my good side...just in case I'm ever the one to put you to sleep should you need surgery one day in the future."

Rosalina gasped. "I do hope you are joking."

Antonio clapped his hands together and laughed uproariously.

Marco rolled his eyes. "He's a pain. Don't believe anything he says. I'd say seventy-five percent of his talk isn't real."

"So does that issue run in the family?" She leaned toward Marco and lowered her voice. Softened the questioned accusation with a wink, hoping he'd realize she only teased.

Marco sent her a glare and jabbed a gentle fist into her arm.

"Ohhh, give me that icepack. Your ten minutes are basically up. I'm getting out of here. Another four minutes and you might be making out, and I don't care to witness that." Antonio snatched the pack from Marco when he limply held it out, then made a hasty exit for the kitchen.

Marco cupped a hand around his mouth. "Don't you think kissing would be a little difficult right now?"

How about we try? Rosalina wanted to say, but she bit her tongue. She didn't want to do anything that might cause Marco undue pain.

Marco's eyes landed on her lips and Rosalina's breath caught. Would he kiss her, despite his injuries?

"I don't know. Mom always kissed my boo-boos when I was little." He still hadn't moved his attention from her lips, and it made Rosalina feel extra self-conscious about her mouth.

She swallowed. "Want me to kiss you?"

Marco's widened eyes popped up to meet hers, his brows raised. Had she shocked him with that question?

He cleared his throat. "Um, no. That's okay."

Disappointing.

"I brought you some orange Jell-O," she said to change the charge of the air between them—which, she wondered if Marco was oblivious to or felt the same as she.

Could he seriously not tell that she wanted to kiss him? That she cared for him? That this wasn't fake, for her at least?

She sighed silently.

"Oooh, my favorite."

"Really? I'm glad I went with that flavor then. Would you like some now?"

"Yeah, sounds good. So long as you didn't put cottage cheese in it."

Rosalina laughed. "I won't make that mistake again. I'd rather not have people spit out my food."

Marco looked properly repentant. "I should be able to manage some, even though it doesn't feel like I have a mouth."

She gave him a sympathetic look. "I'll go get you a bowl."

"Get yourself some too. I don't want to snack alone."

"I will."

"Bring me a plastic spoon too. The hammer claw chipped one of my teeth. I'm not sure if things will be sore in there, so I don't want to accidently hit a tooth with a metal spoon."

"Ah, man. That hammer did a number on you."

"Don't I know it?"

Maria already had Jell-O spooned into two bowls, but had kept them chilling in the fridge, and fetched them when Rosalina entered the kitchen. While Marco's mother went to get the spoons, Rosalina passed along the request for a plastic one.

"Poor dear. I do so hope he can get his tooth fixed." Maria *tsked* and inserted the spoons into the jiggly treats.

"Thank you, Maria."

Rosalina returned to her spot next to Marco on the couch. "Here you are. I hope it works as comfort food."

"I'm sure it will. Jell-O can heal any number of ailments." Marco made quick work of getting a small amount on his spoon and moved to get it in his mouth. He missed and hit his upper lip the first try, sending the Jell-O falling back into the bowl. "Have I said I hate numbing shots?"

She grimaced. "I'm sorry. Would it help if I fed it to you?"

"No, thank you. I'll manage." The response came too fast. Sadly.

I'd gladly do it.

She put the sugary gelatin in her mouth instead of saying those words, however.

"So," Marco said after he finally got his first bite down. "You never answered my question in text. Are you coming to the wedding Saturday?"

"Didn't I? Hmm. I guess I got distracted. Yes, I'm coming. Of course."

Marco swiped imaginary sweat off his brow, momentarily forgetting about the mess that was his face. He yelped. "Remind me not to touch my face."

"Don't touch your face, Marco." She chuckled.

Crinkles appeared at the corners of Marco's eyes and he let out a mirth-filled snort.

They continued to eat their Jell-O in companionable silence for a few beats, until Rosalina remembered she hadn't gotten an answer back from Marco on her question either. "I don't suppose you feel up to babysitting and a Bible study tomorrow now, do you?"

She looked over at him and saw a small trail of saliva running along the crease of the right side of his mouth. "Oh, here." She snatched a Kleenex from off the lamp table next to her and dabbed it away.

Marco hissed, then gently captured her wrist in his. She feared she'd caused him too much pain as he pulled her hand away, but that wasn't what the intensity in his eyes said. "Thank you. Again, I don't like numbing shots."

Rosalina knew she should chuckle at that, but the moment had her motionless and breathless, as they held each others' gaze, Rosalina waiting to see what Marco would do.

She pleaded with him with her eyes to kiss her. Even if it was only her hand, she would be happy.

A whirl of words danced about behind his eyes, she could tell. His lips twitched ever so slightly, as if those words sought freedom.

But in the next second, Marco released her wrist and cleared his throat. The moment gone forever...leaving Rosalina desperately wanting to know what he'd wanted to say.

What made him not say it—whatever it had been?

"To answer your question," his voice sounded tight with—frustration? Discomfort?—Rosalina wasn't sure. "I'll let you know tomorrow if I feel up to it. I'd like to come. I'm not to go back to work until next week. The doctor didn't think it would be wise working on a roof with a concussion. Stupid hammer scored a lot on me."

"Oh my. Certainly, no roof for you. Are you dizzy? Should you be lying down?"

"Nah, I'm fine like this."

Rosalina nodded. "But you should rest. Rest will help you heal faster."

Marco shrugged one shoulder. "You help keep my mind off the discomfort."

A great compliment. One Rosalina took to heart. It was one of—if not THE—nicest thing he'd ever said to her. "Well, I don't want to overstay my welcome."

"Mom would say the door is always open to my girlfriend."

But do you *consider me your true girlfriend?* How she wanted to ask him. Demand him to answer. She almost did, but the front door opened and in walked Guadalupe.

"What's this I hear about an accident?" The smell of asphalt, sunshine, and sweat carried in on him. Rosalina decided she'd rather smell roof tar.

Marco let out a mirthless laugh. "I got in a fight with a hammer and lost."

"Got quite the shiner." Guadalupe's bushy brows waggled—so much like his sons did—then he turned to Rosalina. "Hello, there. I see you're taking good care of the boy."

She looped her arms around Marco's. "Only the best of care."

"I'm gonna go get cleaned up. You staying for supper, Rosalina?" She picked up on a slightly hopeful tone in the question.

How could she say no? "If that's an invitation, then yes."

"Good, good." And with that Marco's dad left the room, although his scent lingered behind.

Marco moaned and rested his head against the back of the couch. "I think the numbing is starting to wear off."

Rosalina rubbed her hand up and down his arm. "That'll make it easier to eat."

"Or more painful. I'm remembering how not fun stitches are."

"Thankfully, I've never had any, so I can only imagine what they must feel like."

Marco's face pinched for a moment and Rosalina found herself holding her breath until he relaxed.

"You know, maybe I will take a little rest. If you don't mind."

"Not at all. Here." She stood and took his bowl, stacked it in hers, and set them on the lamp table. "Let me help you put your feet up."

"You don't have—"

She didn't let him finish, but wrapped her arms around his legs down by the ankles and swung them up onto the couch where she'd been sitting. Then she grabbed a pillow that had been tossed haphazardly on the floor, fluffed it, and carefully placed it behind his head.

"There. Rest well."

"Will you still be here when I wake up?"

What did it say about her when that struck her as a very romantic thing to ask? Did Marco want her to be here when he woke? Or was it the pain medicine speaking...and the tiredness? His eyes were already getting clouded and drowsy.

"Yes, I will still be here. I promise."

He smiled softly and closed his eyes.

Rosalina thought she might cry. It was the first sign of promise she'd witnessed.

Ack, how she wished she could know what Marco was about to say.

Chapter Twenty-Four

It was difficult to get comfortable when he was used to falling asleep on his wretched right side.

It was hard to sleep when his face felt like a pincushion.

And it was impossible to even doze off for a brief moment when all Marco could think about was the look of utter concern on Rosalina's face when she burst into the house.

It'd been a long day—until she'd shown up. Time always dragged when you're in pain. And the night...well, it'd been even longer. Without a wink of sleep.

Marco pushed the button on his alarm clock to light it up. Three in the morning, and he didn't recollect snoozing for a moment.

How did people fall asleep on their back?

Wasn't the medicine supposed to help him sleep?

Marco huffed and dug his fingers in his hair. He hissed when he pulled at the roots, forgetting about his facial injuries. How could a face and head hurt *so* much?

He knew the real reason he couldn't sleep wasn't because of the pain, though.

No, it was because of Rosalina.

Her offering to kiss his injuries. To feed him.

The way she'd dabbed at his mouth with the tissue.

That hadn't been any old touch. It had felt like a tender, loving touch. The kind of fussing a guy could get used to—like, say, coming home from work with a heat headache and half dehydrated.

Marco had been close to telling her he didn't want them to be fake boyfriend and girlfriend anymore. That he wanted it to be real. That he already considered it real. That he...liked her.

But he couldn't get the words to come out.

Why? Why was it so hard to share his feelings? To put them into words? They were up there in his head, so why couldn't they come out his mouth?

Frustrating.

Was it because he'd never said such words before? Ever. Was he unpracticed?

He snatched the bouncy ball, that he'd had since he was a tyke, off his nightstand. He threw it at the wall and caught it upon its return. He continued with the mindless activity to pass the time more quickly.

Maybe he should have tried harder to tell Rosalina, instead of giving up when it felt too abnormal.

Was the problem wholly him?

Or was it also—mostly—the fear of what Rosalina would do?

The way she'd been this afternoon seemed sincere. Authentic. Then again, she'd been doing a top-rate job at their charade since the beginning. How could he know how she'd react to him?

"Ugh."

He supposed he'd gotten what he deserved.

"What's that saying from Sir Walter Scott? 'What a tangled web we weave when first we practice to deceive'."

Marco was feeling tangled. How could he break free from his own web?

The truth will set you free.

Marco threw the ball harder and it made his hand sting on the return.

Yes, he knew the truth would set things right. But he'd lose Rosalina in telling everyone the last several weeks had been nothing but show, wouldn't he?

Now, if he could turn the lie to a truth, he'd gain her. Neither resolution would be easy. Both of them involved speaking truth.

He either had to confess the ruse to everyone, or confess his real feelings to Rosalina. Both options had his mouth going dry and chest getting tight.

"I'm toast." He slapped his hand to his forehead. "Ouch! *Ssssss.*"

He'd never look at a hammer the same again.

He threw the ball to the ceiling this time, missed the catch, and it bounced against his stomach. He left it where it landed beside his body on the bed as he focused on what his options were.

There was only one.

Tell Rosalina.

"I will try. First good chance I get." With that settled, maybe now he could get some shut eye.

A clank sounded from the register on the floor by his bed.

"Are you awake, Marco?" It was Antonio, sounding half asleep.

The bedrooms were wall-to-wall, and Marco could recall many nights when he and his brother had pestered their sister through the connecting vent, or listened in on Isabella's late-night phone conversations with Oscar while they were dating.

Marco turned his head toward the vent. "Unfortunately. Did I wake you?"

"Yeah. You were throwing the ball, weren't you?"

"Sorry. I can't sleep."

His brother cleared his throat. "Is it time for more pain medicine?"

"No. It doesn't hurt too badly right now. Just can't get comfortable." *And I have too many thoughts.*

"You should call Rosalina. Maybe she could help you sleep. She improved your attitude earlier."

Marco snorted. "I'm not waking her up at three in the morning."

"Wish you felt the same way about your brother."

Marco let out a nose laugh. "I didn't mean to disturb you. I think I'll try sleeping again."

"Okay." Antonio yawned loudly. "Me too. Oh, and for the record, Rosalina is gold. I'm kind of jealous. You chose well, bro. And she's crazy about you."

Marco absentmindedly twisted his finger in his ear. "You think so?"

"It's obvious."

"Hmm." That was reassuring. "Get back to sleep."

He heard rustling and knew Antonio was repositioning. Knowing his brother, he'd be asleep in no time.

Now I'm the jealous one.

Because now Antonio had sent his mind back to thoughts of Rosalina and hope of getting any sleep vanished.

No matter if he felt like death tomorrow, he was going to join her and Calvin for babysitting and a Bible study. Maybe they could have a chance for a heart-to-heart if Calvin went down for a nap...or his bedtime. Marco's nerves twitched and sweat broke out on his forehead thinking about it.

He moaned.

If only the night would hurry up and get over.

□□□

Marco regretted wishing away the night. Now a cold sweat broke out over his body as he raised a fist to knock on the Brinkman mansion's door.

Things were going to change tonight. If he could manage to speak. It shouldn't be hard, but there were times he was sure there was a connection missing between brain and mouth.

The door opened wide to reveal a smiling Rosalina with a baby on her hip.

It was a sight a guy could get used to. Only, the baby being one of their own.

Whoa, boy. Watch those thoughts.

"Well, I made it." Pathetic greeting, but it's what he said. He poked the boy in the tummy, pinched his tiny foot, and gave the pudgy leg a little swing. "Hey, Calvin."

Rosalina chuckled and beckoned him in. "I'm glad. Calvin and I would have missed you."

"I brought Coca-Cola and Oreos for our snack this time." He held up the goods.

She sent him a look that said *you shouldn't have.*

"I happen to remember we both like Oreos." He waggled his brows.

He loved the flirty smile and ornery glow in her eyes. "Christmas in July *fiesta.*"

He returned flirty smile for flirty smile, then remembered that shoes were not welcome in the Brinkman home. Marco carefully lowered (fast movement made his head spin) and untied his boots.

Rosalina led the way to the kitchen. "I hope you're feeling better today."

"Yes and no. But I'm vertical and made it here, so we'll say I'm mostly fine."

She gave him a hard look, hand on her hip. Somehow she looked sterner with having Calvin on her hip. "Should you have been driving?"

"I'm fine. Perfectly capable and safe."

She scrutinized him but said nothing. "Do you know where you'll be reading from tonight for our Scripture text?"

Marco set the bag of snacks and his Bible down on the island in the kitchen and claimed a stool. "Nothing specific. Anything you have in mind? Questions about anything?"

Rosalina ticked her head from side to side as she buckled Calvin in his high chair. "I've been studying a lot in Proverbs and James lately."

"Good books."

"Yes. There is a lot to learn from them."

"How about we go over some of the noteworthy things you've come across."

"I'd like that."

While Rosalina fetched a snack for Calvin, Marco opened the package of Oreos and broke the seals on the Coke bottles.

When Rosalina returned and saw the Oreos, she shot him an accusatory look. "A family size package. That sets the limit high."

"I have no hopes of taking any leftovers home. Eat up."

"You're terrible."

"I know. Thanks."

Rosalina tapped her chin and cocked her head, settling on the stool next to him—instead of across the island from him like last time. "I'm not sure I meant that as a compliment."

"But it was received as one, so there."

Her laugh was like a soothing balm to all the irritating pulling of his facial skin from the stitches. If he could stay in her presence, he was certain he'd have a faster recovery process.

Not wanting to stay on that topic when they were supposed to be having a Wednesday night Bible study, Marco flipped his Bible open to James and began reading.

Calvin was fussy tonight, however, and began straining at the stays of his chair and grunting, working up to a cry. Marco found it especially hard to focus on the words, but Rosalina appeared to still be listening, so he plodded on slow and shaky, frustration mounting as the noise continued.

When he reached the end of the first chapter, Rosalina laid a hand on his arm. "Excuse me. I think Cal might be tired. I'm going to see if I can settle him down."

Marco welcomed the break and hoped the kid would fall asleep fast. Reading was hard enough on a good day, but between his pounding head and foggy brain and Calvin's crankiness, it was too much.

He leaned folded arms on the island and laid his head down for a rest while he waited.

He didn't know how much time passed before Rosalina returned, but when she came back she no longer carried Calvin—which provided him the opportunity to speak to her about what he wanted from their "relationship."

"I'm sorry for that interruption. You can start up again." Rosalina settled herself on her stool once again.

Marco straightened his posture. "Is it okay if we stop there for tonight? I don't think I can read any more."

"Oh, I'm so sorry. I forgot about your concussion. You probably shouldn't be reading. I could read a chapter."

Marco started to say no, so they could have The Talk, but a delay didn't sound half bad either. "If you want to. Sure." He slid his Bible over to her.

She took it with reverence and smoothed the pages. "Awww. It's all marked up with references, notes, and underlines."

Marco felt his neck heat up and Rosalina must have noticed.

"I love it, Marco. It tells me you love God's Word."

"I do. It's the only thing I read, and I read it every day. Ever since I got saved as a sixteen year old teaching VBS."

"Interesting. Tell me the story."

"Well, I had all the Bible knowledge since I was raised in church, so it didn't come as any surprise when my youth pastor asked me to help him teach a VBS class of fourth graders. I enjoyed it. But...one night when a student came up asking me how to be saved, I was crushed with guilt and the realization I couldn't honestly help him. I led the kid over to Pastor Jorge, and while the boy—I can't recall his name now—got saved, I also accepted Christ."

Her smile was honey sweet and a twinkle appeared in her eye. "That's wonderful. I got saved at a revival when I was twelve. It was at the same time my brother decided to become a preacher. Have you ever thought about preaching?"

Marco couldn't believe the question had been directed at him. "No! No way."

"Why not?" She clearly couldn't see any reason why he wouldn't.

"Because. I couldn't. I told you I don't like to read. And having to do that in front of an audience...and speak." He shook his head hard. "No way."

"Why do you dislike reading so much?" A V of curiosity formed between her dark brows.

Marco pressed his hands together, fingertips to fingertips, and stared at the formation.

"You don't have to answer if you don't want to. It's none of my bus—"

"It's something I've always struggled with." Marco cut her off, because he, to his surprise, *wanted* to tell her. "And because of my struggles, I suffered a lot of mean teasing. It stripped me of all confidence and took interest in reading away from me. Not that I've ever found it enjoyable. It's work. It's not easy for me like it is for most people."

"Or maybe you haven't found the right book yet to make you fall in love with reading."

Marco shook his head. "I'm dyslexic, Rosalina. I can manage as an adult, but I still struggle."

Her lips formed an O and something like—remorse?—curtained over her features. "Marco, I'm so sorry. Our texting. I-I kept correcting your grammar. You probably thought I was so mean—"

"Not at all. I didn't take it that way. I thought we were having some fun banter. And, really, who cares about punctuation in texting."

Relief softened her features. "I won't be so critical in the future."

Marco waved his hand. "As long as it's friendly nit-picking in texting, I don't mind."

That earned him a face-brightening smile. "I do like this. We're getting along quite well. Think our quarreling is over?"

Marco mentally gulped. If he opened his mouth now about him wanting their relationship to be real—and by real, he meant more significant than merely friends—would the quarreling start up again?

Maybe they should enjoy tonight. They could have The Talk some other time.

"Don't put it off too long," the little voice in his head said.

Tomorrow, then. I'll bring it up tomorrow. He cleared his throat. "Say, Rosalina, would you like to go out for dinner tomorrow night?"

She opened her mouth to answer right away, and by the spark in her countenance he knew it would be a yes, but then her face sunk. "You know, I can't. I have several dogs to walk tomorrow, and I can't skip. I need the money."

There was that comment again. Needing the money. Marco leaned his elbows on the counter and settled his hands against his cheeks, attention fully on Rosalina. "Since we've been having a heart-to-heart here, me sharing a deep, dark secret, do you have anything you want to share with me?"

Rosalina all of a sudden decided she needed to pick up Oreo crumbs off the counter with her finger. "Me? I don't have anything to share. What makes you think I'd have some deep and dark secret?"

"Doesn't everyone?"

She shrugged a shoulder, not looking as nonchalant as she probably hoped.

"Then let me pick a subject."

Wariness crept over her face.

"Why is it so important to be walking dogs and babysitting, on top of working at TPPP all day? You're always saying you need the money. Are you struggling, Rosalina?"

Her crumb collecting finger slowed. "I'm fine. Everything's fine. Life's expensive in this day and age." The answer came too...too thought-out. Carefully calculated. Unnatural. And totally not persuasive. Marco was certain she was hiding something.

"Lina...?"

She glared at him, her feistiness resurfacing. "Didn't I tell you to stop calling me that?"

He lifted his shoulders to his ears and smirked. "You did, but I like it."

She pressed her lips in a fine line. "Well, I guess if you like it, you, and you alone, can call me Lina. But only when no one else is around to hear."

Did he feel his smirk grow? He tried to keep his face passive.

"You're going to ignore that stipulation, aren't you?"

Marco dissolved into chuckles.

Rosalina threw her head back, exasperation evident in the action. She reached for another cookie. Marco did too. Their hands brushed in the process.

Marco about dropped his Oreo. Rosalina stared at him like a deer caught in the headlights. The strangest sensation to reach out and hook their pinkies came over him.

"Rosalina, I—" His true feelings almost tumbled out, but it was as if someone turned the faucet off and they dried up.

"Yes, Marco..." She searched his eyes.

"Rosalina, I—" He tried again, but no more words would come. With a mental shake, he cleared his throat. "It's getting late. I should head home."

"Is there something you wanted to say?"

"Nah." He stuck his finger in his ear.

"I might not be able to accept your offer for dinner tomorrow night, but if you'd like to, you can join me on my walk. If you feel up to it and don't mind being accompanied by three dogs."

Marco couldn't stop a shudder. He could do without the dogs, but he'd like to spend more time in Rosalina's company. "Sure. Walking sounds good. I'd imagine by the time afternoon comes around I'll be stir crazy from sitting around all day—thanks to doctor's orders." He sneered.

Rosalina gave his arm a light squeeze. "It's only for a few days. You don't want to overdo it and have an even bigger setback, do you?"

"Nope. I'll be good."

"Good. Now, you be careful driving home. I don't like the thought of you driving with a concussion."

"It's a mild one. I'm fine."

More fine than Rosalina probably was with her finances. Then again, maybe he was making something out of nothing. How could he know for sure? How could he know if there was some way he could help her?

The way a real boyfriend might.

Would she let him help...if she needed it?

Ugh. So many questions.

"Good night, Rosalina. See you tomorrow. Let me know where you want to meet for the walk, or..."

"My clients are in the neighborhood, so I'll swing by your place once I've collected the three dogs." She winked.

Three dogs. Yay. Please, let them be small ones.

"Sounds good." Not his feelings at all, but the right words to say.

With that, he saw himself to the door. And he was glad Rosalina didn't follow, as he feared it may have been hard to not give in to a goodnight kiss.

Faking it was getting harder and harder.

Chapter Twenty-Five

Tossing and turning took on new meaning for Rosalina.

She doubted she got a wink of sleep last night. While she had much on her mind—pressing matters like needing to pay Truman Scott in four short days—the sleep-stealing culprit for her had been Marco.

The desperation in the depths of his brown eyes as they sat at the island at the Brinkmans', led Rosalina to believe he needed to get out whatever it was he was holding in.

So what kept him from saying it?

Ugh, what was he going to say?

The wondering drove her nuts.

Her mind had thought up at least a half a million ideas during the night...when she should have been sleeping and getting rested up for the busy next day.

And what a day it'd been. The kind Rosalina wished she could undo and start over, but she'd somehow made it through.

Weary, her shoulders slumped as she directed her car down the busy late afternoon streets of Peoria.

A quick ten minute nap sounded like pure heaven, but she hadn't the time for it—since her last client of the day had been unruly and took twice as long to get the bath accomplished than normal.

Figures after the night she'd had that things wouldn't run smoothly today. It always worked that way, or so it seemed.

Thankfully, it wasn't as hot and humid today as it had been the last several weeks. That would make for more comfortable walking conditions for her and the dogs. Rosalina was glad to finally not see strings of days that reached or exceeded ninety degrees. By itself it might not be bad, but with the humidity—*Ick.*

Once at home, it felt like too much work to change her clothes, but Rosalina fueled herself with the fact she would get to spend time with Marco...and maybe get to find out what he'd been about to say yesterday. Then she could sleep better tonight.

Queenie pranced at her feet as Rosalina headed for the door.

"I'm sorry, doll. Not this time. I think Marco will be overwhelmed enough with three big dogs. You be a good girl."

Queenie whined a heart melting whine and Rosalina wanted nothing more than to give in to the darling puppy dog eyes and pleading dance, but she held firm.

Besides, her hands were going to be full enough with Brisco, Brick, and Bri. Rosalina had no idea how the owner kept the names straight, but the dogs were siblings—golden retrievers—and Mr. Hackett had told her he was a sucker for patterns.

Personally, she felt the man had tried a little too hard. Brisco, Brick, and Bri? It's like he kept shortening the name.

That was beside the point. Rosalina blew Queenie a kiss, tossed her a doggie biscuit she'd grabbed from the treat jar at work, and headed on down the sidewalk for her charges...and then Marco.

And that's when pleasure factored into the equation. Despite her tired, aching feet and overall exhaustion, she was looking forward to this job because of *him.*

□□□

Rosalina had a time of it keeping the three goldens to hold still long enough to ring the doorbell at the Mendez house. By the time the door opened, she'd been dragged a couple feet away from the door.

It was Antonio who answered. "Come to see me again, I see."

Rosalina chuckled. "Not you, sorry."

He snapped his fingers in disappointment. "Rats. What brings you here today?"

"Marco and I were going to go for a walk."

"I'll call for him. I think he's helping dad with a project in the garage."

"*Gracias.*"

Rosalina struggled to keep the hyper dogs in line as she waited for Marco.

When he appeared in the door, confusion was written across his face. "We're going for a walk, Antonio says?" The sentence ended with a rising tone of question.

Rosalina crinkled her forehead. "Don't you remember? We talked about it last night."

Marco's fingertip disappeared in his ear.

"Did you seriously forget in such short amount of time?" She plopped a fist, which was full of leashes, on her hip.

"*Tsk, tsk.*" Maria's face popped into view. "Don't fault him for it, dear. If he doesn't write something down or save it as an event reminder on his phone, he's apt to forget anything."

"Oh."

Marco dipped one side of his mouth in an apologetic look, combined with, perhaps, a bit of—shame?

It made her wonder...were adults with dyslexia more prone to forget things?

"It's no problem." She hoped to set Marco at ease.

Right then the three goldens reached their max in patience and they each jerked in a different direction, making Rosalina feel like a human multi-dog plush toy. "Whoa." She knew the smile she gave Marco must have been comical and frazzled. "Ready?"

"Whoa, indeed. Do you need some help there?"

"Just need to get moving. These doggos don't like to hold still."

Marco stepped out and pulled the door shut. "I'm ready to go." He took the steps slowly, eyeing the dogs warily.

"They're big teddy bears. I promise. Golden retrievers are the best family dogs."

When Marco stepped off the last step he froze and stared at the canine trio. "H-hi there, guys."

Rosalina swallowed the laugh that tickled her throat. "These here are Brisco, Brick, and Bri. I'm sure they are pleased to make your acquaintance. Would you like to hold one of the leashes?"

Marco's eyes darted to her and he pointed a finger at his chest. "Me?"

"Sure."

"I—"

"Here." She offered him Bri's leash. The girl was as tame as a pet rabbit. She wouldn't even get hyped up over a squirrel.

"I'm not so certain—"

"She won't bite."

His raised brow said he didn't believe her.

"You can't look at every dog as if they're the enemy and untrustworthy. Haven't you heard that dogs are a man's best friend?"

"I have heard. And might I remind you I have a dog. I trust Luigi because I know him. I don't know these beasts."

"They are not beasts." Rosalina let her extended arm that was holding Bri's leash fall lax at her side with her exasperation.

"Something that big is considered a beast in my mind." He pointed at Bri.

"Okay. Well, Beauty fell in love with the Beast, so here." Not knowing what possessed her—other than her strong drive to help him overcome his fear—Rosalina uncurled the fingers of his right hand, looped the braided leash in place, and closed his fingers once again.

"There."

He stared at his hand, then the dog. Hand. Dog.

Rosalina wished she could know what was going on inside. What his thoughts were.

"All good?" was all she asked when there was so much more she could have.

"Yes." She'd never heard a word so dryly spoken.

Give the man some water. If she had a water bottle on her, she'd hand it over.

Marco lowered the sunglasses on his forehead to cover his eyes.

Rosalina was dead.

My, but he looked like a movie star.

She cleared her throat. "Let's go."

"Yeah. Let's."

"You could sound more excited about it." Rosalina, Brisco, and Brick began walking and Marco and Bri fell in step beside them.

"If it were a walk with just you and me, maybe I'd be a little more *excited,* as you put it."

"Then pretend like the dogs aren't here."

"That's an impossible suggestion."

"Humph." He could pretend most anything else.

They walked in silence for a couple blocks, Rosalina surreptitiously stealing glances at Marco in those sunglasses.

He caught her once when her gaze lingered a little too long.

An amused expression lifted one side of his mouth. "Looking at something?"

"Your sunglasses."

"Like them, huh?"

"On you, *sí*. Very much."

"Thankfully my nose was spared any injury, so I can handle wearing glasses."

"I have to ask you something."

"Okay." He voice was starting to loosen, leading Rosalina to hope he was growing comfortable with their canine walking companions.

"How come you don't have a suntan around the frames? I mean, you work in the sunshine all day. And I know you've mentioned wearing safety sunglasses while working."

Marco chuckled. "I'm not particularly fond of a permanent look of sunglasses on my face. I wear a sunhat."

Rosalina rolled her lips in to fight a mirthful grin. "That I have to see."

"It's not a glamorous sight."

They shared a laugh.

"Perhaps, I shall visit you while you're working sometime." She tapped her chin.

"That won't be necessary." He shook his head.

"It'd be fun."

"You wouldn't know where I'm working. My job isn't in a factory that never moves."

"No, but I live with your boss, so I can ask *Tío* Juan where you are any day." She added a little sass to her tone.

Marco snorted. "True, and I wouldn't put it past you. And I guess I can't tell you no. But maybe you could leave Queenie at home." There was no rising inflection in his voice to indicate a question. No, this was a suggestion.

"Ha! No. Where I go, Queenie goes. We're a package deal."

Rosalina found herself halting, not sure if she'd stopped walking first or if Marco had and she'd followed suit.

He stared deep in her eyes. "Is that so?" The words were husky, spoken slowly.

Rosalina swallowed in an effort to put some moisture back in her voice. "Y-yes." She was surprised by her slip into English on that one affirmative word she always said in Spanish—and probably would no matter how long she remained in the States.

"Hmm."

She couldn't decipher the meaning of that tiny response for anything. And he turned away, so she couldn't read what his face might say.

Another couple blocks passed in silence, save for the sound of a cardinal boasting about his prettiness in the treetops, and a squirrel chattering from somewhere in their vicinity. Rosalina tightened her hold on the leashes and scanned the area to see if she could spot the creature, for she knew Brisco and Brick would try to pull her arm off if they saw the tree rodent.

Her search came up empty, so she relaxed her hold. When the silence grew irritating, she decided to ask what was at the forefront of her mind.

"Marco?"

"Mmm."

She glanced at him. He looked wholly at ease now. His stride was confident, his shoulders relaxed, his face at peace. In fact, he looked to be enjoying himself.

Rosalina knew the feeling well. It was a sort of therapy to walk dogs in God's creation. It was a good time to be alone with thoughts, breathe deeply of fresh air. Almost energizing...even after an exhausting day.

"Marco, what were you going to say last night right before you left?"

"Oh. Um..." His finger went into his ear, which told Rosalina it was something important. Something hard for him to get out.

Why was it hard for him to say some things? She wondered if it had anything to do with the dyslexia, but she didn't know much about the condition. She would have to do some research so she could better understand him.

"You can take your time. This is a one-hour walk."

He let out a breathy, mirthless laugh. "I doubt that will even be enough time."

"Well, try."

He slanted her a slightly annoyed look, and she wondered if pushing him—no matter how kindly or encouragingly—was the wrong way to approach this.

His steps slowed and he stared at the ground. His jaw rocked. Rosalina patiently waited.

Marco cleared his throat. "Rosalina, I..." It's as far as he always got.

"Please, Marco. Whatever it is, you can tell me." She kept her voice soft, as if she were soothing baby Calvin.

"I-I...I can't get it out." He sighed and his shoulders slumped.

Rosalina frowned. "Then, can you at least tell me what it is about?"

He shook his head. "Maybe some other time."

She didn't want to accept that, but maybe he was dealing with anxiety with having the dogs. "Okay." She would choose to be gracious, but it wasn't easy.

"Th-thank you."

Rosalina took a left turn when they reached the end of the street, so they could start doubling back. It was then she noticed Marco wore work boots. She screwed up her face. "You're walking in work boots?"

"Yeah." He looked at her as if that were the most normal thing in the world and couldn't reason why she would think it something to point out.

"Don't your feet hurt?"

"No. They'd be screaming if I had tennis shoes on. I hate tennis shoes." He twisted his face in disgust. "Work boots are the best footwear ever designed, in my opinion."

"To each his own, I guess." She shrugged. For some reason the topic of footwear called to mind the wedding on Saturday. "Say, since we're on the subject of clothing, what are we going to wear to the wedding?"

"Come again?"

"We are going as a dating couple. I think we should color coordinate or something."

He shrugged one shoulder. "It's outside and going to be hot. I'm dressing for comfort."

"Which is...?"

"Nice blue jeans and a clean shirt."

Talk about a brief description. Rosalina laughed through her nose. "Blue jeans? To a wedding? I don't think so."

"That's dressing up for me. It works for church, so I don't see why it wouldn't be fine for an outdoor wedding."

Rosalina sighed, deciding there was no point in arguing the matter. "Okay. I'm going to wear a more formal dress."

Marco just looked at her.

"What color shirt are you wearing?"

"I don't know. It's not Saturday yet. Orange, maybe."

Rosalina threw her head back. "You always wear orange."

"What can I say? I'm partial."

"Is your entire wardrobe orange?"

"Mostly."

Rosalina shook her head and *tsked*. "I don't have much orange, and not anything that would pass for a wedding. You're right it's going to be hot. I have a yellow dress I think would work well. Do you have anything yellow?"

"Probably."

"It's settled. We'll wear yellow."

"Is it necessary to match?"

Rosalina turned to him, slack-jawed by her frustration at him. "It is. And it won't hurt you, I promise."

Marco rolled his eyes. "I never thought it would hurt me." And then something changed about Marco, although Rosalina couldn't put her finger on it. Was it talk of the wedding? Or was she imagining the difference?

The rest of the walk passed relatively quietly, but for a few remarks here and there, which solidified Rosalina's hunch that something had changed.

She tried to tell herself that it could be his face was starting to hurt him. After all, it was warm and he wasn't supposed to sweat with the incisions. Were his wounds stinging? Was he ready to go home?

She picked up the pace, and Marco adjusted his to match. She studied his face a moment to check for any sweat. He didn't appear to be perspiring, which surprised Rosalina, for she was wet in places she'd rather not be. Maybe he didn't sweat much, since he was used to working in the heat, she reasoned.

At last, they reached Mr. Hackett's and the three goldens started getting excited—even calm Bri.

She heard Marco's slight intake of breath beside her, and his whole body went rigid as Bri strained against the leash for the last few steps up to the house.

"Here, I can take that now." Rosalina tried to take the leash from him, but he had a death grip on the handle. "Marco, loosen up."

He appeared to be looking at her, but not seeing.

"Marco, the leash. Release it." She spoke sterner than she intended, but it worked.

"Oh." His eyes cleared and his fingers went lax, and Rosalina was able to slide the leash from his hand to hers.

She took the remaining steps up to the house and rang the bell. Mr. Hackett was as grateful as always, passed her a check, and led his dogs inside with as much excitement in his voice as one would expect of an owner who hadn't seen their pet in two weeks.

It brought a pleased smile to Rosalina's face. She loved seeing people in love with their animals. She tucked her payment in her pocket, turned around, and strolled to where Marco had stayed rooted after handing off Bri.

"Ready to go home? Sorry about dragging you all the way to Mr. Hackett's. We should have swung by your place first. It was on the way. I didn't think of it."

Marco plunged his hands into his front pockets. "It's fine."

"I hope I didn't wear you out. An hour of walking can be a lot if you're not used to it."

He shrugged and they started down the sidewalk once more. "I'm holding up." But his somber countenance was less than persuading.

"Are you certain? You look a little tired, or down."

"I'm fine."

Sounded like a lie to her, but Rosalina didn't press. "I'd say we're closer to your house than mine, so I guess we'll part at your place." She wasn't about to make the only-two-days-post-injured one do the extra walking.

"We don't have to. I can walk you home."

"No, I insist."

"Well, if you insist."

She shouldn't be disappointed that he gave in so easily. But the softer side of her that had recently realized how much she was interested in romance and affection felt insulted. And it only drove home the truth that Marco still viewed this as fake—despite how strongly she wished it were real.

Would everything be over after Saturday?

It was looking likely.

She wasn't ready to part ways with Marco. To not have a reason to do things together. She enjoyed their "dates." Especially their Bible study and babysitting.

But, no doubt, all that would come to an end once there was no longer a need for the charade—only two days away.

Rosalina wanted to cry.

Chapter Twenty-Six

By Friday, Marco was about to go stark crazy with not being able to work. His whole body was restless from doing nothing all day and he was snapping on everyone in the house.

"Why don't you go somewhere?" His mom suggested, who'd had enough.

Marco almost rubbed a hand down his face, but caught himself. "Want me out of your hair, huh?"

"For a bit." She winked to soften the truth.

Marco nodded. "I might not be able to work, but I think I'll pay the guys a visit. It's almost lunch break."

"That would be good. Here." She handed him a grilled cheese sandwich. "For the road."

"I see you were prepared. Thanks, Mom."

Marco wrapped the sandwich in a paper towel, checked the work schedule on his phone app to see where the guys were working, grabbed a coconut water, and headed out for his truck. It'd be nice to talk with José.

He arrived at the jobsite in short order—on the nose at noon—and his coworkers were climbing down from the roof for lunch break.

"Hey, *amigo!*" José waved and gave him a bubbly smile. "Good to see you, man. You're vertical and looking good."

Marco gave him a doubtful look. "I may be vertical, but I've looked in a mirror recently. Good is not the word that comes to mind."

José stepped close and scrutinized his face. "The bruising is going down and you don't look swollen. That's an improvement."

Marco shrugged. "I suppose. Can't say incisions make a nice statement piece. I wish it wasn't my face that got assaulted. I can't hide my face."

"No, you can't, but you can smile real pretty to make up for it."

He rolled his eyes. "How's it going? Managing without me?"

José filled his cheeks with air and let out a puff of breath. "Barely."

Marco gave him a little shove. "Cut it out."

His friend laughed. "So, tomorrow is the big day, right?"

Had to bring that up. He gave a stiff nod. "Lillian's wedding."

"You ready for it?"

"As ready as I'll ever be." Marco walked along with José as his friend headed for his lunch box, stored in the utility truck.

"Rosalina still going with you?"

"As of the last time we spoke, anyway."

José turned a mirthful expression at him. "What's that supposed to mean?"

"We get into arguments every now and then. She's already threatened to not come once. I wouldn't put it past her to threaten me again."

"So, don't get into any arguments between now and tomorrow afternoon."

"You make it sound easy. Do you know your cousin?"

José snorted. "She's sassy, but she's not unreasonable."

"I wouldn't go so far as to say she's unreasonable, but she can sure be difficult and stubborn and—"

"Hey, this is my cousin you're speaking of."

Marco groaned. "I know. I had no idea we would butt heads so much. I thought it would be...easier."

"No relationship is easy."

"This isn't a real relationship, José. Remember?"

"Hmm. I thought you two might kick it off." José studied him.

Marco turned away and said nothing.

A huff from José. "I guess I'm a failure as a matchmaker then. Or maybe it's the way it all began. I should have kept quiet about the whole thing and let you meet her for the first time at my and Regina's wedding."

"Don't quit your day job, man."

This time José gave him a shove. "Don't worry. I don't claim to be a cupid."

"Bah. I don't believe in all that cupid junk."

"Neither do I. Regardless, I obviously don't know how to make a good match."

But maybe you do...

Marco didn't believe he and Rosalina were incompatible. The whole thing between them was just muddied because of the deception surrounding it.

No wonder the Bible had so much to say about lying. It made things difficult.

He sighed deeply.

"Whoa. What's that for?" José paused in taking a bite from his sandwich.

"Nothing."

"Something, I think. Actually, I know something is bothering you. You have those tortured crinkles at the corners of your eyes."

"I'm not tortured."

"Not physically. But I think there are some unsettling thoughts going on inside your head."

Marco chewed on the inside of his cheek instead of admitting that his friend was right about that, at least. If only he could make sense of all the thoughts swirling up there. If only he could put his feelings into words.

José threw his arms up. "I'm trying to help you, *amigo*. But do you want it?"

Marco shook his head and stood. "I don't think you can help me." He walked back to his truck and headed home, where he locked himself in his room so he couldn't irritate anyone and no one could bother him.

To get his mind off everything he didn't want to frustrate himself with, he pulled out his phone and began looking at motorcycles and boats.

□□□

Later that night, Marco's phone went off with a text from Rosalina.

He'd done such a good job of distracting his mind and had finally gotten himself into a better mood for the remainder of the day, but now his troubled thoughts and frustration at himself ramped up once again.

Rosalina: Remind me, what time is the wedding?
Marco: 3:00
Rosalina: Am I meeting you there, or…?
Marco: I will pick you up.
Rosalina: <thumbs up emoji> What time?
Marco: Idk. 2:15?
Rosalina: Sounds good. See you then.
Marco: <okay emoji>
Rosalina: Did you have a good day?

She had to go and ask that. He couldn't classify his day as "good," but if he told her he had a bad day, she'd probably make a fuss and he did not want that right now. Didn't think he could handle it.

Marco: It was fine. Ready to get back to work next week.
Rosalina: I'm sure you are.
Marco: How was your day?
Rosalina: Busy, but good. Looking forward to the weekend. Is there anything I need to know about tomorrow?
Marco: Nope. It's just a wedding.
Rosalina: Just a wedding? Haven't we been preparing for this the last 3 weeks?
Marco: Just keep up the act you've been doing. It's working.

The dancing trio of dots that told him Rosalina was typing didn't show up right away as had been the case for every response so far. Marco stared at the screen. Waited. Waited some more. And waited some more.

He let out a disgruntled grunt. Had he said something wrong? Typed a wrong word? He reread his message to make sure there were no errors and that he'd typed what he'd meant.

No problem there.

"Maybe Queenie needed something." Or her aunt. That would make sense. It's not like she was a teen who had nothing to do but stay glued to her phone.

At last, the dots appeared and Marco became the one glued to his phone.

Rosalina: Will do.

Will do.

That's it. He had expected some kind of flirtatious message back. Like when she'd gone on about the couch cuddling for Christmas in July.

But...nothing. There'd been no banter at all. Marco found himself disappointed.

He poised his fingers to type a message, but words escaped him, so with a sigh he set his phone, screen down, on the nightstand and readied for bed.

He hoped for a better day tomorrow.

□□□

The dreaded day arrived, but, surprisingly, Marco didn't find it as dreadful as he thought it would be.

To be honest with himself, he believed he was truly over Lillian. His revelation that night when he and Rosalina had gone bowling had done wonders in helping him work through his feelings for Lillian.

Because he could see it clearly now. He'd never loved her. Not in a husband-wife kind of way. They'd simply been good friends and he'd been too attached to that relationship. Too sad to see it end with Lillian finding the friend—love—of her life.

But he'd found something better.

He'd found Rosalina.

She made him feel things he'd never felt before. He could only reason it was the stirrings of love. He was ready to explore a relationship with her even deeper than what they were in this fake dating charade. Because, if he cared for her this much when it was a "lie"...how more amazing would it be if it were for real?

There was one problem.

It was always a problem.

It was the wall that stood between him and so many things throughout his life. He couldn't speak his heart.

If only he could find the key to unlock whatever was barring the escape of those words.

And just like that, yesterday's sour mood returned to him, as he grew frustrated with himself.

Today was not going to be a better day, after all.

Chapter Twenty-Seven

Rosalina couldn't remember the last time she'd spent so much care on her appearance, but by the time she stepped away from the mirror on her dresser and faced the full-length one on the wall beside her closet, she was satisfied with the end result.

Her hair she'd curled and left loose down her back, with plenty of hair spray to hopefully fight against the straightening humidity and knot-tying wind. She'd also added a thin pearl headband to fancy it up a tad.

The yellow sheath style linen dress wasn't so tight to be immodest, but paid compliment to her figure, and the matching yellow heels were delightfully fun and made Rosalina smile. She didn't wear heels often, but she loved the opportunity to. It at least put her at five feet tall then, and maybe helped her look her age more. She did hope Marco wouldn't mind them being practically the same height, though.

With only ten minutes to spare, she changed into a clutch purse and sprayed on some of her favorite cotton scented body mist.

It was then her nerves kicked in and Rosalina pressed her hands to her middle.

She had no idea what to expect from today, but she prayed it would go well...and end on a good note. A hopeful note.

She still had a hunch Marco had been about to share something important Wednesday night. The intensity of his gaze had led her to believe he did have feelings for her and was about to declare them. But, she'd given him another chance on their walk Thursday and he'd not taken it. Would he ever say the words inside him? Was she going to have to make the first move?

She hated the thought of that. She was old-fashioned at heart, and it felt wrong to make the declaration first. How could she get Marco to speak? It was easier to train dogs to do so.

Perhaps, the extra time she'd spent to pretty herself would help him open up—not that she was so vain, mind you. But it couldn't hurt, could it? Men appreciated beautiful women, that was a fact.

Rosalina didn't consider herself a real beauty, but she did feel extra feminine with the little makeup and lip stick she'd applied—something she rarely did.

Before she could primp or nitpick her appearance any more, Rosalina strode out to the living room and stood a few feet away from the big picture window, where she watched for Marco's arrival.

"I do hope he isn't late." She found herself nibbling on a nail and stopped herself before she could harm the fresh yellow nail polish she'd painted on early this morning.

An appreciative whistle sounded from behind her.

Rosalina spun around, a hand to her chest. "*Tío* Juan, you startled me." He was sitting in his favorite chair with a thick hardcover book.

"You look lovely, Rosalina."

"*Gracias.*"

He returned to his reading, not one given to many words—most unlike cousin José.

Would Marco think she looked lovely?

She peered out the window once again, and hoped he wouldn't be late.

Blessedly, she had nothing to fear. In a matter of a few short minutes, his white Dakota parallel parked along the road. Rosalina didn't bother waiting for him to come to the door, but grabbed her clutch, gave Queenie a pat on the head, and threw the door open.

Marco was headed up the walk then. Their eyes met. His mouth parted, his eyes widened, and he tripped on his next step.

"Marco, are you al—"

"I'm fine. I...wow. You look amazing, Lina." She couldn't deny the pleasure that stole over her at the compliment, and surprisingly, she found that the nickname no longer made her grimace. She gave credit to the fact that Marco liked it, and that's all that mattered to her.

She looked down at herself. "You think so?"

"I do." His throat sounded dry.

She ducked her head with gratitude. "I see you got...dressed up." She couldn't keep the silly smile from emerging.

Marco let out a dry laugh. "I'm woefully underdressed, aren't I?"

Rosalina waved a dismissive hand. "I'm glad you wore the yellow shirt." She had expected a button-up at the very least, but— How had she not figured he'd wear a crisp T-shirt? The man did not know how to dress up. And it came as no surprise to her that he wore his work boots.

"Here." Marco raised his right hand, which had been conspicuously hiding something behind his leg.

"Aww." Rosalina's heart warmed at the plastic box that contained a yellow rose corsage with a sprig of baby's breath. "This is so nice. *Gracias*, Marco."

"You did say roses were your favorite flower."

"They are." She about melted to a drop of dew that he had remembered.

There might be hope after all.

She pinned the corsage in place and set the box inside the house. Queenie peeked her head out and let out one of her high-pitched barks at Marco.

"I didn't forget about you." He dug in his pocket and produced a milk bone. "Here you are, little dev—doll."

Rosalina gave him a stink eye and he had the decency to look guilty.

"Are we ready?" she asked.

"If you are."

She smiled. "I am." And she walked to the truck with more optimism than she'd first woken up with.

Thank God for little reassuring blessings.

□□□

Some blessings, apparently, are short lived. It didn't take long upon arriving at the outdoor venue that Rosalina noticed Marco was in a mood.

He was stiff beside her, short with everyone who came up to talk, and a smile barely graced his face when necessary.

Rosalina could tell something had him preoccupied, and it clearly bugged him. She worked with children enough that she could read body language to know when things were not right on the inside. While Marco was far from the age of the kids she babysat, some human responses never really changed—no matter how old.

Not until they settled in white plastic folding chairs on the bride's side, did Rosalina tap Marco's arm. "Are you okay?"

"I'm fine."

If she heard him say he was fine one more time...

She pinched her lips together. "You're sure?"

He nodded stiffly.

Rosalina studied his face for a moment. He was tightly wound up. Definitely bothered. Were the pain medicines affecting his mood? Were they making him constipated and grumpy? Did his face hurt? Was he too hot?

Or...was his mood sour because today was the day the woman he loved was getting married and Rosalina had gauged every one of his reactions over the last couple dates entirely wrong? He had loved Lillian, still loved Lillian, and would never have room for *her* in his heart and life.

It took great self control to not slump in her chair as disappointment sent her heart in a dip. So much for hope.

How long until Marco put an end to their ruse?

How painful was it going to be for her poor heart that had finally learned how amazing it was to care for a man?

She prayed the let down would be easy and she could recover without too much heartache.

But she feared it was too late for that. Her heart was already dangerously, deeply involved.

□□□

The ceremony was one of the most beautiful and unique ones Rosalina had ever witnessed. She loved that Lillian wore Vietnamese wedding garments and that the music honored her heritage. The lavender purple had looked absolutely breathtaking with Lillian's tan skin and black hair. It made it easy to see how Marco would have fallen for the woman.

But there was no denying Lillian and Clint were madly in love. The way they looked at each other... My, but it put tears in Rosalina's eyes.

She longed for Marco to look at her like that. She thought she'd seen hints of it at times. But today...well, she had more doubts than anything.

As the reception commenced and dancing began, Rosalina somehow got separated from Marco. No matter how hard she searched the crowd, she could not spot his bright yellow shirt.

"Looking for something? Or someone?"

Rosalina recognized the voice spoken from behind her shoulder and she turned about. "Hello, Antonio. I seem to have lost your brother."

"He's easy to misplace." He laughed.

Rosalina frowned, not at all happy with the joke.

Antonio sobered. "Have a dance to share with the brother of the boyfriend?" He held out a hand in a princely fashion.

She sighed. She'd wanted to dance with Marco, but maybe he didn't dance. The way he'd reacted when Lillian had mentioned dancing at Heritage Days made her wonder. Rosalina found herself nodding. "*Sí*, I think I can share a dance with you."

"Sweet." He settled her hand in the crook of his arm and led her up to the dance floor.

Rosalina laid her hand on his shoulder, while Antonio's settled on her waist. Their other hands joined, and she took care to keep plenty of space between them.

"So, tell me, Rosalina, how much longer will it be before we hear of an engagement?"

"Oh." Flustered by the surprise question, Rosalina missed a step and Antonio crushed her toes. "Ouch."

"Sorry." He cringed.

"I-I don't know, Antonio. We've only been dating for three weeks." After she said it she realized her slip. Three weeks would not match up with what they'd told people about when they'd first met. The story was that by the time Rosalina met Marco's parents, they'd already been dating for two weeks, so to be accurate with that timeline she should have said five weeks.

The truth always comes out... But, thankfully, it didn't appear as though Antonio noticed the inaccuracy.

"For some that's more than plenty of time to know. My parents were engaged after a month of first meeting, and married two months later."

"Oh my."

Antonio laughed. "It's not so unbelievable when you're truly in love. At least, that's what Dad always tells me when I start complaining about not having a girl and fear I'll be an old man before I ever get married."

Rosalina questioned how much she should share with Marco's brother. Could she confide in him? "Can you keep a secret?"

"Me? Of course. I'm going to be a nurse anesthetist. I know all about HIPAA rules."

"But that's for patient protection in the medical world. This is normal day-to-day life."

"On my word of honor, anything you say will be kept in the strictest confidence."

"How can I be sure?"

"You can trust me."

For some reason that was all the reassurance she needed. His gaze was unwavering, his expression gravely serious.

Rosalina sighed and had to focus on her footwork lest she miss another beat. "Very well. You see...there is a bit of a problem where Marco and I are concerned."

"In the middle of a tiff?"

"It's nothing like that." Although she had to wonder if she'd done something wrong with the way Marco had disappeared after the ceremony. Weren't they supposed to be together? She was his plus-one, after all. If not for him, she would not be here.

"Then tell me, please. If I can help, I want to."

She chewed her lip a moment as she debated the wisdom in sharing the truth. But the pull to speak truth felt like the very medicine she needed. To get it off her chest... "Marco and I aren't boyfriend and girlfriend."

"What?" Antonio stumbled and Rosalina stepped on his toes this time. He didn't flinch though, probably because he was too flabbergasted.

"We've been fake dating so people would believe we were a...couple, and he could prove to Lillian he was over her. The only reason for us spending time together was for the sole purpose of me coming to the wedding with Marco."

"You mean, after today...you and him...are no more?" He looked like he might tear up at the news.

Tears burned at Rosalina's own eyes and she looked away for a moment, lest the disappointment on Antonio's face make her emotions unable to be held in check. "I'm afraid so."

"Wait, wait, wait. You're afraid so. Does that mean...? Do you like my brother? Do you wish it were real?"

"¡Sí! With all my heart!"

"Then tell him."

"I'm afraid to."

"Why?"

"Because, this wasn't supposed to happen. What will he think?"

"You don't think he cares for you and wants it to be a real relationship?"'

As the conversation went deeper, their steps slowed, not at all keeping in rhythm with the waltz being played on a keyboard by an Asian man who looked almost identical to the groom.

"I don't know. There have been moments where I believe the feeling is mutual, but today... Have you noticed how he's been?"

Antonio wrinkled his nose. "Definitely not one of his better days."

"Is it because he is still in love with Lillian?"

Antonio shook his head. "No. I think it's something else. He hasn't been acting forlorn over Lillian for quite some time. In fact, if I remember right, that stopped shortly after he met you."

"Really?" Hope started to flutter in her heart again.

"Yeah. Honestly, he's been extra on edge since the pain medicine. I don't think it agrees with him."

Rosalina nodded thoughtfully. "So what should I do? If you and I are both right and he does care for me?"

"You could tell him how you feel."

She frowned and furrowed her forehead. "I've always felt the man should make the first move."

"Even if it means you lose him?"

"You have a point."

Antonio smiled proudly, as if he found it a great honor to be the helpful little brother. It made Rosalina laugh. Antonio joined in too.

And that was the moment in which Marco stormed up to them. "I do believe you've danced with my girl long enough, Tony." Marco's voice was icy cold.

"It's Antonio." He used a haughty tone.

Rosalina rolled her lips inward as she witnessed the tension between brothers.

"It's my turn to dance." Marco bumped hips with his brother.

Antonio released Rosalina and raised his hands in surrender. "Sure, Cocoa Bean. Sure."

"Don't call me that." Marco ground out.

"Then don't call me Tony."

Marco glowered and Antonio retreated.

Rosalina attempted a smile.

Marco's gaze was piercing. "Looked like you two were having a good time."

"Your brother was being friendly. He saw me standing alone and the dancing had started. Where did you disappear to?"

"I just...needed a moment."

Apparently, that was all the answer she was going to get.

She rested her hand on his shoulder as she had with Antonio, but this time her mouth went dry with the human contact. And when Marco placed his hand on her waist, her knees about gave out on her.

Oh...my. She felt the pull to reduce the space between them— so unlike her reaction to Antonio.

She worked to moisten her mouth and then when she could talk said, "I didn't realize you danced."

"Why's that?"

"You didn't seem to like the idea of dancing at Heritage Days."

"Because I don't know anything about that *courting dance* you and Lillian were talking about. But I do plenty of dancing."

"Really?" That was something she'd not yet learned about him. It must be true, for they moved perfectly in sync, and Rosalina believed they were made to be dance partners. She doubted there would be any stepping on toes for them.

"Mostly on the job when we've got the music blaring, or bopping in my car. I have some moves."

Rosalina chuckled. "I'd love to see them sometime."

"Maybe when you pay a surprise visit to a jobsite, like you said you would do."

She smiled. "I must do that now."

The song ended, everyone clapped, and another one began. This one a modern song played over speakers rather than a waltz by the pianist.

Only a few lyrics in and Rosalina recognized it as "Crazy girl."

Something changed in Marco then. A twinkle in his eye and a smile curving his lips upward. "May I have this dance too?" His eyes were pleading, as if he feared she might refuse him.

How could she? Why, she would dance the entire night away with him. Few other—okay, no other—experiences in her life had ever made her feel so...alive. "Of course."

He surprised her by moving her arms to hug his neck, while his hands clasped behind her at the small of her back, removing any remaining space between their bodies.

Oh...my. Oh my. Oh my.

Rosalina was getting dizzy, and it had nothing to do with the heat, but the effect the man had on her. She closed her eyes and rested her cheek on his shoulder. She fit there just right.

There was no way she could have feelings for anyone but Marco.

Did Marco feel it too?

Rosalina raised her head to look at him. Their eyes connected and her lungs quit working, and everything disappeared from around her.

Was he going to kiss her?

Marco's mouth parted.

He's going to say something. That could prove better than a kiss. And she already knew firsthand he could kiss a girl breathless.

Then something that looked like frustration curtained over his brown irises, he swallowed, and he dropped his gaze. It looked like he was studying her corsage, as if it could supply him with the words he sought.

While she tried to patiently wait for him to, hopefully, speak, she allowed herself a moment to look out over the pond, which had been the backdrop to the wedding arbor. The venue was beautiful.

Somehow, she could feel Marco's eyes on her face again, then felt one of his arms come up and a finger make a gentle trail down the length of her neck.

Her breath caught.

"What's this?" His words were the softest they'd been all afternoon.

"What?" Rosalina moved her hand from his neck to feel where his touch had been and then she remembered. "Oh, it's just a scratch. I had an unruly dog yesterday. He didn't want a bath. He was a new client."

Concern softened the face that had been taut all day. "He didn't bite you, did he?"

"No, only a scratch."

"Clear up on your neck?" He shuddered.

"Roscoe is friendly. Nothing to worry about. He's a gentle Labrador retriever. Didn't want to be given a bath by a stranger in a strange place, but I eventually got him calmed down and made comfortable."

The song ended and Lillian's father's voice boomed through the microphone telling everyone it would soon be time for some bride and groom games, but that everyone could take a moment to get refreshments and whatnot.

Despite how dreamy dancing with Marco was, Rosalina was glad to get off her feet. Her heels were pinching and rubbing and making her want to cry.

When Marco stepped away from her, she missed the warmth of the embrace, the feel of his strong arms around her.

"If you'll excuse me." He ducked his head and took off, down the stone steps of the dance platform, and Rosalina lost him to the crowd.

What's with all the sneaking off?

Rosalina sighed but wove her way through the assembly. Her throat was parched, so she went to the beverage table and got herself some punch.

She took a sip and noticed the floral table scatter. She picked up one of the blooms and began pinching off petals.

He loves me.

He loves me not.

He loves me.

He love—

Feminine hands gripped her upper shoulders, startling Rosalina to the point she dropped the flower. She turned to see who'd come up to her. "Lillian!"

"Hi, Rosalina. I'm so glad to see you again."

"You are an absolutely gorgeous bride."

Lillian's face beamed. "It's the happiest day of my life."

"I can imagine."

"I do hope your day will come soon."

Rosalina looked out over all the heads of people in search for a glance of Marco, feeling wistful. "Hope. If only it were so simple." She hadn't meant to say it out loud.

She must have, because Lillian let out a compassionate, "Aww, don't you worry. Things can happen so fast it'll have your head spinning. Why, I only met Clint in April, and here we are in August and married!" She showed off her wedding ring.

"You make it sound easy."

To Rosalina's surprise, Lillian snorted. "Don't be fooled. Clint and I have our fair share of battle scars we received along the romance road."

"Battle scars? Romance? Are we talking about the same subject?" Rosalina drew her brows downward.

Lillian chuckled. "Most definitely. We'll have to get together some time and I'll tell you the whole story."

"I'd like that a lot."

Lillian smiled. "Well, I need to get back to Clint. I have no idea what kind of games they are going to make us suffer through, but I hope they're not embarrassing."

"Congratulations, by the way."

Rosalina doubted a woman could look more radiant than Lillian did at the moment. "Thank you. And might I say how cute you and Marco are together."

She ducked her head. "*Gracias*—I mean, thank you."

Then Lillian leaned in close. "For the record, in case you hadn't noticed, Marco isn't good about speaking his feelings. It's hard for him. Be patient with him, but not too patient. Sometimes he needs a little push. Don't be afraid to be bold and make the first move. In fact, he would probably be glad you did." And with that Lillian breezed away, her lavender purple silk Vietnamese gown flowing in a beautiful silhouette with each step.

Rosalina picked her cup back up and stared in the depth of the punch. Had God used Lillian to tell her what to do?

Chapter Twenty-Eight

The wedding festivities died down, the bride and groom were sent off with much fanfare and thrown dried lavender flowers, and only a handful of hours remained until midnight's arrival, and, with it, the end of their fake dating agreement.

Marco felt frantic to do something about it, yet at the same time he was afraid to. How would Rosalina react?

Had she been counting down the days to when she could finally quit the playacting and be on her merry way? To wash her hands clean of him?

Or had those tender, charged moments between them been as real for her as they had been for him? Did she feel the chemistry between them? Did she—*ahem*—love him like he...yes, loved her.

Was it possible to love a person you've only known for three weeks—and that under false pretenses? How had it happened? It was supposed to have been strictly superficial. For show. No chance of the heart and emotions getting involved.

That was not so. Rosalina held his heart, and he loved that crazy girl like....well, like *crazy*. If he'd had any doubts before, they'd vanished as they'd slow danced to "Crazy Girl." He would never hear the song the same again. It was their song.

But how could he get the words out to tell her? Was there another way he could express his true feelings? Some way that didn't involve using his mouth and hoping his brain would cooperate? He'd tried practicing speeches in the bathroom multiple times this afternoon—whenever he could sneak away—but nothing ever came out sounding right.

He plunged his finger into his ear and gave it a dramatic twist.

"Why do I have to be this way? Why can't I be normal like everyone else?"

You're not everyone else. You're my child, and I made you special. In your weaknesses, My strength is glorified. Through Me, you can do all things.

Marco stilled. The world stilled. No longer did he notice all the chairs and tables being folded and carted away. No longer did he search the crowd for Rosalina's bright yellow dress and long dark hair.

It wasn't every day a man felt God speak in his spirit.

Hadn't God proved His faithfulness, His strength *every* single day throughout *every* school year, with *every* test?

He might not have graduated top of the class, but he hadn't failed either. That could not have happened with his own feeble mental functioning "strength."

One of Marco's favorite stories in the Bible came to mind. The one of Gideon. When Marco lacked courage and doubted himself (which usually happened every time he had to take a test in school), he started his morning in Judges and read that account. It was in those words he fought his way through to read that he would be reminded that in God's strength, with God on his side, he could do, what seemed like, impossible things. And succeed. Not because of anything of his own doing. But God.

In that account there was also the fascinating scenario of the fleece, where Gideon asked a sign of God when facing a big decision.

Marco was up against a big decision. While he didn't think a person should be in the habit of asking God for a sign, he didn't want to mess things up more than he already had in initiating a lie in the first place—which, mind you, quit being a lie for him July twenty-fifth and that mistletoe kiss Rosalina had about killed him with.

So, standing in the middle of wedding clean-up chaos, Marco presented a fleece. He would release Rosalina from the agreement, but ask her to be his plus-one for José's wedding next Saturday, and they would continue to date all week. With the ruse dropped, if her actions toward him remained the same, he would know it'd not been merely for show, but that she had real feelings for him.

Boy, he prayed they were real.

And with that, Marco pulled from his trance and found Rosalina talking with the pianist, who looked so much like the groom a person could think Lillian left the venue alone.

He walked over to them and listened to Rosalina's words: "I've always wanted to play a piano. We never had one growing up. Our church didn't either."

"Well, go ahead and play around on the keyboard. I can wait to pack it up. In fact, I might go get me some more punch and those little mints before I lose my last chance."

Rosalina chuckled. "Thank you, Josh. If you don't mind..."

"Not at all. I've unhooked it from the speakers, so you don't have to worry about everyone hearing you."

Rosalina looked momentarily horrified at the thought of everyone being able to listen in to her "playing around."

When Josh turned to go, Marco stepped up to Rosalina and placed a hand at the small of her back. "Hey."

She smiled up at him. "Hey." It was breathy and her eyes twinkled.

Had to be a good sign. Or, she missed her calling and should have been an actress. Certainly, she was pretty enough.

She settled on the padded bench. "Wanna join me? I really don't know what I'm doing. I don't know a thing about the piano."

Marco seized the opportunity to squeeze onto the tiny bench next to her. There wasn't even room for a piece of paper between their legs. He cleared his throat and wiped his sweaty hands on his denim-clad legs. "I can tell you where middle C is."

"That's more than I know. Show me."

He placed a finger down on the key.

"So what do I do from there?" She pointed at the binder of sheet music on the holder. "Can you read music?"

Marco laughed through his nose. "No. But I do know how to play 'Chopsticks'. Everyone can do that, though."

"Not I. So can you play piano?"

"Mom tried to force lessons upon me as a boy. I only had but a handful before she realized it was useless."

"Ah, I had you pictured as a trouble maker."

"Takes one to know one."

Her jaw dropped and he wrinkled his nose playfully at her. Then she smiled. "Okay. Show me how to play 'Chopsticks'."

Marco, unable to pass up such a grand chance, gently closed a pincer grip around her index fingers and settled them on the correct keys and, in essence, played through it for her.

The smile she sent him at the end was purely delightful and felt like a bubbly carbonated beverage in his belly. He could get used to the feeling.

"Can we do it again? But, this time, you play *with* me?" Her excitement was contagious.

"Sure."

"You'll have to coach me."

Marco nodded and slowly played through the song with her, Rosalina giggling her way through.

"Do you know any more?" She asked when they'd played several repetitions, until Rosalina was able to play it without any fumbles.

"Um, one more. If I can recall all of it."

"What is it?"

Marco cleared his throat. "It's, uh, 'Heart and Soul'."

Rosalina's lips rolled inward and her chin dipped as a pretty rosy color brightened her cheeks.

She eventually returned her gaze to him. "Is it hard?"

"Nah. But let's switch places. It might be easier for me to play the melody."

"Okay."

He rose so Rosalina had only to scoot over. A little more coaching was involved with this song, but Rosalina picked up on it quickly. Marco wished he could learn that fast.

When they finished, Rosalina clapped her hands. "This is *so* fun. Now I can say I've played the piano. *Gracias*, Marco."

He could live his whole life making her happy—if she'd let him.

And now it was time to lay out his fleece. He managed to twist a little on the bench so he didn't have to crane his neck to look at her.

"Rosalina?"

"*¿Sí?*"

"I'm releasing you from our agreement now. The wedding is over. There is no need to...pr-pretend any longer." He paused. "Thank you for going along with it."

The shine left her face and a V formed between her brows, but the rest of her expression remained passive. She merely nodded.

"But, if you wouldn't mind, I'd like you to be my date for José's wedding," he hurried to add.

She licked her lips and took her time responding. "I —*sí*...I mean, no...I don't mind. I'd be happy to. After all, I'll be there anyway."

I'll be there anyway. Not the response Marco had hoped for. He forced a smile, which probably produced the kind Rosalina thought irritatingly fake.

She touched his arm. "I also wanted to ask if you'd like to come to church with me tomorrow. We're having a special potluck after the service in honor of José and Regina. I wasn't sure if José would have already invited you or not." She lifted a shoulder.

"I'll be there."

"Great. You know which church we go to?"

"Yes."

"Good. Service begins at ten forty-five."

"Okay."

Her smile didn't quite reach her eyes, and the light that had been in those beautiful browns had been snuffed out.

Was that a good sign then? Because if she was disappointed about being released from their agreement...

Marco was finding her to be as hard to read as a page full of words. Utterly confusing, all her differing reactions.

He stood and offered a hand to Rosalina. "I guess it's time to be going."

"I guess. Looks like we missed out on helping with the clean up." She made a silly cringey face, like she didn't mind because she'd had fun at the piano.

"Looks like." At that moment Marco was hugged from behind and a kiss planted on the back of his head. Only one person would do that. He turned around. "Hey, Mom."

"You two are adorable in your matching yellow. Let me take your picture by the arbor before it gets any darker out. I need a good photo of you guys on my phone."

His mom was going to be disappointed if things were over between them. That picture could be worth nothing but sadness in a matter of a few days, but he obliged.

As they walked over to the arbor, Marco noticed Rosalina was half limping.

He leaned toward her ear. "You okay?"

"Ready to be out of these shoes. I think my entire feet are nothing but blisters."

"You need a good pair of work boots."

She laughed. "I'm pretty sure I wouldn't look as good in them as you do."

"So you admit I look nice in them."

Her smile was too cute, her lips pinched in the start of a fish face. "They suit you."

"Now let me get you in position," Mom said as she took one of each of their arms and guided them into a pose she liked.

Marco wasn't distracted by his mom, but said to Rosalina, "I think they'd suit you too. You'd look cute in some Carhartt women's work wear."

"Ha, that is so not my style." She wrinkled her nose and pinched her eyes shut, but happiness bloomed over her face.

Marco soaked in every inch of her, had no idea what expression he might have been wearing, but he heard his mom's phone snap an unprepared picture. He jerked his head toward her. "Hey, we weren't ready."

Marco could tell Mom was already zooming in on the picture. "It's perfect. Completely natural. Completely you two. I might blow this one up on canvas and put it on the wall."

"It is a nice picture," Dad said, who'd showed up behind mom and peered over her shoulder at the phone screen.

"I demand a retake," Marco thrust a finger toward his parents.

Rosalina buried her face in his shoulder, snickering.

"I'll gladly take another one." Mom sing-songed.

Sure, she would.

This time they faced the camera and smiled prettily, but Marco could already tell his mom was wholly in love with the first one. He hoped he didn't look like a love-sick dog.

But, maybe, that was the most accurate capturing of him. Because, yes, he adored—loved—the crazy girl beside him.

And next Saturday he would make it known to Rosalina...depending on the results of his fleece, that is.

Would it be wrong to pray for the results he desired?

□□□

Weddings were exhausting. Marco had to force himself out of bed the next morning. If not for church, he would have slept in, which made him wish there was another weekend day in-between Saturday and Sunday.

He moved about his room with only one eye open as he gathered his church clothes—a pair of black jeans (since his good denim ones were dirty from wearing yesterday) and an orange button-up.

The cold water he flicked on his face, along with brushing his teeth, went a long way in ridding of the last bit of tiredness, but still a big yawn stretched his mouth...too wide. He winced as stitches pulled.

Marco made a conscious effort of breathing in and out until his face relaxed again. Then he wet his hair, passed a brush through it, and used some hairspray...since it was Sunday.

His eyes drifted to his alarm clock. Nine forty-five. He needed to—

"We're leaving for church!" His dad bellowed from down the hallway. "Don't be late, and don't forget to pin Luigi up in the laundry room."

"Okay. I'll be a few minutes behind you!" He hollered back and proceeded to turn his phone on the *do not disturb* setting like he always did for worship. He had enough trouble focusing on the pastor's words without the device vibrating in his pocket.

Marco heard the front door shut, and as he hurried about grabbing his wallet, keys, and Bible, there was a strange niggle in the back of his mind that he was forgetting something.

Something important.

He paused for a moment and clenched his fists. He'd heard once that could help you remember something you forgot.

Unfortunately, there were no remedies for his forgetfulness. When Marco forgot something, it was lost forever.

Such was the case today.

With a dismissive shrug, he went to the kitchen and grabbed a breakfast bar and a coconut water, and headed out to his truck.

All the while hoping he hadn't forgotten anything.

Chapter
Twenty-Nine

Rosalina awoke Sunday with a smile on her face as she looked forward to attending church with Marco.

Would he rest his arm on the pew behind her?

What did his singing voice sound like?

Might he let her hold his hand, if she tried, while they stood to sing the hymns?

"It's going to be a good day."

She swung her legs out of bed and when her feet touched the floor, she was bombarded with the remembrance that Marco had called off their agreement yesterday.

There was no more need for pretending.

So what, exactly, did that look like for her—for them—now? She hadn't been pretending since the first few dates.

But did Marco expect her to be...different now?

She couldn't.

How could she? Especially after slow dancing with him and basking in the feeling of being held in his arms. Oh, what a tender, beautiful, wonderful moment.

No, things could not be different. She loved Marco—silly, bubbly smile and all. She would prove to him that the last three weeks had not been a charade on her part. Surely, he would be able to see that. If not, that was okay too. Because she was determined that, today, she would tell him, face-to-face how she felt about him.

She was going to take Lillian's advice to heart and put it in action. She didn't yet know how she'd go about it—wanted it to be special—but no matter what, she was telling him today.

Rosalina took extra care with her appearance and selected a dress she thought Marco would especially like. It wasn't as fancy as what she wore to the wedding, but she felt the mauve color of it did amazing things for her complexion, and with a little matching lip gloss...

Sí, now she looked ready to declare her love to Marco.

Queenie, who finally woke up (always the last to rise) stretched up at Rosalina's leg, asking for some good-morning attention.

"Careful, doll, or you'll snag the lace on my dress."

As if she understood, the dog lowered to all fours and looked up at Rosalina with a smile.

"It's going to be a wonderfully awesome day, Queenie. I'll be sure to tell you all about it when I get home. If things go well, it could be late, though. We might not get our afternoon walk in. But you'll be a good dog for *Tía* and *Tío*, won't you?" She booped Queenie's little leathery black nose.

The dog pranced and licked her lips.

"*Sí*, it is time for your breakfast."

Rosalina measured and poured some kibble into Queenie's bowl, then joined her *tía* and *tío* for their special Sunday breakfast of orange sweet rolls.

Orange...

It made Rosalina think of Marco, causing her stomach to tingle. Time for church could not get here soon enough.

"You look positively happy this morning, Rosa," *Tía* Carmen noted.

Rosalina's smile only grew as she took a bite of the orange roll. She chewed it thoroughly and swallowed before dabbing some orange glaze from her lips and responding. "I am. Marco is joining me for church this morning."

"How lovely." *Tía* Carmen's eyes took on a knowing glow.

"Marco, you say?" *Tío* Juan pointed his fork at her. "As in Marco Mendez, one of my employees?"

"*Sí*, I thought I'd told you about seeing him lately."

Tío grunted, and Rosalina could only assume which meaning it held this time. It was hard to believe how much a man could express with grunts and mumbles that made no sense to her, and yet all men were able to decipher. They had their own language.

Rosalina was first to finish her two rolls and she quickly washed up her dishes. "I'd like to arrive at church early, in case Marco happens to as well. So I'm going to leave now."

"Okay, dear."

Rosalina kissed her *tía* on the cheek. "It's an exciting day for José and Regina too."

"Don't tell her that," *Tío* Juan lamented. "If you only knew how long she cried in bed last night now that we're in the last week before their nuptials."

"Oh." Rosalina covered her mouth with her hand. "I'm sorry." Her *tía* hadn't shown any emotions up to this point, so she'd assumed it wasn't a teary subject. After all, José had been moved out of the house since he turned nineteen.

Tía Carmen waved a hand. "Ack, I'm fine this morning. It just hit me last night that my baby boy is going to be a married man. Every mother has the right to cry over such a milestone."

"Absolutely. Now, I'm gonna run."

As she bustled out the door, Rosalina couldn't help but add an extra skip to her step to think it might not be much longer before she'd be the one getting married. She wondered if *Tía* Carmen would get emotional about it. *Tía* was like a mother to her.

They'd developed a special relationship. In fact, as Rosalina thought about it, she might see if *Tía* Carmen would be her matron of honor—should a wedding be in her future.

She prayed so.

And soon.

If it was God's will...

□□□

Marco did not arrive to the church early.

That's okay. I didn't expect him to.

Not once had Marco been early for anything, so why would it change now?

But Marco did not arrive in time for worship service to start either, and Rosalina grew concerned. Had he forgotten what time she'd told him? She inconspicuously pulled out her phone and sent him a text to make sure everything was okay.

By the time the pastor took to the pulpit, she had not received a reply, nor had Marco arrived. Rosalina was no longer concerned, but stewing on the inside.

Be patient. Something could have come up. Don't jump to conclusions.

But he was late.

Very late.

And it hurt.

Because this was not the first time. It wasn't the second time either. But the third, and at a point where it cast doubt in Rosalina's heart and head.

Doubts she did not want to have. Not when she'd been so happy and sure of everything this morning.

The sermon was a long one. Well, not by terms of the clock, but it felt like it dragged on for eternity to Rosalina as she checked her phone every couple seconds. It was no surprise she got nothing out of the message, and she hoped no one asked her what the preaching had been on. She hadn't the faintest idea.

After they'd sung the final hymn, Rosalina knew she was probably hypertensive. And she didn't need a mirror to know her cheeks matched her dress.

Marco never showed up.

Unless...

Unless he'd arrived so late he snuck in and sat in the back.

Rosalina gathered her purse and Bible up in a flurry and squeezed past her *tía* and *tío* to get out of the pew and into the aisle. She scanned over heads and past suits, knowing she would find Marco in more casual attire, but her search came up empty.

Her shoulders slumped and the tiny flicker of hope that had risen was thoroughly doused.

"I guess we're back to ground zero." Her whispered words shook with the tears burning her eyes and throat.

Back to where they'd been on their first dinner date. Mere acquaintances. Nothing special.

Honestly, they probably never were *anything*. Rosalina had let her heart get involved where it never should have. Her pain now was entirely her fault.

She shoved the church door open with great force. "I never should have gone along with a lie."

With a huff, she stomped across the parking lot to her car, where she opened the door and sat on the seat, her legs out and feet planted on the asphalt. She pressed her fingers into her forehead and willed the tears to not flow.

She sniffed.

"Something wrong?" It was José.

Rosalina blinked several times in quick succession before looking up. "Hey, José."

"What's wrong? I saw you barrel out of the church like only you can when you're upset."

"Humph. Should I be offended?" She hated how pitiful her voice sounded.

"None was intended." José tugged at his pants at the thighs and squatted before her, then touched a finger to her chin, forcing her to look him straight in the eyes. "Now, tell me what's got you upset."

She sighed deeply. "It's that frustrating man!"

"By man, am I to assume Marco?"

"*Sí*. I never should have let you talk me into going on the dinner date with him."

"Why? I mean, why does it matter at this point? Lillian's wedding is over. That was the only reas–"

"Stop it!"

José's eyes widened and he leaned back at her sharp interruption. "What...?"

"I care about him, José, but he doesn't share my feelings."

"Why do you say that?" His tone was quiet and gentle, the same way Rosalina comforted Queenie when the first few storms of spring frightened her.

"I invited him to church today. And, well..." She waved a hand over the parking lot. "He never showed up."

"Hmm. Maybe he had a good reason."

She snorted. "It better be a very good reason."

"Have you told Marco how you feel?"

"No." It came out sounding like a lamentation.

José made one of those indecipherable male grunts (something he learned from *Tío* Juan), and circled a hand over his jaw. "Look, I need to get back inside before the potluck starts without me."

Rosalina looked away. "I'm not hungry."

"Then might I suggest you pay Marco a visit?"

"Why should I?" Now she sounded hard and unreasonable, but she couldn't help it. Her heart was sorely aching.

"Because I think you need to get some things settled with him before any more time passes. Besides, you aren't going to enjoy the potluck in this...mo—er, state."

She sent him a stink eye, knowing he was going to say mood. But it was the truth. Marco had a way of putting her in a mood at times. If only he weren't so frustrating.

She sighed. "I think you're right. I'm sorry. Maybe I'll make it back before the celebration is over."

José cupped her elbow. "Don't worry about it. This is more important business. I already know you love me. Marco needs to know. Go set your heart at ease, Rosa."

She gave him a soft smile, warmed by his sweetly spoken shortened form of her name. Nobody said it quite like José did. She hugged his neck. "Thank you. You really are the best cousin."

"I like to think so."

Rosalina jabbed him in the biceps and they both chuckled.

"Now, go get him tiger." This time José jabbed her in the arm.

She twisted on her car seat and pulled her legs inside the vehicle. "Pray for me."

"I will be."

With that, Rosalina pulled her door shut, started the engine, and headed for home first. She wanted to be calmed down before she saw Marco, so she planned to get Queenie and they would walk over to the Mendez house. Nothing like walking a dog to set her at ease.

Her legs started bouncing and her hands grew clammy on the steering wheel.

"Don't chicken out now, girl. You've got a man's heart to win."

□□□

Rosalina didn't bother changing her dress, but did slip into her favorite pair of tennis shoes—which happened to have dark pink stitching, so they almost matched.

Queenie was more than happy to be getting in the Sunday walk that had been debatable earlier this morning.

The pounding of Rosalina's feet mixed with the *click, click, click* of Queenie's nails on the pavement worked to soothe her frayed nerves. By the time they reached the block where the Mendez house stood, she felt in a better mood to be about the task of declaring her love.

She paused at the end of the walkway leading up to the house and took in a confidence-boosting breath, slowly letting it out. As she went to take her first step, the front door burst open, and a frantic-looking Marco stepped out, although he was unaware of her presence as his head was down.

Before he could pull the door shut behind him, Rosalina called out. "Marco."

He froze and his head whipped up. "Rosalina!" He dashed down the three porch steps. "I'm so sorry. I forgot about today. When I got home a few minutes ago, I saw your text. I was going to head to the church now." She wondered what her face registered, as he quickly added, "You have every right to be mad."

And just like that, she was irked all over again. "How could you have forgotten? It was only yesterday I asked you."

He hung his head.

And now that she'd started off on her rant, she couldn't stop. Her intentions regarding this meeting were forgotten as she let the hurt inside do the speaking. "You know what? You can forget about me attending José's wedding *with* you. Our agreement was over last night. As far as I'm concerned..." Her voiced wobbled as a tight wad of emotion lodged in her throat. "We're...through."

She stomped a foot and wheeled around.

Marco grabbed her elbow. "Rosalina, wait. I didn't—"

She flung his arm away. "Forget about it. I-I..." She slipped into Spanish, then took off at a jog, Queenie doing a good job of keeping up.

"Rosalina! Rosalina!"

She didn't stop. She didn't look behind. She did slow down, however, as it grew hard to see past the sheen of tears in her eyes. How had she messed up so badly?

And with that outrage, she knew she might as well give up on Marco returning her feelings. She'd ruined everything, if there'd been anything to begin with.

Her stupid, stupid tongue.

Why hadn't she controlled it?

I should go back and apologize.

She didn't think she could right now. Maybe never. Could she ever face him again?

"I've lost him." She choked on the lament and pressed a hand over her mouth...but her sob turned into a gasp when a pounding accompanied by vicious growling came upon them.

Rosalina's heart lurched into her throat as the ugly, teeth-barring pit bull stopped to take their measure.

She swallowed. "Be a good dog. I like dogs." She held statue still, talking calmer than she felt. "You be good now and go home. Right?"

Queenie growled and started barking as she jumped and strained against Rosalina's hold.

"Queenie, no," she whispered and gave a tiny tug on the leash.

The pit bull lunged.

Rosalina screamed.

Chapter Thirty

"I love you, don't you see it?"

At least, that was the translation Marco came up with from Rosalina's parting words.

Had it only been his ears turning her words into what he wanted to hear, or had she declared she loved him?

Marco stomped up the porch and froze before he could enter the house when he saw Antonio glaring at him through the open door.

How much had his brother witnessed?

Why couldn't his brother have not been home? Like their parents, who had gone to help at some mission right after church.

He growled. "Get out of my way." He tried to shove past, but Antonio clasped the doorjamb with a death grip and widened his stance.

"You aren't coming in here until you make things right with Rosalina."

"What's there to make right? You heard her. We're through."

Antonio rolled his eyes, complete with a head roll too. "Did you not hear her say she loves you?"

"I'm not sure if that's what she meant to say."

Antonio threw his arms up. "She loves you, you idiot."

Marco was taken aback.

Idiot?

A muscle in his neck ticked. *How dare...*

"She loves you, Marco. She told me. She's just upset. You have to go after her. Don't let her leave like this."

"Why would she tell you she loves me, but not me."

"She was afraid how you might take the news."

"Why?" His tone was harsh and clipped.

"Because this whole *thing* between the two of you was fake, and she feared what you might think if you knew she'd fallen in love with you. It wasn't supposed to happen."

"She told you everything?"

"Yep. I'm the trustworthy brother."

He growled and plunged his finger in his ear deeper than he ever had before and twisted as if he could drill clear through to the other side. "I-I wouldn't know what to say to her."

"The truth, man! The truth."

"But..."

"It's not that hard."

"Yes, it is!"

They both fell silent. Stared at each other.

Antonio shook his head. "I'll never understand you. They're just words, Marco."

Frustration mounted—at himself, at Antonio—and emotion burned his chest. "I'm not smart with words like you." He hated having to say it, but Antonio knew it was true.

"Speak from your heart, not your head. There's a difference, and if you could figure it out, you'd find it's not so hard."

Since when did his brother know so much about love?

Marco ran a hand over his hair as he considered his brother's words.

Speak from his heart and not his head. Was that it? Was that the bridge he'd been searching for the last couple weeks?

He opened his mouth to tell his brother he was right, but his words dried up when a scream split the air.

Marco couldn't know for certain, but something told him that was Rosalina's scream. His heart stopped and he took off at a sprint.

"Rosalina!"

Sure enough, she was a block and a half down, screaming, her movements puzzling. Frantically jumping up and down.

Attempting to reach her arm out, jerking it back to herself again. Flailing her arms as if she felt helpless and scared.

What was she doing?

What was going on?

Then he came to a standstill, petrified, when the scene clarified for him and brought back a slideshow of memories.

The pit bull. The vicious growls. The terrifying teeth. Painful bites to his face. The stinky dog breath. Heavy weight upon his torso. His using every ounce of strength to push back and scream, while the attacks kept coming.

The yelps.

The yelps?

That wasn't a sound from the past. That was...

"Queenie!"

He shook himself out of his nightmarish memory and took off at a sprint again to cover the remaining distance, but not before Rosalina—devout dog lover that she was—tried to help her little "doll" one too many times, drawing attention to herself this time.

His blood turned to ice when the dog bit Rosalina's hand, drawing a yelp out of her too.

"No." Marco didn't yell, but used a stern, commanding voice when he arrived at the scene, hoping the dog would recognize the tone and stop.

Poor Queenie was no match against the pit bull, and Marco could see the fight draining from her little body.

There was no time to spare. His adrenaline pumping and his past trauma forgotten, Marco gave a mighty kick to the attacker's throat, sending the dog rolling over several times, away from Queenie.

The dog growled angrily, wiggled off its back, and prepared to rise again, but with quick movements Marco lodged his knee in the middle of the beast's back, rendering it immobile...and decidedly angry.

He was glad he'd read every article he could find on how to handle dog attacks from the age he was allowed to use the internet.

The devilish growls made him wince and he flinched every time the mad dog twisted its head around and attempted to bite at his thigh. He kept his hands fisted and elbows tight against his body so there were no protruding limbs that would be easy targets for the blood-thirsty mouth. Marco pressed down with more pressure on his knee. He cared not if he broke a rib. That dog had attacked what was his.

His...

Yes, his. And he didn't mean that in a selfish, possessive way, but a loving, protective way. Rosalina had his heart (and she had his if she'd still have it) and, thus, she was his to protect. And, yes, that pert little Queenie too—because Rosalina and dog were a package deal.

"Marco, be careful!" Rosalina cried from where she stood, stunned or shocked, or both, her tortured eyes darting from him to Queenie over and over again. She started shaking.

If only he could comfort her.

Pounding footsteps shook the ground and Antonio jogged up, phone in hand. "I called the police and they should be here any minute. They said they have someone in the neighborhood."

No sooner had Antonio finished speaking than a Peoria Police SUV parked haphazardly along the curb. Shortly thereafter another one arrived...and animal control.

What happened next Marco couldn't process. His body shook now that the adrenaline had worn off, and the fear from so long ago attacked his heart and head. So much happened so fast, his brain couldn't keep up with all the flashing scenes before him.

Eventually, the dog was hauled away, Marco was standing again, and all was quiet...except for Rosalina's soft crying—in Antonio's arms.

Feeling numb, Marco walked over to where his brother, Rosalina, and Queenie were. The fluffy dog was more red than white, one leg quivering, and little nose whines escaping the tiny creature.

Marco had never seen or heard a more sad sight. As much as he wanted to go to Rosalina and take her in his arms, he did what he knew Rosalina would want more than personal comfort.

He dropped to his knees before the injured and adored pet. "You've got to be okay," he whispered to Queenie, who looked up at him with weepy but trusting eyes.

She trusted him. After all the dates, the little nips, the peace offerings of dog biscuits...now the bichon trusted him. It wasn't the way Marco would have asked to earn that trust, but, well, here they were.

And it was enough to make a grown man cry.

"Let's get her to the animal hospital," he said loud enough for Rosalina to hear, hoping she didn't detect the waver in his words.

She hiccupped on a sob. "Queenie, my baby..."

"Shhh." Antonio soothed.

As carefully as he could, Marco slid one hand under Queenie's neck, and the other hand under her rump. Gently, with slow movements, he lifted the dog, whose little exhales of pain tore at his chest.

"It's going to be okay, little one. I've got you."

He'd never known he could have such fighting love for a dog that had disliked him—which had been mutual. But, man...he'd do anything to save this dog from death at the hands of such a beast. For Rosalina. She would be heartbroken if Queenie didn't survive.

One policeman remained yet and he offered to drive them to the animal hospital.

"Please." Rosalina was quick to accept.

The policeman ducked his head and reached for the door handle on his vehicle. "Get in."

Marco had never ridden in a cop car before, and he couldn't say he enjoyed the experience, but it got them where they needed to go...quickly. That's all that mattered.

The next several minutes went by in a flurry. Queenie was whisked away, he and Rosalina were questioned, paperwork was handed over to be filled out, and, at last, they were sitting and Rosalina began working through the necessary papers.

Marco just sat, trying to process everything that had happened, unable to say anything at the moment, or be of any help.

That is, until a strangled cry emerged from Rosalina's throat.

He jerked his head to her. "Lina...?"

Fresh tears trailed down her cheeks and pure pain was etched in every line along her forehead, and the little dip in the middle of her chin that he'd not noticed before. "I don't know what I'm going to do."

Sympathy welled up in him and he draped his arm on the chair behind her, curled his hand around her arm, drawing her to his side. "About what? Queenie is going to be fine." He believed it. Prayed it was so. She was in good hands here.

She pressed wobbling lips together and shook her head. "My business."

"Your business?"

"I can't afford this emergency."

Marco drew his brows down and waited for her to continue.

"I have a meeting with my landlord tomorrow and I owe him a hefty sum. If I don't pay in full, he won't renew my lease. I'll lose TPPP. But I can't *not* have Queenie treated. She is my baby." She sniffed.

So that was the reason behind all the remarks about needing the money with the babysitting and dog walking. She hadn't been truthful when she'd said everything was fine. She *was* struggling.

Why had she kept it to herself?

"Ah, Lina, I'm sorry."

She used the back of her hand to wipe at her nose, and that's when Marco noticed a familiar hankie tied about her hand. It was Antonio's church hankie. He gently took her wrist and pulled her hand over to him.

"You were injured."

She nodded but kept her gaze down.

"We have to get it tended to. Dog bites can be dangerous. Infection and all. Once Queenie is stable, we need to get you to the ER."

Rosalina shook her head. "An ER visit is too expensive."

"I'm not letting your wounds go untreated. Prompt Care, at least?"

She nodded, albeit grudgingly. Then her face crumbled. "I've lost. I've failed. I'm no businesswoman. I can't even pay my bills." She choked on a sob, started crying again, and it broke Marco's heart.

If only there was something he could do—

Do...

Yes. There was something he could do.

And he'd see to it first thing tomorrow.

Rosalina finished filling out the paperwork, carried it up to the counter, and returned. Marco watched her every move and frowned at the blood stains on her dress. A dress the same color as the dark shade of pink his sister's bedroom walls used to be painted. Somehow, on Rosalina, the color looked anything but disgusting.

She looked right pretty in that lacy dress. He hoped it would come clean. Anger knifed through him at the beast that caused such harm to his girls.

Marco left his arm draped over the back of Rosalina's chair, and when she settled back beside him she angled toward him and snuggled into the corner of his shoulder.

She searched his face and he found himself holding his breath, wondering what she was looking for. What she saw.

"Thank you, Marco. You might have saved Queenie's life."

He rolled his lips inward in a show of sympathy. "I'm sorry it happened."

"It must have been hard for you. With your...history."

He nodded once, gently. "I can't deny I had a wave of memories I'd just as soon forget, but something else, much stronger, came over me."

"Which was?"

"The need to protect. That dog was attacking, hurting, and I needed to do something about it."

"It was a heroic thing for you to do."

He ducked his head. "Thankfully, I've researched and watched informational videos on what to do in the event of a dog attack, or when approached by a dog that appears to be bent toward harm. That knowledge was strength and courage for me today."

"I didn't think you liked Queenie. You called her a devil."

Marco exhaled a laugh through his nose and pulled at his ear. "I did. But...well, I guess the little fluff ball has grown on me." *As has her owner.* Confound it, but he felt a burning behind his eyes then when he remembered the dog's weepy, trusting eyes. "Lina, when I bent to help Queenie, she...I just knew she trusted me. She wanted me to help her. She accepted my touch."

Twin tears trailed down Rosalina's cheeks and Marco wiped them away with the thumb not currently rubbing comforting motions on her arm.

"She has to be all right," her words sounded purely tortured.

"Shhh. They'll take good care of her. And we're praying for her."

"You're praying for her?" She searched his eyes.

"Of course."

The look Rosalina gave him made Marco want to kiss her lips. He couldn't explain what the expression was, but it mirrored everything he felt for her right now.

He didn't kiss her, though.

Regretfully.

But there would be time for kissing—and soon, he hoped.

Chapter Thirty-One

Rosalina woke the next morning with a splitting headache, puffy eyes, a raw throat, and a nose as red as Rudolph's.

"Ugh." She pressed the heel of her hand to the top of her head. "Why does crying have to leave such awful side effects?"

Or maybe it was all the stress.

She couldn't believe she managed to steal a few winks of sleep last night. Must have conked out from sheer exhaustion.

She let out a sorrowful sigh when she got out of bed and saw Queenie's was empty.

Her chin took to trembling and she bit down on her finger. A pitiful mewling sound reverberated in her throat.

"My baby. Oh, my baby. Queenie, you have to be okay."

By muscle memory only, Rosalina changed out of her pajamas, slipped into an easy-on faux denim summer dress, and carelessly passed a brush through her hair.

She needed to get to the animal hospital. She needed to see Queenie.

Realizing then she'd yet to check her phone, Rosalina snatched it off the nightstand. What if the hospital had called during the night and she'd slept through the ring?

What if Queenie hadn't made it through the night?

What if...

"No, no no! Don't think about the what ifs." They were too painful. Too awful.

Rosalina breathed a sigh of relief when there were no missed calls from the hospital.

No news is good news.

She sagged against her bed until she lowered to her bottom, knees pulled up to her chest, where she let a few more tears fall as she lifted up a prayer for her dog.

Surely God would hear her prayers. Some might think Queenie *only* a dog, but her heavenly Father knew how much Queenie meant to her, and she chose to trust Him like a little girl does her *pa-pá.*

With a sniff, she grabbed her purse and phone, and rushed out the door—not caring about breakfast. She hadn't had an appetite since breakfast yesterday.

At the hospital, Rosalina received encouraging news about Queenie, although she wasn't out of the woods yet. Her injuries were extensive, but the most concerning was that she'd suffered serious bites to her back which had caused some damage to internal organs.

Rosalina found it hard to breathe throughout the explanation, but when the technician walked her back to visit Queenie, she pasted on a smile of encouragement for the recovering dog.

"Hi, doll."

Queenie's tail twitched the tiniest bit, but her eyes still drooped with misery and it was heartbreaking to see a cone around her neck and in such a sterile-looking stainless steel pen—Rosalina refused to call it a cage.

"My baby." Rosalina's throat filled with emotion. "I'm sorry this happened to you." She wanted to reach out and pet Queenie, but feared causing any undue pain. She hoped her presence and voice alone would bring comfort.

"You fight for me, doll. You hear me. Don't give up. You're a strong and feisty girl. And I...I need you." She couldn't go on. Didn't want Queenie to see her tears, but one leaked out regardless.

Queenie let out a little whine, minutely moved her head, and gently licked Rosalina's finger.

"Oh..." It was exactly what she needed. "I love you too, Queenie. So, so much."

And hard though it was, Rosalina swallowed her emotions and started talking in happy tones, encouraging her little princess to fight through. She would be sure her visits to Queenie were positive and healing.

"Oh no!" Rosalina gasped and slapped her hands to her cheeks when she arrived back at home shortly after one o'clock.

She tossed her purse on her bed and dropped into her desk chair, her hands instinctively rising to rub her aching temples. "I forgot about the meeting with Truman Scott."

How could I have forgotten?

Easy for her to answer.

Queenie. Stress.

And yet...she doubted her landlord would be understanding. She'd missed the twelve-fifteen appointment. But the day wasn't over. Maybe he would meet her this afternoon and she could at least pay him what she could—which, unfortunately, wouldn't be the full amount like she'd have been able to pay before the attack.

Maybe she should have forced herself to go into work today. Then she might have remembered the meeting. She'd called Haven yesterday and told her to cancel all appointments for today, because there was no way Rosalina could have worked with dogs while aching over her own. Not to mention it would have been nigh impossible to bathe dogs with her wrapped hand.

Not letting another second go by, Rosalina rushed to her purse, got her phone, and quickly scrolled through her contacts. As the call rang in her ear, she gathered up her checkbook and a pen.

"Hello." Brief as always, Truman Scott answered.

"Mr. Scott, I am so sorry about missing the meeting over the noon hour. I had a family emergency and—"

"There's nothing to discuss, Miss Torres."

Noooo.

Rosalina fell to her knees.

I lost the building. God, help me be calm.

The last thing she should do was lash out at her landlord, when what she needed was mercy.

"I can explain. I can pay you, Mr. Scott. It won't be the full amount like I could have—"

"Miss Torres." She was getting tired of his interrupting, and she was about ready to butt in, but his next words rendered her speechless. "Your bill is paid in full."

"My— What?"

"Your bill is paid. I've renewed your lease. In fact, your rent is covered for the next six months. I'm sorry about your unfortunate emergency, but know you have one less worry."

This man did not at all sound like the Truman Scott she'd come to know the last couple months. He was being...*nice*. What changed?

She swallowed and tried to make sense of the conversation, which made her shake her head.

There was no making sense of it.

"I don't understand. I didn't make a payment."

"No, you didn't. But your boyfriend did."

"My boyfriend?" What was he talking about?

Boyfriend!

"Wait, you mean...Marco?"

"Ooooh, I, um, uh...I wasn't supposed to let that slip."

Rosalina's heart started pounding. "Was it Marco?"

"I'm not—"

"Was it Marco?!" Pardon the scream, but she had to know.

"If that's your boyfriend's name."

It was Marco. She knew it. The tone with which Truman answered the question was a total yes.

"Bye, Mr. Scott, and thank you." She disconnected the call before he could say anything more.

"I have to see Marco."

Rosalina snatched her purse up once more and ran out of the house, a different kind of tears pouring down her face.

Her bill paid. Her rent covered for six months. That was a large sum. How could Marco have paid it?

His motorcycle money.

"Oh, Marco..."

How was she supposed to see to drive?

□□□

"He's not home," Antonio said when he answered to Rosalina's pounding.

"What do you mean he's not home?"

"He went back to work this afternoon."

Rosalina exhaled loudly through her nose. "But I have to see him. Do you know where he's working?"

"No, I don't. Why do you need to see him? Is everything all right? Is Queenie okay? You look like you've been crying."

Rosalina sniffed at the mention of crying. At this point, she could start back up again at simply stepping on a roly-poly.

"Do you know anything about Marco making a big payment today? For me?"

"Ahhh..." Antonio rubbed the back of his neck and averted his gaze.

"You do, don't you?"

He remained silent and avoided looking at her.

"So, Marco did pay my landlord."

Slowly, Antonio raised his head and gave a barely perceptible nod.

"He used the money he'd been saving for his motorcycle, didn't he?"

Another silent nod.

"Why? Why would he do that?"

"Because, Rosalina, he loves you."

"He loves m— But he's never said so."

"Marco doesn't share his feelings easily. But if anything says 'I love you,' I'd think what he did today does."

Rosalina's lips slightly parted as she rolled those words around in her mind, and, with a cry, she spun around and rushed to her car.

She would call *Tío* Juan and find out where Marco was working today. This couldn't wait until later.

□□□

Rosalina's hand shook when she reached for the gear selector to put her car in park. She gazed at the house to her right and did a quick scan of the utility truck and van, the dumpster in the driveway, and a ladder leaned against the house.

She followed the ladder with her eyes all the way up to the roof, where she studied each of the workers. Her heart galloped when she recognized Marco's familiar frame toward the front of the roof. She should be able to holler up at him.

As she got out of the car, a smile stretched her face at the fact she got to see Marco in his sun hat after all. She was paying him that surprise visit at work—although with a far more important purpose than just seeing him, and hopefully catching a glimpse of him dancing to the Mexican music blaring from a radio somewhere.

Rosalina doubted Marco would be able to hear her holler over the music.

She stopped halfway across the yard and took in a shaky breath. So many emotions going on right now. She felt like a mess, probably looked like a mess, but it didn't matter.

Marco stood and moved over a few paces, and as he did she got to witness a few of his "moves."

The sight of him wholly lost in the beat was endearing. The silly man who, clearly, had a heart of gold.

She drew closer to the house, cupped her hands around her mouth, and yelled, "Marco!"

Not one of the workers turned.

She pursed her lips and eyed the ladder. She supposed she could climb up there, but she never had liked ladders. She got wobbly knees using a three-step stepstool.

She waited out the song, and when it came to a pause before commercials started up, she tried again. "Marco! Marco!"

His head whipped up and turned. Surprise widened his expression as his work came to a halt. He set down whatever tool he'd been wielding and, like a monkey, he scaled the roof and shimmied down the ladder.

The sight was quite...enamoring.

And that sun hat.

It made her silly, bubbly man look even sillier, but it only made her love him more.

Go figure.

It was crazy how feelings could change.

Love was an incredible, wonderful, life-changing thing.

"Rosalina." He sounded shy. "What are you doing here?"

She closed the distance separating them, until she stood so close she could see tiny black flecks in his dark brown eyes. Could count the stitches on the right side of his face.

"Why'd you do it, Marco?" She used a soft and loving voice.

"Do what?"

"Don't play clueless with me. You know what I'm talking about. My bill. Six months of rent." Maybe utilizing a little sass would help.

There went his finger into his ear. "You weren't supposed to find out about that quite yet."

"How'd you find out who my landlord is?"

He shuffled on his feet. "I called Haven and she gave me the contact information for Mr. Scott so I could set up a meeting with him. Wow, is he a grumpy man. I gave him a little what-for with a Bible lesson on greed. I was kind about it. I promise."

Marco's lesson must have touched Mr. Scott's heart. He'd acted like a different man on the phone. "I can't thank you enough. You...you saved my business from closing down. You didn't have to. You were saving that money for a motorcycle. Or a boat. Instead, you saved The Pampered Poochie's Parlor. That's...I don't understand."

Marco came a step closer. So close she could feel his warm breath when he spoke, although it took him some time to speak. "You are more important to me than a dumb motorcycle or boat."

"I-I am?"

"Yes." The intensity in his dark eyes was all the validation she needed. "And since TPPP is important to you, it's important to me."

She smiled softly and pressed a hand to his cheek. "Thank you, from the bottom of my heart."

He ducked his head in a brief nod, then gently pulled her hand away and kissed her knuckles, bandage and all. And leave it to her silly man to break the serious moment by saying, "I need to shave." She knew he hadn't since the hammer accident

She choked on a laugh, the abrupt change surprising her. "I don't know about that. I kind of like the scruff. Gives you an *almost* serious look."

"Are you insulting my fake smile again by saying that?"

"No. I've found I love your smile. I could see it every day."

Another step closer. Marco cupped her elbow in his hand. He had to tilt his head so their noses didn't collide. "The first thing that caught your attention about me, eh?" He wouldn't let her forget about that, would he? "Then you will see it every day." He smiled for her.

Was she only imagining it, or was there an unspoken promise of some kind in the way he spoke those words? She found herself unable to respond or breathe.

"Come on, Marco, it's not break time. Let's get to work!" Someone hollered from up on the roof.

Marco grunted and muttered a name that sounded like "Santiago" under his breath before saying to her, "I guess I better get busy." His tone was reluctant, though.

Rosalina felt a measure of disappointment that the heart-to-heart, almost intimate moment, was coming to an end far too soon.

Would she ever hear Marco say "I love you?"

She sighed, then said, "And I'm sorry about blowing up yesterday. It was not my shining moment. Rest assured, I will attend José's wedding with you."

A pleased grin spread across his face. "Good."

Good? That wasn't the response she'd been expecting.

She raised a brow at him, pleading with him to expound, but he only grinned larger and waggled his brows.

She did so love it when he waggled his brows. When he did, it felt flirty and warmed her middle.

"You're slacking on the job, man!" That same voice called out from the roof.

Rosalina was getting irritated with the guy. He was interrupting precious time with Marco. But she had high hopes they'd be spending a lot of time together. Meaningful time. Not fake.

"I better get back up there. Santiago and Javier are already giving me a hard time for starting late and having all of last week off."

Rosalina nodded. The last thing she wanted was to cause him any trouble.

But, because she felt the impulse to do it, she said, "*Te amo,*" and kissed him on the corner of the mouth before dashing away, not looking back to see if Marco was left standing there stunned by the kiss or not, or if he understood what she'd declared.

Chapter Thirty-Two

Marco thought he'd be a bundle of nerves when he woke the morning of José and Regina's wedding, but with Rosalina's clear declaration still ringing in his head, he felt nothing but confidence. He'd translated those words straight over to English. There was no doubt, not like there had been on Sunday afternoon when he'd wondered if he'd heard her right or not.

"Rosalina loves me."

Knowing that for certain made it easier for him to do what he was going to do today. The results from his fleece were in. God had answered his prayers. Every day between Tuesday and today had reassured him even more, as they spent every evening together walking dogs or sharing picnics, and tending to Queenie, who had finally been released from the hospital Thursday afternoon.

During the hours when they weren't together, they were texting. And Marco made good on his promise about her seeing his smile every day. Silly though it might be, he took a selfie each morning and texted it to her with some cheesy caption that always received a laughing emoji in return.

As confidence-boosting as all that had been, now he especially needed God's grace and strength to carry out his plans for today— because, well, truthfully, he was a little nervous after all. But he was going to follow his brother's advice.

Speak from his heart, not his head.

His brain had a tendency to mix words up, and he feared he'd say the wrong thing. The last thing he wanted to do was make a mess of what he wanted to convey. So, maybe, if he spoke from his heart, where his strong feelings for Rosalina abided, he wouldn't screw up.

He hoped.

At least he didn't have to write it out. He doubted Rosalina could read his writing if he did. His penmanship was sloppy at best, but that couldn't be helped.

He finished tying his shoes in the room where all the groomsmen were changing and picking on José, but all he could think about was his girl. Rosalina.

His real date.

Man, that changes everything.

He felt like a prisoner let loose when they finally left the room to have pictures taken by the professional photographer. Marco managed to spot Rosalina right away when the bridesmaids and bride joined them.

His heart skipped a beat at the first sight of her, a beautiful rose of a woman. He tugged at the collar of his too-tight shirt, suddenly feeling stifled. Why did people like dressing up? He did not envy bankers or office workers in the least.

His job might be sweatier and more labor intensive, but that's the way he liked it.

But, by the way Rosalina's eyes roamed over him from head to toe with obvious pleasure at his wearing a black suit and tie, and crisp white shirt, he decided he could dress up from time to time.

As he walked toward her, she appeared to be as speechless as he. All he could do was take her in. Her cheeks were pink and her eyes shimmery like morning dew. Sparkly earrings dangled from her ears almost to her chin, and she wore a silk dress of deep red that messed with a man's mind and breathing. It was more ravishing than the dress she'd worn for Christmas in July, and it hugged her in all the right places.

The biggest surprise for him, though, was that all her long dark hair was up in a bouncy style around her head. There were curls everywhere with dainty roses scattered here and there. Marco had never seen her neck exposed before, and it ignited a fire inside him. Made him want to kiss her slender neck.

He let out a whistle. Rosalina ducked her head and her cheeks turned darker, matching the shade of her dress.

How long were they going to stand there without saying anything?

Marco cleared his throat. "You look amazing."

"And you look like a stranger. Are you truly Marco Mendez?"

He bowed. "The one and only."

"Wow." It was all she said, but it contained everything he saw in her eyes and face.

He felt the need to lighten the moment, lest he kiss her then and there. "Although...I might be walking like a penguin at the end of the day thanks to these horribly uncomfortable dress shoes."

Rosalina laughed. "I'm surprised you're not still wearing your work boots even in a tux."

"I didn't get a choice." He shrugged. "But, here." He reached in the pocket of his suit coat and pulled out a single sleeve of Oreos. "*America's* favorite cookie for my favorite girl." He winked.

She sent him a side eye, although a smile of adoration blossomed on her face. "You're not going to let me forget that, are you?"

"Nope. The package clearly reads '*milk's favorite cookie.*'"

"Well, I'm sure it's America's favorite too."

"Probably the world's favorite."

That made her smile get bigger. "Thank you. I know what we'll be snacking on after the wedding."

"We? Wow, you're going to share them."

She slapped him playfully in the arm. "Of course, I will share them. But only with you." She batted her lashes. "Now, put them back in your pocket and keep them safe for me. I don't think I can stow them away in my bouquet."

Marco took the cookies back and their fingers touched. *Delightful.* His eyes fell to her lips.

Not yet.

It was getting harder and harder to wait. But then they were required in the next several pictures, which had them separated— sadly. Although, Marco kept stealing glances at Rosalina, the two of them swapping smiles.

After that, the wedding commenced and there was no more time for talking—which, for the first time, was the only thing he wanted to do with Rosalina.

At last, they moved onto the reception, but it wasn't the occasion he had expected. Instead of sitting with Rosalina, he had to sit at the head table with all the groomsmen on José's side of the table, while Rosalina was far down on Regina's side.

It was downright rotten. The only thing that made it tolerable was that the menu featured tacos. Now, that was Marco's kind of wedding reception.

When he was about to go crazy with the waiting to get to what he was most excited about today—sorry, José and Regina—finally, the bride and groom left in a limousine, and Marco dashed up the church stairs, hoping his brother would follow through with his side of things.

He hadn't a need to worry. Right when he was ready, and not a second sooner, Rosalina parted the double doors of the sanctuary and took a slow step inside, looking all around.

"Hello? Marco? Are you up here? Antonio said you wanted to meet me in the sanctuary."

Of course, she wouldn't expect to look where he was situated.

All part of the plan.

Tonight, Rosalina would learn something new about him. Something few people knew. It was his creative outlet. His *thing* when he needed help with concentration. It brought peace to his frustrated mind when he'd had enough with words.

Before Rosalina could say anything more, he put his fingers in action upon the keys of the church's gleaming baby grand, and played the most fitting Elvis song: "Can't Help Falling in Love."

He watched Rosalina as she searched the sanctuary looking confused, but then her eyes met his and he saw rather than heard her gasp, and she stared with slack jaw and eyes full of astonishment.

Oh, so slowly, she padded down the carpeted sanctuary, but not once did they lose eye contact.

When she stopped at the piano, Marco shimmied to one side of the bench and invited her to sit beside him with his head motion.

She slid into place. Fit perfectly.

Marco continued to stare into the depths of her eyes. Eyes that glistened with unshed tears, and were filled with unanswered questions.

As the last note of the song faded, he leaned over and kissed her on the cheek, causing her to blush a pretty rosy color.

"Hi." It was a lame start, but it's all he could get out at the moment, feeling as if he were in a trance. The best kind. Rosalina held him spellbound.

"I thought you couldn't play the piano."

"I never said I couldn't, just that lessons didn't work out."

"Then how...?"

"Lillian opened up the world of playing by ear—or, by heart as I like to call it—when we were in high school."

Rosalina abruptly dropped her chin and toyed with her fingers. Marco could only reason it was because of the mention of Lillian's name.

He lifted her chin with a curved finger, but she refused to raise her eyes. "There is no competition, Lina. I realize now I never loved Lillian."

That brought her eyes up. "Truly?"

"I only recently learned that I've never experienced true love—the kind God created to be shared between a man and a woman."

"Only recently?"

"Yes. And you were the teacher."

"Me...?"

"Rosalina, I-I'm sorry for...well, everything. I'm sorry I dragged you into the whole fake dating thing." She made a noise, as if to interrupt, but Marco hurried on. "I can't help but wonder how different things might have gone had I not taken things into my own hands and fabricated a lie, and just met you for the first time today." She looked horrified at that. "But...I can't say I've regretted the last four weeks. They were...more than I ever could have imagined."

"Oh, Marco..." She laid a hand on his arm.

"I know I made many mistakes in the short time we've known each other. But the truth is, asking you to be mine was the smartest thing I ever did, despite it starting out as a deception. It wasn't long before I realized I didn't want our relationship to be fake."

"I couldn't agree with you more. Oh, Marco, I'm so sorry about all the fighting we did. And for..." She dropped her gaze. "For the mean things I said to you. The insults."

He caressed one of her cheeks and rubbed his callused thumb across the soft skin. "I have to admit, I like your bluntness. I never want you to change that. I always want you to say what's on your mind. It's easier than me having to guess what you're thinking."

She laughed. "First time anyone has ever told me that."

He smiled. "Can I be the first to, hopefully, tell you something else?"

She leaned toward him. "What?"

"*Te amo, mi amor.*"

Rosalina took in a sharp breath and tears pooled in her eyes and fell over. "My love? You love me?"

"*Sí.*"

"Y-you speak Spanish?"

He gave her his biggest grin and nodded.

"So you've known everything I've said...?"

Again, he nodded, his smile somehow getting bigger.

She covered her mouth with her fingers. "Oh...my."

"Including what you said upon waking after the movies at the Christmas in July *fiesta.*"

She scrunched up her nose. "What did I say? I don't recall."

He snickered. "Wouldn't you like to know." He waggled his eyebrows.

"What did I say?" She jabbed him in the arm.

"You were sleeping on my shoulder and when you woke up you said I was very comfortable and wanted to stay all night."

"I didn't!" She slapped her hands to her cheeks.

Marco laughed. "Oh, but you did."

"Ohhh." It was a sound of aggravation at herself. "I cannot believe—"

"I didn't mind, Lina. It was that night everything changed for me."

That had her hands dropping to her lap. "It was quite the night."

"Our first kiss."

She rolled her lips inward, creating an adorable, ornery smile. "I wondered how you would react to me all but throwing myself at you. I'll admit I was horrified with my actions when I got home. Afraid you'd think I was a wanton woman."

"Whatever that means." Marco waved a dismissive hand. "All I know is that you are the perfect girl for me—that is, if you'll be my girl." His chest constricted as he waited for her response.

She gently cocked her head to one side and her mouth moved in a way that led him to believe she was fighting emotions. Then she took in a breath. "Marco, I'd love nothing more than to be your girl."

He let out the breath he'd been holding. "I want you to know my intentions are honorable. I'm not toying with you. I want this to be serious. Lead to...to marriage."

Pleasure blossomed on her cheeks.

A good sign.

"But I know I can't ask that of you right now. Propose, that is." He paused as he struggled to find the right words to continue. "I don't feel it's been honorable the way we've been interacting the last four weeks. I took things into my own hands and lied. Lying is never the solution to any problem. I recently read about Abraham and Isaac in the Old Testament, telling the king their wives were their sisters. That turned out kind of messy and could have been really bad. So, however long it takes, I want to prove to you I am a man of honor. That I can live up to my name—"

"Your name?" She interrupted with a curious tilt of her head.

"My middle name is Honor."

"Marco Honor Mendez. I like it. You've already proven to me you're a man of honor. The way you saved Queenie and me from the pit bull. Using your money to keep me in business. That takes integrity. Character. And admitting you were wrong and apologizing...that's the kind of man I want to spend the rest of my life with and have father my children."

Marco tugged at his tie and undid the top button of his dress shirt. It was getting mighty hard to breathe in here. "So, you'll accept my court?"

"Absolutely. And you don't even have to do the Mexican Hat Dance."

He snorted out a laugh. "Good thing."

Her laugh was prettier than anything he could ever figure out how to play on the piano.

"Then, this is for you." He pulled from his inside breast pocket the slim, rectangular jewelry box he'd been keeping safe all day. He opened the lid and Rosalina sucked in a breath.

"Marco, it is beautiful."

He gently lifted the necklace from its velvet bed. "May I?"

She nodded, turned on the bench so her back faced him, and went to move her hair, but stopped awkwardly when she realized it was all atop her head.

Marco fumbled with the clasp of the necklace and his fingers lightly grazed her neck a few times, shooting fiery tingles up his arms. "There," he finally said when the little gold loop fit inside the clasp.

She looked down at the pendant sitting against her red silk gown. "I love it, Marco."

He did too. On her. The gold heart shimmered, and the little rose set in the center was perfect for his Rosalina. "It was my *abuela's*."

"I will treasure it always."

"And I will treasure you... Man!" He gave a fast jerk of his head. "I never would have guessed that what started with a verbal fight outside a restaurant would end up here. All I can say is...I'm full of wonder at the hand of God. He made good of my mess. More than good." His eyes dropped to her lips. My, but he wanted to taste them. They were so red and glossy.

She raked her top teeth over her bottom lip, which had him raising his gaze to ask her permission with his eyes.

A barely perceptible nod was her response.

Scooting closer, Marco cupped Rosalina's face in his hands and lowered his lips to hers.

He felt her melt as her hands settled at the nape of his neck.

This was nothing like their mistletoe kiss, charged though it may have been. This one was gentle, full of promise, and it curled Marco's toes in a most delightful way.

He wasn't sure who pulled away first, but when they did Rosalina looked more radiant than ever. "Wow."

He laughed. "Yeah. Wow."

She touched her lips with the back of her hand and one of her dark brows rose with question. "If everything changed back then, why didn't you say anything?"

He slid his finger in his ear. "I didn't know how to tell you how I felt, and feared how you would react—considering the way you were when I asked you to fake date."

"Oh." There was a hint of shame in the one word. "I acted badly."

"I don't blame you. I handled it all badly."

"I hope you'll feel free to tell me your feelings from now on."

"I'll try. It's difficult for me. I don't have much practice. I mean, don't take this wrong, I know my parents love me, but we've never been ones to speak about our love for each other. So, it just feels...awkward."

She laid a hand on his uninjured cheek. "I'll help you overcome that."

"It's already getting easier."

She smiled, then slanted a look at the piano keys. "Can you play anything else?"

"I can, but I'd rather do this."

"What?" She gave her head a curious tilt.

He slid his phone from his pants pocket, where he already had the music player pulled up to a specific song, a cover of "My Girl," by a classical crossover group he enjoyed listening to on occasion. He pushed play, stood, and watched Rosalina as she followed his every move.

He knew when she recognized the song, as she melted before his eyes.

Marco held out a hand. "May I have this dance?"

"*Sí.*"

In the front of the church they slow danced to another of *their songs*, whispering words of endearment in a mixture of Spanish and English, basking in the wonder of a mess turned blessing.

Epilogue

Three years later

After almost two-and-half years of marriage, Rosalina was used to making sure Marco had every important date and event plugged into his phone calendar, lest he forget. But she never would have thought he'd need a reminder about her birthday.

Yet here she was, alone at home, and cleaning up after Marco. It hadn't taken long to learn he was an untidy sort, but after researching as much as she could on dyslexia in adults and living with one as your partner, she'd discovered it was a common issue for the dyslexic to be disorganized—which was fine. She didn't mind. But today, well, it was her birthday—and a Saturday. Everything was rubbing her the wrong way.

Maybe it was childish to expect something special from Marco for her birthday, but she had to admit she was downright disappointed.

He never had to work on the weekends, and yet that's what he said he was leaving to do.

"I need to work," he'd stated matter-of-factly as he kissed her on the cheek and left, not saying one word about it being her birthday.

Well, she was about ready to call up *Tío* Juan to find out where the crew was working today. It must have been an emergency or something for them to be called in on the weekend.

With a huff, Rosalina straightened from picking up *another* pair of forgotten socks off the floor.

"It's fine. I'm fine. It's just another day."

Telling herself wasn't helping.

A hard kick pressed against her abdomen and Rosalina laid a caressing hand over the spot.

"Ah, little one, not much longer before I get to meet you. Two more weeks."

She couldn't wait. Marco was going to be a wonderful *pa-pá*. She'd known that from the first time she'd seen him interact with Calvin Brinkman. And she was quite pleased to be giving Marco a son as their first child.

She could see it now, little Rosalio and Marco best buddies. She'd better be sure she had plenty of space on her phone for all the photos and videos she'd be taking.

Rosalina fondly rubbed her large belly and ambled down the hallway to drop in the hamper the armload of socks she had tucked against her side.

As she passed the front window, movement caught her eye. Marco was home, pulling in the driveway.

With a squeal, she waddled to the door and undid the locks. Before she could close her hand over the handle, Marco swung it open—narrowly missing her—and emerged with his big, silly smile. The one she adored.

"I'm home!" His bubbliness did not make her forget about the more than half day of her *birthday* she'd spent alone and cleaning house.

"*Sí*, I can see that. Where have you been?" She planted a fist on her hip.

"Working on some— Working."

Peculiar how he changed his wording. "Do you realize what time it is? It's almost three o'clock. And have you any idea what day it is?"

He rubbed his chin. "Hmm. Saturday, I believe."

"Saturday? Saturday! That's all you—"

Marco let out a belly deep laugh, circled her waist, and pulled her to him. "I know what today is. It's my favorite girl's birthday." Then he stole a most heavenly kiss from her that robbed her of any more thoughts of scolding.

She relaxed against him and savored the moment. "You remembered," she whispered when their lips parted and she laid her cheek against his chest.

"I would never forget your birthday."

She sent him a doubtful look.

"Hey!"

She snickered.

"Now, come with me. Oh, hold on. Queenie!" He clapped his hands together. "Queenie, girl!"

The dog came bounding down the hallway and skidded to a stop at Marco's feet, her little tail going a mile a minute. No longer was there a trust issue, but mutual love between the pair.

Marco pulled something out of his back pocket and squatted before Queenie. "Here's a little something for you, doll. Yes, I got something for you." It was cute to hear him talk in a high-pitched voice. He proceeded to slip a red bow around her neck, which sported an adorable print of sombreros and little dancing Mexican women in full skirts.

Then he stood and placed both hands on Rosalina's shoulders. "And I have a surprise for you."

"A surprise?"

"Mm-hmm." He held out his hand and she placed hers in his and let him lead her out and help her into the car. "Come along, Queenie." The dog obeyed without a second thought.

"Where are we going?" Giddiness bubbled inside Rosalina.

He slanted a mischievous expression at her. "You'll see."

"Ack, but you know how much I can't handle suspense when it comes to surprises."

Marco shrugged as he backed out of the driveway. "You'll have to deal with it this time."

"Humph."

He chuckled, which made her smile. She could never stay mad at the man—which was kind of, well, *maddening*. Especially when she wanted to prove a point. For that reason, their arguments never lasted long. She couldn't remain serious when he was so silly and happy-go-lucky.

Oh, but he could be plenty serious about the things that mattered. Like her and baby Rosalio. And...one of the things Rosalina loved most about her amazing husband—his love and zeal for Jesus.

Marco had never forgotten about her telling him he should consider preaching. While he wasn't comfortable with standing behind a pulpit, he did a fantastic job with teens. For over a year now he'd been the teen group leader at church, and Rosalina had the joy of serving alongside him. It came as no surprise his signature lessons were on lying and courage in God's strength.

She perked up when Marco flicked on the turn signal and pulled in at the church. "What are we doing here...?"

He held up a patient finger. "No questions. You. Will. See."

She sent him an annoyed look. Patient was the last thing she wanted to be right now.

He picked Queenie up, lovingly helped Rosalina out of the car, and pecked her cheek with a kiss before they crossed the parking lot. Rosalina started to look around to see whose cars were there, but Marco stopped her by using his finger to turn her head toward him.

"Uh-uh-uh. You just look at me."

"Well, that's not too hard to do."

He grinned. "You can count all my facial scars."

She chuckled. "Have I told you that you're handsome?"

"Yep. You have. But I don't mind hearing it again." He waggled his brows.

Rosalina slapped him on the arm. "You're—"

"Incorrigible. I know. You've said that before too."

Oh, but that brought back good memories of their early texting days.

At last, they made it down the hill to the basement entrance. Marco prepared to open the door, but first raised a finger at her. "Now, close your eyes. No peeking."

"Marco..." She giggled, but complied.

She heard the door handle click and allowed Marco to direct her through the threshold, and then her eyes burst open at the yelled:

"SURPRISE!"

Queenie took to barking maniacally.

"Kids!" She smiled at all of them, lined up in front of her. Behind them the basement was decorated in red, yellow, orange, and turquoise, with a *piñata* hanging from the tile ceiling, and Spanish words dangling from swirly doo-dads. She pressed her hands to her cheeks.

"Happy birthday, Mrs. Mendez!" They chorused.

Her heart did a delightful dance. She'd never grow tired of hearing Mrs. Mendez. She leaned into Marco.

He rubbed his nose over her temple. "Happy birthday, Lina."

"This was so thoughtful of you all. Thank you."

"Oh, but this isn't the whole surprise." Marco bobbed his head with each word, excitement dancing in his eyes.

"Well, I'm dying to know what else you could have possibly—"

The teens spread like the waters of the Red Sea for the children of Israel, and sitting in chairs were two familiar figures of tanned skin, black hair, stocky build, and loving eyes.

"*Ma-má! Pa-pá!*" Rosalina rushed forward and threw her arms around both parents. Tears spilled from her eyes.

Oh, it had been so long since she'd seen them. It'd broken her heart when they were unable to attend her and Marco's wedding, but 2020 had not been a good year for such an event, and certainly not friendly to travelers. She knew she was squeezing too hard, but, oh, she couldn't let go.

Between the three of them there were a lot of whispered words of love, although only half of them understood, and yet Rosalina didn't have to hear them to feel the effect of her *ma-má* and *pa-pá's* love for her, and knew they felt the same of her.

Only when Rosalina's back started complaining from her bent position did she finally pull away, and her husband was right there beside her.

Husband.

That still amazed her.

Queenie, who had been let down, now pranced about her feet, no doubt concerned about Rosalina's tears.

She wiped at her wet cheeks. "This is the best birthday surprise ever. Even if I had to spend most of the day by myself."

Marco ducked his head sheepishly. "About that. Things didn't go as planned. Your parents' flight got delayed. Dora dropped the cupcakes when we got to the church and we had to get new ones. I misplaced the candy for the *piñata*. The list goes on. I'm sorry."

"None of that matters. No need to apologize. This was worth the wait."

He pulled her close, his hands on her waist, and Queenie started shoving at their legs with her nose—she always wanting to be in the middle. Marco paid the dog no mind, though. "I hope you know you're too special and I love you too much to possibly forget about something as significant as your birthday."

She smiled softly, her heart warmed by his words. "What did I ever do to deserve you?"

"Well, I know I don't deserve you. But I love you with all my heart. You and only you, my Lina. My crazy girl."

How something as incredulous as a lie could have turned into her greatest blessing, Rosalina would never know. But of one thing she was certain about. She had won Marco's heart. His love. And there was nothing fake about it.

"*Te amo,* my forever love." She laid her palm against his cheek.

And she would forever be full of wonder at God's amazing way of taking a lie and turning it into something good.

That was something only a wondrous, gracious, and merciful God could do.

THE END

ACKNOWLEDGEMENTS

No book makes it to print without the love, help, and support of family and friends, and this is the place I get to give them the credit they so deserve.

First and foremost, I thank God for His faithfulness in giving inspiration and feeding me the words to write another book. There were times I wanted to give up on this story, but He wouldn't let me. He gave me the courage to keep punching away at the keys and gave me the wisdom I needed to re-work ideas—a few times requiring me to even go back to the drawing board. In the end, I love Marco and Rosalina's story and I'm thrilled to get to share it with you.

Thank you to Marie D. for her excitement about this book when I wasn't sure it would ever come to existence. She kept asking me about my writing and it encouraged me to know someone was out there waiting for the next book in the *Wonders Never Cease* series.

I can never fail to thank my family for their patience, love, and support for yet another writing project. Especially my mom for being a listening ear when I needed to vent my frustration.

A big thank you to my awesome beta-readers: Kaelin, Drew, and Marie. They are the absolute best and provided me with great feedback that strengthened the story even more.

My sincerest thanks to my editor, Korinna, who makes editing enjoyable (as much as it can be. Haha!), and lovingly tells me the truth even when it isn't always easy to swallow. And yet, she's always right. ;)

Thank you, also, to Sharp-eyed Shari for her assistance with my most dreaded part of any project: writing the blurb. Somehow, Shari makes even that task fun, and I am always amazed at the finished product.

And, thank YOU, dear reader, for taking time out of your busy life to spend with my characters. That is literally the most heartwarming thing to me, that you choose to read my book when there are so many other things vying for your attention. If you loved this book, I would appreciate it if you left a review. And if you'd like to read about Clint and Lillian's story, you can do so in *The Tuner's Discordant Heart,* book 2 in my *A Melody of Love* series, which can be read as a stand-alone.

Until next time, friend. God bless you and happy reading! ☺

ABOUT THE AUTHOR

B.M. Baker currently resides with her family in Central Illinois. When not writing or working her medical transcription job, she can be found making memories with her family, or playing with her Yorkshire terrier, Snoopy. She enjoys crocheting, and is a lover of music; playing the piano, violin, and flute. She has been writing stories from the time she was old enough to hold a pencil, and has forever been a bookworm. She began writing her first novel as a teenager, and has since written twenty-plus books. A few have been self-published, with more to come, Lord willing! Her love of Jesus, music, and medicine is evident in her writing. Her greatest desire for her books is that her readers will be blessed, and be pointed to the Author of the greatest love story of all time.

Made in the USA
Columbia, SC
21 June 2023

18526999R00167